MW01006481

GREEN MOUNTAINS, DARK TALES

ALSO BY JOSEPH A. CITRO

Shadow Child, 1998

Passing Strange, 1996

Green Mountain Ghosts, 1994

Deus-X, 1994

Dark Twilight, 1991

The Unseen, 1990

Guardian Angels, 1988

Vermont Lifer (writer/editor), 1986

GREEN MOUNTAINS, DARK TALES

Joseph A. Citro

University Press of New England

Hanover and London

University Press of New England, Hanover, NH 03755
© 1999 by Joseph A. Citro
All rights reserved
Printed in the United States of America 5 4 3 2
CIP data appear at the end of the book

I would like to hear your stories of Vermont and Vermonters. I would also like to be made aware of inaccuracies or additions to the tales of this book. You can contact me in the care of the publisher or by email. My web address is: <jacitro@vbimail.champlain.edu>.

Contents

THINGS

For Diane,

beloved spirit

who manifested

not a moment too soon.

I will not take you far or detain you long. But I will lead you into what at first sight would pass for a region of enchantment.
—**Franklin S. Harvey,** *The Money Diggers*

A Strange Tale

A Strange Tale stands head and shoulders
above New England's best legends and tales.
—Roland W. Robbins

The Mysterious "A. M."

Long before they began enjoying the luxuries of Caribbean vacations and second homes in Florida, certain Vermonters practiced a unique method of getting through the grueling winter months—they slept through them.

Tales of Vermont's "human hibernation" have been told for over a century. The secret practice was first revealed in a December 1887 issue of the state's largest newspaper, the Montpelier *Argus and Patriot* (circulation 6,000). The article was titled simply *A Strange Tale*.

The reporter, who signed himself only as "A. M.," had discovered information in an old diary written by an eyewitness. The entries—presented almost like an exposé—focused on the efforts of an isolated family of wretchedly poor hill farmers from up around Calais. Their problem was how to stretch a far too meager food supply through the long, terrible winter months.

Their solution was a mixture of Yankee ingenuity, colonial witch-craft, and gothic horror. Impossible as it sounds, this secluded clan had somehow developed a process whereby the elderly and the infirm were actually frozen alive. Then, like hibernating bears, they would sleep the winter away to be revived again come spring.

I have been to the place . . . , and have seen the old log house where the events . . . took place . . . and talked with an old man [whose] . . . father was one of the parties operated on.   —A. M.

Though the exact ingredients of the chemical concoction have been lost, the process began by drugging four men and two women, who were either "crippled" or "past the age of usefulness."

At night the unconscious individuals were stripped and carried outdoors. They were packed side by side on beds of straw in ten-by-six-foot wooden boxes. Then, partially protected by a ledge, they were left to freeze in the bitter cold mountain air. Their noses, ears, and fingers turned white beneath the full moon. When their upturned faces assumed a tallowy look, they were judged "ready." Cloth was placed over their heads and more straw was packed protectively around them. Last, the boxes were sealed to guard against predators.

The diarist watched, frozen in horror until he ran inside to escape the nightmare.

I piled on the wood in the cavernous fireplace, and, seated on a shingle block, passed the dreary night, terror-stricken by the horrible sights I had witnessed.

In the weeks to follow, twenty-foot snowdrifts would bury the sleepers for one quarter of a year.

On May 10th, just as the Green Mountains were beginning to warm up, the other half of this odd ritual was performed. The writer returned to the cabin to witness the sleepers' liberation from their icy crypt. This time the process involved placing the frozen individuals in troughs made of logs. Hot water and a hemlock-based potion were poured around them.

Slowly, color brightened their features. Muscles twitched, fingers moved, vitality returned. In time they were taken inside where they were warmed by blankets, fire, and a hearty meal—completely revived after their long winter's nap.

Mr. Elbert S. Stevens

This fascinating story hibernated for about half a century until it was picked up in 1939 by *The Rutland Herald*. Then *The Boston Globe* followed suit (May 28, 1939), as did *Yankee* magazine, *The Old Farmer's Almanac*, and a fair number of books, periodicals, and newspapers, giving it wide—eventually worldwide—exposure.

By the early 1950s people from all over the globe knew Vermont's darkest secret.

As colorful as the freezing ritual may have been, the primitive techniques described—not to mention the operators' apparent indifference to human life—cast Vermont and Vermonters in an unsavory light.

Because the story's lurid details seemed the product of a horror writer's imagination, most people dismissed the whole affair as an especially grisly mountain myth. But a fair number of sensible people—including some scientists—believed it. Researchers like Dr. Temple S. Fay of Philadelphia suggested this arcane Vermont "folk medicine" might someday be applied to curing cancer and heart disease.

Experiments at the University of Toronto buttressed the story when researchers demonstrated that a dog could be kept alive after stopping its heart by freezing. The American Medical Association revealed details of recent experiments in which humans were frozen so that all bodily functions were suspended for hours. An Illinois newspaper reported, "A man was restored to life after having been frozen in an unconscious sleep for five days and nights."

But Elbert S. Stevens of Bridgewater Corners *knew* the whole thing was true; he had the original newspaper clipping to prove it.

Elbert had often told his neighbors about the odd arctic ritual. That's how word got to Bob Wilson of *The Rutland Herald*. It was Wilson who examined the original newspaper article and once more brought the story to the public's attention in May 24, 1939.

Alton Blackington, famed chronicler of New England curiosities, tracked Elbert Stevens down and got a look at the original clipping. It had been saved by Mr. Stevens's mother, who filed it among the pages of an old book. Unfortunately, she had made no note of the date or source of the article. At the time Mr. Blankington examined it, the article was more than half a century old, its origin still a puzzle.

Roland W. Robbins

The real Sherlock Holmes of this Vermont mystery is writer, archaeologist, and honorary detective Roland Wells Robbins.

His "sleuthing" credentials were impeccable. He had, after fifty years of controversy, finally determined the exact location of Thoreau's cabin at Walden Pond. And he had located and begun the restoration of America's first iron works in Saugus, Massachusetts.

But Vermont's human hibernation was, he said, the strangest story he'd ever heard. Determined to discern whether it was the "figment of an energetic imagination" or legitimate local history, Robbins set out to get to the bottom of things once and for all.

He began exactly where Alton Blackington had left off—by visiting Mr. Elbert Stevens in Bridgewater, Vermont.

When he examined the newspaper clipping he found that the printed columns were unusual. They were wider and longer than those used in most newspapers of that era (the late 19th century). A visit to the state library in Montpelier and a file search brought exceptionally quick results: the paper in question was the Montpelier *Argus and Patriot*. Though he had to flip a lot of pages to do it, he finally located the story on page one of the December 21, 1887, edition.

But there the trail seemed to end. He found no more information about *A Strange Tale*, no additional articles by the mysterious A. M., and, in subsequent issues, no letters to the editor regarding the unusually provocative piece. Why had no one bothered to write? Hadn't the story seemed sufficiently out of the ordinary at the time it was printed?

So, in the winter 1949 issue of *Vermont Life* magazine, Mr. Robbins published an article called, "Was Human Hibernation Practiced in Vermont?" He concluded that most likely it was not.

But the mystery still wasn't solved. The mysterious "A.M." was still a writer without an identity. Who could he (or she) have been? And what had become of the original diary from which the chilling "facts" had been taken?

Not long after the article came out, so did the rest of the story.

Allen Morse

In response to the *Vermont Life* article, Mr. Robbins was contacted by Mrs. Mable E. Hayes of Agawam, Massachusetts. She was able to fill in many of the holes, including the identity of the elusive "A.M." He was Allen Morse, her grandfather, an authentic Vermont yarnspinner and dairy farmer from Calais, who lived from 1835 to 1917.

She recalled how at picnics and family reunions Grandpa and the other men would take to "yarnin'," that is, competing to top each other as storytellers. Allen Morse had been something of a local champion. And, she recalled, he had frequently told his macabre masterpiece, the tale of the hibernating hill folk.

Apparently Mr. Morse had been an intelligent man with a wide spectrum of interests. In addition to his practical attention to farming and politics, he was fascinated with Spiritualism and enjoyed relating his own encounters with the supernatural, both imagined and, presumably, real.

Clearly he had a highly developed sense of fantasy.

His daughter, Mrs. Hayes's mother, talked him into putting "A Strange Tale" on paper. Then, as a surprise, she secretly arranged to have it published in the Montpelier *Argus and Patriot*, where she was employed. It appeared in print on December 21, 1887—her father's fifty-second birthday.

It was a wonderful birthday present, I'm sure, but there was a bigger surprise, one that Allen Morse would never know about: His story made him immortal.

*

Today there is little in modern Calais to recall the secret ghastly rituals of a century and a half ago. One can still visit the spots mentioned in the story. The cabin is long gone, of course, but Eagle Ledge is right where Mother Nature put it. And locals will tell you that during the harshest winter months wind-driven snow still piles up to a depth of twenty feet.

Even now people occasionally ask me if the events Mr. Morse described ever really happened.

I'm sure it happened, I tell them. But of course I don't know for sure. Allen Morse described Vermont's cryogenic events so vividly and so convincing that the story took root in our folk memory and was frequently confused with fact. Even today some people argue that it is true. Supposedly, the University of Vermont still gets occasional inquiries from cryonics researchers from around the world.

In his book *Inside New England*, *Yankee Magazine* editor Judson Hale relates an anecdote that perfectly illustrates *A Strange Tale*'s unique position between fact and fantasy. He says, "I once asked an old Vermont farm couple in the Montpelier area if either one of them truly believed the 'Frozen Death' story.

"'Certainly do,' the husband answered emphatically, without hesitation.

"Then the wife added, 'The only part I doubt is the thawing out.'"

*

Just for fun, and for perhaps the first time in years, what follows is a complete, verbatim copy of the original story, exactly as it appeared more than a century ago. The only change is that this time I will give it a proper byline:

A STRANGE TALE
By Allen Morse

I am an old man now, and have seen some strange sights in the course of a roving life in foreign lands as well as in this country, but none so strange as one I found recorded in an old diary, kept by my Uncle William, that came into my possession a few years ago, at his decease. The events described took place in a mountain town some twenty miles from Montpelier, the Capital of Vermont. I have been to the place on the mountain, and seen the old log-house where the events I found recorded in the diary took place, and seen and talked with an old man who vouched for the truth of the story, and that his father was one of the parties operated on. The account runs in this wise:

"January 7.—I went on the mountain today, and witnessed what to me was a horrible sight. It seems that the dwellers there, who are unable, either from age or other reasons, to contribute to the support of their families, are disposed of in the winter months in a manner that will shock the one who reads this diary, unless that person lives in that vicinity. I will describe what I saw. Six persons, four men and two women, one of the men a cripple about 30 years old, the other five past the age of usefulness, lay on the earthy floor of the cabin drugged into insensibility, while members of their families were gathered about them in apparent indifference. In a short time the unconscious bodies were inspected by one man who said, "They are ready." They were then stripped of all their clothing, except a single garment. Then the bodies were carried outside, and laid on logs exposed to the bitter cold mountain air, the operation having been delayed several days for suitable weather.

"It was night when the bodies were carried out, and the full moon, occasionally obscured by flying clouds, shone on their upturned ghastly faces, and a horrible fascination kept me by the bodies as long as I could endure the severe cold. Soon the noses, ears and fingers began to turn white, then the limbs and face assumed a tallowy look. I could stand the cold no longer, and went inside, where I found the friends in cheerful conversation.

"In about an hour I went out and looked at the bodies: they were fast freezing. Again I went inside, where the men were smoking their clay pipes, but silence had fallen on them; perhaps they were thinking of the time when their turn would come to be cared for in the same way. One by one they at last lay down on the floor, and went to sleep. It seemed a horrible nightmare to me, and I could not think of sleep. I could not shut out the sight of those freezing bodies outside, neither could I bear to be in darkness, but I piled on the wood in the cavernous fireplace, and, seated on a shingle block, passed the dreary night, terror-stricken by the horrible sights I had witnessed.

"January 8.—Day came at length, but did not dissipate the terror that filled me. The frozen bodies became visible, white as the snow that lay in huge drifts about them. The women gathered about the fire, and soon commenced preparing breakfast. The men awoke, and, conversation again commencing, affairs assumed a more cheerful aspect. After breakfast the men lighted their pipes, and some of them took a yoke of oxen and went off toward the forest, while others proceeded to nail together boards, making a box about ten feet long and half as high and wide. When this was completed they placed about two feet of straw in the bottom; then they laid three of the frozen bodies on the straw. Then the faces and upper part of the bodies were covered with a cloth, then more straw was put in the box, and the other three bodies placed on top and covered the same as the first ones, with cloth and straw. Boards were then firmly nailed on the top, to protect the bodies from being injured by carnivorous animals that make their home on these mountains.

"By this time the men who went off with the ox-team returned with a huge load of spruce and hemlock boughs, which they unloaded at the foot of a steep ledge, came to the house and loaded the box containing the bodies on the sled, and drew it to the foot of the ledge, near the load of boughs. These were soon piled on and around the box, and it was left to be covered up with snow, which I was told would lie in drifts twenty feet deep over this rude tomb. 'We shall want our men to plant our corn next spring,' said a youngish looking woman, the wife of one of the frozen men, 'and if you want to see them resuscitated, you come here about the 10th of next May.'

"With this agreement, I left the mountaineers, both the living and the frozen, to their fate and I returned to my home in Boston where it was weeks before I was fairly myself, as my thoughts would return to that mountain with its awful sepulcher." Turning the leaves of the diary to the date of May 10, the following entry was found:

"May 10—I arrived here at 10 a.m., after riding about four hours over muddy, unsettled roads. The weather is warm and pleasant, most of the snow is gone, except here and there drifts in the fence corners and hollows, but nature is not yet dressed in green. I found the same parties here that I left last January, ready to disinter the bodies of their friends. I had no expectation of finding any life there, but a feeling that I could not resist impelled me to come and see. We repaired at once to the well remembered spot, at the ledge. The snow had melted from the top of the brush, but still lay deep around the bottom of the pile. The men commenced work at once, some shoveling away the snow, and others tearing away the brush. Soon the box was visible. The cover was taken off, the layers of straw removed, and the bodies, frozen and apparently lifeless, lifted out and laid on the snow. Large troughs made out of hemlock logs were placed nearby, filled with tepid water, into which the bodies were separately placed, with the head slightly raised. Boiling water was then poured into the trough from kettles hung on poles over fires near by, until the water in the trough was as hot as I could hold my hand in. Hemlock boughs had been put in the boiling water in such quantities that they had given the water the color of wine. After lying in this bath about an hour, color began to return to the bodies, when all hands began rubbing and chafing them. This continued about another hour, when a slight twitching of the muscles of the face and limbs, followed by audible gasps, showed that life was not quenched, and that vitality was returning. Spirits were then given in small quantities, and allowed to trickle down their throats. Soon they could swallow, and more was given them, when their eyes opened, and they began to talk, and finally sat up in their bath-tubs. They were then taken out and assisted to the house, where after a hearty dinner they seemed as well as ever, and in nowise injured, but rather refreshed, by their long sleep of four months."

Truly, truth is stranger than fiction.

Green Mountains, Dark Tales—An Introduction

> But I am so obviously offering everything in this book, as fiction.
> That is, if there is fiction.
> —Charles Fort, *Wild Talents*

Truth *is* stranger than fiction.

Between the years 1985 and 1994 I wrote a series of five suspense novels—fiction—all based on legitimate oddities of Vermont folklore and history. I dealt with topics like the Lake Champlain Monster, the Underground Railroad, Bigfoot, the *Daoine Sidhe*, and the possibility of ancient Celtic settlements in the region.

Admittedly, such tales have always held a certain fascination for me. Growing up here, I couldn't help encountering their most conspicuous and venerable examples. In my youth I developed a strong affection for them; in time I dared take a crack at synthesizing them into fiction for modern readers.

What I hadn't anticipated is the hydra-headed quality of my research: the moment I investigated one story, a dozen more would spring to my attention. In time I had collected scores of wonderful tales of magic, suspense, and horror, many thoroughly documented and far, far stranger than fiction. I'm convinced that our state is a veritable treasure trove of history and mystery. I could never write novels enough to keep up.

And so this volume: a book of stories.

Some may be true. Others may be deceptions—deliberate or, like Allen Morse's, accidental. Most, I suspect, lie in the vicinity of "real" history books, somewhere on that indistinct continuum between fact and fabrication.

What they all have in common is this: even the most outrageous has always been told as if it was swear-on-a-Bible truth, unimpeachably etched in Vermont granite.

None of them are my stories. I am merely the collector, the editor, a teller of someone else's tale.

My role is that of conservationist, striving to protect representatives of a potentially extinct species. As if they were the fading words of a dying language, I want to record them before they are gone forever.

Some appear in print here for the first time ever. They are family stories never before shared with a general audience, gifts to me by living Vermonters.

Others are seeing the light after a century in hibernation. I resurrected them from overlooked and long-forgotten sources.

Each—from the least well-known to the oldest chestnut—is as much a part of today's Vermont as our green epidermal mountains or our marble spine. And the Yankee "yarners" who perpetuate them are Vermonters of the first order. Like our more conspicuous forefathers—say, Ethan Allen or Calvin Coolidge—the people in these tales, and the people who tell them, are instrumental in molding our state's unique character.

The fact that most stories in this selection reflect a certain peculiarity of world view is the contribution I bring. In accord with some inexplicable editorial instinct, I chose some and set others aside. The process was irrational; the resulting uniformity is obvious. They are "Dark Tales." Eccentrics, ghosts, monsters. The unexplained and the unexplainable.

PEOPLE

The Autograph & The Gazetteer

A Remarkable Fellow

Seems to me Vermont has always had an extraordinary number of newspaper, magazine, and book publishers. But by far the most individual, and perhaps the most eccentric of all was Mr. James Johns of Huntington. If writers and publishers were to put out calls for patron saints, Johns could easily do double duty, representing both groups.

This minor miracle man was born September 26, 1797, the son of Jehiel and Elizabeth Johns, Huntington's first settlers. Perhaps being almost as old as the town gave him a unique perspective. No surprise then that he should become the town's pioneering historian and newspaperman.

With tremendous singleness of purpose he produced his first newspaper, *The Huntington Gazette*, when he was just thirteen years old. He wrote it by hand on a 6½ by 8½ piece of brown wrapping paper. He then went on to write nonstop: histories, fiction, short stories, poems, political essays, and local interest articles.

Apparently Johns had some trouble finding publishers for most of his early work. His *Green Mountain Muse*, published in 1828, didn't sell a single copy. Like many writers, he blamed the publisher and printer. Thereafter, he was determined to self-publish.

In 1832 he started his own newspaper, a five-times-a-week journal called *The Vermont Autograph and Remarker*. As he said in something of an editorial mission statement, "As it is composed wholly of original matter, it is of course the channel through which we occasionally expound our sentiments on political and moral points which we intend to express boldly without fear or favor of any man or act of men."

A number of things about this periodical were completely unique: First, his habit was to print only one single copy of each issue.

Second, since Johns had no use for the printing press, each issue was lettered entirely by hand. "And the reader may be assured," Johns wrote, "that every paragraph is composed and written by the Editor himself, and that too without having first to draft it on another piece of paper, which is more than can be said hundreds and thousands of . . . royal and imperial folios issued from the press."

Third, the quality of his penmanship was so good that at a glance his publication was indistinguishable from typeset copy.

And last, there was the one-of-a-kind quality of Johns's eccentric writing style.

Johns used *The Vermont Autograph and Remarker* to chronicle all the notable happenings in the town of Huntington: births, deaths, weather, accidents, and more.

On October 10, 1834, he felt moved to explain the title of his publication. "We have more than once since our paper was published under its present title been asked what was the meaning of the word *Autograph*. Although we would think that any person might by consulting a dictionary easily satisfy his mind on that point, still as we are willing to give information as to the meaning of words which we may use, we will condescend to explain it for the edification of those of our readers who may wish to know its meaning. Know then that Autograph means a person's own handwriting on any copy or work executed with one's own hand, in distinction from that which [is] struck off upon type at a printing office. We have adopted this word as part of the title of our little paper as being most characteristic of the manner in which it is executed for there is no one who is at all experienced in reading but can readily perceive that this was done with a pen."

Each issue contained about a half-dozen articles, totaling about 1,500 words. "I can fill out one in half a day," he said, and he used only a quill pen to do so. He would then take his one-page, single-sided gazette to the center of town where he would post it for all to read. On rare occasions he might condescend to create a special hand-lettered duplicate if someone wanted a souvenir copy for some very good reason.

Johns didn't really hate the printing press. In fact, he acquired one in 1857 in order to expand his operation. But—finding hand printing faster than typesetting—he continued to put out the *Autograph and Remarker* completely by hand.

Somehow he also found time to keep a diary, hand pen a forty-four-page history of Huntington. And, with the new press, he also wrote and printed his *Green Mountain Tradition, Remarkable Circumstances,* a book entitled *A brief record of the various fatal accidents which have happened from the first settlement of the town of Huntington to the present time,* and *The Book of Funny Anecdotes.*

Despite his individualistic publication habits, Johns was arguably one of the most prolific American writers. It is surely no surprise that he never married—he was just too busy, too preoccupied, and no doubt too strange. Surviving photographs show an intense-looking man with bushy eyebrows and thick, white sideburns. Contemporary accounts describe him as having a swarthy complexion and speaking with a deep bass voice.

But to be fair, the way to get to know him is through his writing. His literary voice is unique, his opinions unfettered. He even ventured into some highly opinionated investigative journalism, political shenanigans and secret societies being favorite targets. For example, on June 15, 1823, he reported a meeting of the Freewill Baptists that he attended in Richmond. "Saw & heard much noise and wildfire. . . . His Freewill Highness Pope Ziba was present, and tried to see how much noise he could make."

"September 21d . . . Trespass committed by our worse than no neighbor Roswell Stevens in cutting down a bee tree on our land and taking the honey."

Then there was the stolen potash caper that occurred on the night of April 5, 1824: "Information supposed, or known to have been given the thieves concerning where the potash was, given by that most abandoned of all villains, Gail Nichols, the curse and bane of society."

Sometimes he'd be reporting on a bit of local news and, if he were so inclined, he'd switch unpredictably from prose to poetry. One report, reproduced in *Huntington, Vermont 1786–1976,* tells of the time Huntington residents were spooked by the continual screeching of a catamount. A bunch of armed men banded together to hunt the thing. Johns writes:

> O'er rock and knoll they scour'd the hill
> Ransacking every quarter;
> Until at length they came upon,
> A little run of water.
> And here they found the catamount,
> That sent forth all the screechin'
> Who in the shape of water wheel,
> Complained he wanted greasing.

His total literary output was uncanny. His hand-printed *Autograph and Remarker* came out five days a week, for over forty years. He ceased publication just four days before his death in 1874. His legacy: an extraordinarily vivid picture of early life in a small Vermont town.

Abby's Gazetteer

In an attempt to demonstrate that men have no monopoly on monomania and Vermont chauvinism, let's consider the case of Abby Hemenway and *The Vermont Historical Gazetteer*.

The *Gazetteer* is one of my favorite sources of material for books and commentaries because it is full of stories that haven't been seen for decades. Believe it or not, this 6,000-page compilation of Vermontiana is the brainchild and product of a single person: the remarkable Miss Hemenway.

Because I—and everyone who writes about Vermont's past—owe her so much, I'd like to tell her story. For if it were not for Miss Hemenway's monumental independence, eccentricity, and drive, much of Vermont's most intimate history and folklore would have been lost forever. She anticipated that loss and set out to prevent it.

In 1828 Abby Maria Hemenway was born in a two-room log cabin in Ludlow, where she lived with her parents and nine brothers and sisters. When she was just fourteen years old she began a career as a schoolteacher. In 1842 she took a better teaching post at Ludlow's Black River Academy, Calvin Coolidge's alma mater.

At thirty, when most women were married and raising families, Miss Hemenway was busily working on a literary anthology called *Poets and Poetry of Vermont*. Maybe that editorial effort inspired what was to become her life's work and her obsession. By reading verse it is likely she came to appreciate the power of the individual voice, the poetry of personal perception, and the singular nature of an individual's recollection.

As a historian she realized that many significant events were never recorded in conventional history books. While the grand affairs of war and political posture inevitably found their place, the stories of individuals and communities were routinely overlooked—just the sorts of details that give history breath and life. As a staunch Vermonter she feared losing colorful local lore. She said, "Our past has been too rich and, in many points, too unique and too romantic to lose."

This became her mission: Abby was determined to record these endangered Vermont chronicles before they became extinct. In Vermont—a rather youthful state by New England standards—frontier days were within easily accessible memory; Abby's own father could even recall a time when there was but a single house in her native Ludlow. So her plan was to visit every town in the state, seeking out the sons of Revolutionary War veterans and the descendants of Vermont's original settlers. Along with their personal histories, she'd also collect supernatural stories, treasure tales, religious anecdotes, and Indian data.

Abby soon realized the project was way too big for one person alone. So she decided to recruit town historians, local clergymen, teachers, and elderly residents to write the stories of their own towns—in their own words. (It should be no surprise that Mr. James Johns prepared the section on Huntington.)

Then her plan was to publish the material in a series of quarterly magazines, town by town, according to the alphabetical order of the counties. She'd sell the magazines at twenty-five cents a copy, thus raising funds for the next batch.

When finished, the individual magazines would be combined into one vast historical encyclopedia, the comprehensive literary equivalent of the founding and flourishing of the state of Vermont, told from the point of view of its citizens.

Of course, the formidable project couldn't be accomplished on a schoolteacher's salary. And fundraising was especially difficult at that time because of the Civil War. Worse, many so-called experts tried to discourage her. Professors at Middlebury College said her project was impractical and unsuited for a woman. They asked how she expected to do what forty men hadn't accomplished in sixteen years.

How? Well, by God, she'd show them!

In Bennington she enlisted the support of ex-governor and historian Hiland Hall. He endorsed the idea, vowed his support, and even helped her gather material.

Through sheer will and tenacity, she managed to produce six issues before war expenditures and other drains on public interest and finance caused her to suspend publication.

When she was thirty-nine, a Methodist minister from Burlington proposed marriage, promising to help with the *Gazetteer*. She declined, forsaking the restrictions of marital security. After all, there was no time for romance; she had a job to do.

In the late 1860s, while she was working on Volume Four, the state legislature finally began to recognize the value of her effort. They offered some expense money, but the conditions they imposed, just like marriage vows, were far too confining. Again—independent as ever— Abby forged ahead on her own.

When she couldn't pay her bill, printers in Montpelier seized her magazines. Undaunted, she entered the print shop one night and seized them back! It was the only reasonable thing to do: in order to pay the bill, she'd have to sell the magazines.

All this showed that she had to economize further. Since she couldn't afford a printer, she'd do the job herself. Abby rented a large room in Ludlow and partitioned it off with curtains. In one division she worked, in another she slept, and in the third she received visitors. With the help of relatives and occasional part-time employees, Volume Five began to take shape.

It's hard to imagine the force of this woman's determination or the extent of her obsession. Nothing would keep her from her work. When she was run down by a sleigh in the streets, she got up and kept working. When she was penniless and hungry, she kept plugging.

It was the creditors who finally did her in. Their harassment drove her from the state. In 1885 she moved to Chicago. There she set up shop again, editing the manuscript by night and setting type by day.

But tragedy soon followed. In 1886, when she was almost a thousand pages into Volume Five, her building burned down. She lost everything. Apparently the fire was the final roadblock in a journey strewn with obstructions. Abby took ill. Three years later she died of a cerebral hemorrhage, alone and poverty-striken, in a meager rented room a thousand miles from home.

Sadly, the volume containing her own county, Windsor, was never printed.

Though Abby Hemenway died a debtor, things have changed: today we owe a great debt to her. *The Vermont Historical Gazetteer*, is still—by far—the most comprehensive history of the state she loved.

The Shepherd of Vermont

In earlier books I have written a good deal about William and Horatio Eddy and their ramshackle farmhouse in Chittenden, Vermont. There, night after night, legions of ghostly visitants performed in vaudevillian splendor.

The Eddy manifestations in the 1870s were so dramatic that it was easy to overlook equally strange goings-on in the nearby city of Rutland.

There, in 1873, Dr. Solomon W. Jewett was about to revolutionize communication between this world and the next. The doctor's extraordinary credentials seemed to make him just the man for the job. An exceptional individual in an era of eccentricity, Solomon Jewett was a peculiar hybrid of chauvinistic Vermonter, successful businessman, and Green Mountain mystic.

He entered this world in Weybridge on a Sunday morning, May 22, 1808. According to his own account he was born with a veil, which was believed to be a sign of "second sight." It was at a time when, he wrote, "all planets but Saturn were ascending." As if that were not enough to herald lofty spiritual development, Solomon was the *seventh son* of parents Samuel and Lucy Jewett.

In spite of, or maybe because of, his occult attributes, Jewett became an extremely successful Vermonter. By age twenty-six he owned the largest flock of sheep in the state. He also had a second huge sheep farm in Oakland, California. He was so prosperous in his sheep-raising enterprise that he awarded himself the title "the Shepherd of Vermont and California" and sometimes more grandly, just "the American Shepherd."

His drive and determination were briefly impaired in 1838, when his wife Fidelia died in Weybridge. It is likely this sad incident exacerbated his preoccupation with the mystical side of human nature, but being a true Vermonter, he tended to business.

In 1851 Jewett won the distinction of being Vermont's representative at the Great Exhibition in London, where he purchased farm animals from Prince Albert himself. Over the years he made several trips to Europe, bought hundreds of French and Spanish Merino sheep, and, through careful breeding, improved the lines.

Solomon Jewett might have been remembered in Vermont history as nothing more than a clever businessman. But he had always had a mystical side to his nature, and eventually it compelled him to become a shepherd of men.

Some time along, probably the late 1850s or early 1860s, Jewett got caught up in the American phenomenon of Spiritualism. He began attending seances, frequently at the Eddy homestead in Chittenden.

Solomon came to believe he was tied in closer than most men to the primary life force. It was a common supposition at the time that anyone who was successful with animals was likely to have unusual healing powers. So Solomon turned his talents to healing.

He took to calling himself *Doctor* Jewett and advertising his "magnetic healing" skills in various newspapers. Never lacking confidence, he guaranteed he could cure a wide range of diseases, anything from "Milk Legs" to "Tape Worms," from "the tobacco habit" to "cancer." His prices, ranging from $10 to $20, were steep in an era when $10 was a week's pay for most workers.

In 1861 he left for California, where he and his children lived on his expansive sheep ranch "among Indian Settlements."

On his way back in 1868 he detoured through New York City, where he met Wella and Pet Anderson.

This psychic couple had a particular niche within the realm of Spiritualism—they produced life-sized paintings of dead people, whom they believed they could see.

The Andersons did a few pictures for Solomon, including one of his dead wife Fedelia. The inquisitive Vermonter then got it into his head that this would be a good way to get a look at historical personages whom no one had ever seen. How fine it would be, he thought, to see what Jesus had actually looked like. Or Jesus's mother. Or the founders of Free Masonry. Or even the regal Solomon after whom he was named.

Sure enough, Wella Anderson was able to produce just such likenesses. Not only did Solomon receive a portrait of Hiram Abiff, an early Mason, but the experience launched a friendship: the man and the spirit began a correspondence—via medium—that would last for years.

It was also during this stop in New York that something terrible happened.

Raising the Dead

On February 25, 1882, Solomon reported the events in a fascinating letter to *The Saratoga Eagle*.

He says that in the fall of 1868, for reasons about which he is not too precise, he was arrested and incarcerated in a New York City jail. His letter implies that the reason could have been any of three things: a bad debt, a lawsuit, or something to do with his "medical cures."

Anyway, while locked up at 70 Ludlow Street, he was presented with the opportunity to prove once and for all, at least to his own satisfaction, that he was a mystical healer of biblical proportions. For on March 17, 1869, Solomon Jewett proved that he could do more than simply summon spirits from the Summerland. He could actually raise the dead. In the presence of one hundred witnesses, he restored life to the dead body of John Cronham.

Jewett had been behind bars for nearly five months "breathing the same air with 150 other debtors and criminals." His "time and mind" were generally occupied with good books, continued fasting, and a diet of "pure" honey and milk. He had also requested, and had been granted, a smoke-free cell.

Two doors away a "German Jew" by the name of John Cronham was admitted. Around midnight of Cronham's second day of incarceration, Solomon heard groans coming from the newly occupied cell. Then came the sound of a body falling.

The attendant, who was with Solomon at the time, hurried to the man's assistance, with Solomon in tow. They found Cronham on the floor of his cell experiencing severe convulsions, his face distorted in pain.

Jewett's immediate reflex was to help. "I will boss this business," he said as he rushed to the man's side. As he began his "magnetic" maneuvers, the stricken man began to relax. Jewett explained to those around him, "Just as long as I hold him in this position he remains quiet."

But the prison doctor had arrived on the scene and didn't take kindly to Solomon's assistance. He said, "Go back to your cell, sir; what business have you here?"

Guards hauled Solomon back to his cell, but by the time he got there Mr. Cronham was again moaning in pain. For the next five days Solomon listened to the man's agony and watched the comings and goings of various medical personnel, all trying to ease Cronham's suffering. Word got out that the poor man was dying.

Finally, in the presence of "Keeper Tracey" and five ineffectual physicians, John Cronham passed away.

Dr. Jewett was permitted to pay his final respects. The fallen man, covered in a pale white sheet, lay motionless in the dim cell. One doctor said, "The man is dead; all hope of life has passed." Another doctor told Mr. Tracey to have the body removed to the morgue.

Solomon wrote, "Rapidly I felt a circle of spirits, or angels about me; my whole system seemed to loom up with light and power."

He then spoke to the people who surrounded the corpse. "Move out and leave me here alone." And to the doctors, "Grant me this request of only forty minutes of time, and this body shall be raised to life."

Although they laughed at him, he was nonetheless given forty minutes to try his magnetism. He attributes this unusual opportunity to the warden's predicament: a man had died needlessly while in the warden's care. If nothing could be done to correct the situation, the warden was in danger of losing his position and a substantial annual salary.

Prison guards were posted at the door to keep curiosity seekers from interrupting Solomon's ministrations.

Solomon describes his ordeal in some detail. First he fell to his knees and begged for divine aid as he examined the corpse. Its mouth hung slack, a wide dark cavity. Enlarged pupils blackened the staring eyes. Purple veins covered the hands and arms. Solomon wrote, "The same death sign presented itself under each finger nail."

But he saw himself as "a chosen instrument in the hands of God and angels," so he set to work:

"After making upward passes without touching the body, I then moved to the feet, grasping the ankles, drawing all downwards, so that the feet hung over the bed frame of iron. Dropping down upon my knees, and placing the soles of both feet against my naked and warm magnetic body, in this peculiar position, holding on at the wrists (this connection forming the most thorough magnetic battery between the living and the lifeless, a regular circuit or current of magnetic, not electric, life forces were at work)."

By this time about six of his forty minutes had passed.

Solomon uttered another prayer to God, closing with, "If you raise this body to life, you remove your servant [i.e., Solomon] from the hands and ignominy of scornful bigots."

He continued the resurrection: "After following repeated upward passes over the form, then stretching myself over it, I breathed with force into its gaping mouth several times."

Soon he noticed both eyes twitch and move toward the left. Then, after pausing, they looked straight ahead again. Dr. Jewett said they moved with a "mechanical precision" that told him "the wandering spirit of Cronham was about to return to the house it had left!"

He continued forcing breath into Cronham's mouth until the body began to tremble and choke.

About fifteen or twenty minutes into the process, independent respiration returned and Cronham's face began to show expression and life. Dr. Jewett pulled him into a sitting position and called in the others.

The silent crowd realized they had witnessed a miracle. William Muller, a prison employee, recorded the reanimated man's first words. "I have been a great way off," Cronham said in a whisper, "I have seen many things. . . ."

Shortly afterward Cronham's wife arrived at the prison and she took her husband home.

One of the officials said, "Well, Doctor Jewett, you are King in this house."

Less than a month later, on April 6, 1869, Solomon W. Jewett was granted an unconditional release from prison by the order of Judge Brady.

*

Two years later, in 1871, Solomon was to be reunited with the spirit-artist Wella P. Anderson. While again traveling to California, Jewett was summoned to the home of Spiritualist Marshal Curtis in San Jose. Anderson was there, but he was not painting. He'd been struck down with some unnamed affliction that caused paralysis of his right arm and leg. From brief descriptions, one suspects a stroke, but it doesn't really matter—within ten minutes Dr. Jewett had produced a "perfect cure."

To reciprocate, Mr. Anderson did a sitting for Dr. Jewett during which he produced "the picture of Fidelia [Bell Jewett, Sol's first wife], attired in the costume she wore in A.D. 1838, at the time of her decease, at Weybridge, Vt."

Not long after that—and perhaps influenced by his experience with Wella Anderson—Dr. Solomon Jewett returned to Vermont. He settled in Rutland, where, at the specific request of the spirits, he began construction of *Shepherd Home*.

Shepherd Home

It was to be a unique building. As far as I know, nothing like it existed in Vermont. But its purpose was a bit mysterious, even to the builder. As *The Banner of Light* reported on September 20, 1873, Dr. Jewett, "is directed by the spirits in his work, and building for he knows not what."

The mysterious enterprise was an "octagonal house, of good proportions."

It was two stories high with a circular seance room that occupied the entire first floor. The ever-present "spirit cabinet" was built directly into the wall.

Upstairs a second circle room included a gallery of spirit portraits, mostly completed by Wella and Pet Anderson.

By this time Solomon had taken a second wife, Mary L. Jewett, who was "not only a regular and excellent physician, with a good practice, but one of the best magnetic healers."

Rutland townspeople speculated about the purpose of this mysterious octagonal house on East Street. So did Sol and Mary Jewett. The best guess was that somehow the peculiar design was supposed to facilitate clearer communication between this world and the next. Many people were prepared for something big—perhaps earth-changing revelations.

But whatever the monumental event might have been, it never rivaled the strange goings-on in nearby Chittenden, which had turned into a virtual Spiritualist Mecca.

Mainstream Spiritualists took little interest in Dr. Jewett's activities. After all, Spiritualism's goal was to improve the present and the future, so the relevance of an elaborate portrait gallery of people long dead was questionable.

As one correspondent wrote: "Nine of [the paintings] purport to be Bible characters, whose existence to us is a matter of debate, but as we are not and never were acquainted with any of them, not even Jesus and his Mother, we shall not say they are not *good* likenesses. Of the other still more ancient names, we know as little and care as little, so they may be all right; but to us they have no value save as curiosities. We are looking *at* the present generation and for *its* future and its successors, and care little for the opinion of the ancients, whose surroundings were so unlike ours."

In short, Dr. Jewett was not taken seriously by Spiritualists or lay-persons in the Rutland community.

On November 20, 1874, the venerable *Rutland Herald* reported an incident the tone and content of which might illustrate Dr. Jewett's status in the community.

Several young men showed up at Shepherd Home, feigning an interest in Spiritualism. Dr. Jewett, known as an outgoing and hospitable sort, invited them in and showed them the "circle room."

One of the young men pretended that he was able to function as a medium. Delighted, Dr. Jewett eagerly ushered him into the spirit cabinet where the young man pretended to go into a trance.

Meanwhile, one of his cronies sneaked up to the second floor while the rest stayed downstairs with Dr. Jewett.

The man upstairs made a lot of noise as his confederates secretly tossed objects around, mimicking spirit activity to impress the good doctor.

One youth struck Jewett in the head with an apple, almost knocking him out.

The man upstairs lowered a rope through a hole in the ceiling. There was a noose tied in the end which the "spirits below promptly slipped . . . over the head of the spiritualistic proprietor."

Above, the ethereal force began its work. "[T]he slack of the rope was soon taken up; then it began to grow a little tight around the victim's neck, and in a short time he began to ascend. The old fellow was almost strangled, and the spirits becoming alarmed, loosened the rope and let him go."

Dr. Jewett wheezed and coughed for a while. When he had recovered sufficiently to speak, he said, "Boys, the spirits appear to be a little rough to-night, but you see they are genuine."

The boys agreed that yes, they were genuine. After a number of equally absurd performances, they threw a pail of water at the doctor and left.

The *Herald* went on to say that Solomon Jewett "concluded to hold no more seances for the present."

I'm not sure if that was the end of Shepherd Home, but it is clear that soon after the incident, Dr. Jewett resumed his travels around the country, conducting his own business and that of the spirits.

Solomon and George

For example, during a visit to Philadelphia in 1884, Solomon began his association with George Washington.

A medium named M. R. D. Lewis called upon Dr. Jewett at his hotel to deliver a message from the former U.S. President. Washington wanted the Vermonter to visit a photographer's studio so the two dignitaries could be photographed together.

Jewett was unable to comply at the time, but he found Washington to be a persistent president.

Later, on February 21, while participating in a seance at the home of a Dr. Ruggles in Brooklyn, Jewett received another spirit communication through automatic writing. It simply said, "Solomon, I am here," and was signed George Washington.

This time, at Washington's request, Solomon Jewett made an appointment with a photographer. A spiritualist magazine called *The Medium and Daybreak* reported the story in August 1884. Dr. Jewett, they said, "called on Mr. William Keeler, a photographer who was an entire stranger to him, and who could know nothing of the message received in Philadelphia."

The article continued, "Three [photographic] plates were exposed in succession at the one sitting, each one having a likeness of 'George Washington' in addition to Mr. Jewett."

As an aside, I have to step out of the narrative and tell you that I have examined one of these "spirit photographs"; it is reproduced quite clearly in Ida Washington's *History Of Weybridge*. The photo definitely shows Solomon Jewett sitting back to back with a transparent image of George Washington—who looks pretty much as he does on a one dollar bill. The photo is so obviously phony that one wonders how anyone could be so easily fooled.

I suspect it's all a matter of timing. During the age of Spiritualism, those who believed the dead could return were eager to prove it. To a degree, Spiritualism and photography developed together, both becoming popular in the mid-1800s. Photography was in its infancy. It wasn't universally understood. And there was something pretty mysterious—maybe even mystical—about photographic images captured on tin or paper. At the same time, people presumed that the camera did not lie.

Charlatans all over the United States and Europe made fortunes concocting phony spirit photographs. Thousands of such photos survive today. One famous example shows the ghost of Abraham Lincoln standing protectively behind his grieving, and believing, widow.

It is difficult to say after more than one hundred years whether Dr. Solomon Jewett of Weybridge, Vermont, was, in reality, a spiritual pioneer or merely a shepherd with the wool pulled over his eyes.

Most of the surviving documentation about him was originally produced by him, so we can conclude with some certainty that at the very least he was a tireless self-promoter.

*

The most recent interview I could find with him was published in the *San Francisco Chronicle* on July 21, 1883.

At that time he was living in a single room in the Snyder Block, 475 Ninth Street, Oakland, California. The reporter, who had no byline, described Jewett as "Plainly dressed in a well-worn suit of black."

He estimated Jewett's age to be sixty-five, a good ten years younger than his actual age, and found something in his aspect that suggested he had been "a wiry, well-made and energetic youth. A somewhat massive head, with bushy, iron-gray hair, might not attract particular attention, but for the steel-like glitter of his gray eyes."

The reporter said the room was clearly that of a reclusive and eccentric person. He remarked on the plainly covered bed, the table "littered with papers and writings and scraps of miscellaneous articles," a bunch of packing boxes, a small wardrobe, a shelf and a few chairs. "The walls of the room are literally studded with nails, but no pictures hang from them."

Most of this interview was devoted to inquiring about Dr. Jewett's career as a seer. "You, then, are possessed of a prophetic spirit?" the reporter asked.

"They come to me. I have had communications from the spirit life. When such things come to me I tell them for the good of mankind."

Dr. Jewett's success ratio wasn't sufficient to make him remembered as one of the great prophets of our time, but he apparently did accurately foresee the assassination of President Garfield (which made way for a Vermonter, Chester A. Arthur). He missed the mark with predictions about labor revolts, a great American business depression in 1883, and independence for Ireland by 1885.

Dr. Jewett died in Santa Barbara, California, in 1894 at the age of 86. Shepherd Home, well disguised by many structural modifications, still stands in Rutland, Vermont. The Rutland Historical Society and the building's current owner knew nothing about its colorful history.

Achsa and the Angels

If Calvin Coolidge becoming President hadn't put the village of Plymouth Notch on the map, chances are it would be there anyway. It was already famous because of an equally colorful but far less taciturn Vermonter—Achsa W. Sprague. In fact, Achsa was the first citizen in town to enjoy widespread fame.

Unfortunately, Ms. Sprague is all but lost to history. But during that brief period of the mid-nineteenth century when she was active, she quickly became a powerful and influential reformer who, among other things, battled for the rights of women, advocated the elimination of marriage, campaigned for improved treatment of prisoners, promoted abolition, and tirelessly traveled around the country in an effort to elevate the spiritual development of all who met her.

She was also a wonderfully prolific essayist and poet, yet much of her verse remains unpublished. And the women—even here in Vermont—for whom she so vigorously campaigned have for the most part forgotten her name. (Or maybe they simply can't pronounce it. It's AK-sa.)

The big—and perhaps mysterious—question is: Of all that she accomplished in her relatively short life—just thirty-four years—what was the true source of her power? Was it natural, or supernatural?

Well, the jury is still out.

Achsa White Sprague was born November 17, 1827, on a farm at Plymouth Notch, the sixth of eight children. The family was not well-to-do but was respected. Her father was the best educated man in town. All who knew him valued his opinion, though he had a reputation for occasional intemperance. In fact, there seemed to be a strain of ill health in the family. As historian Leonard Twynham points out, "[Achsa] had two sisters and one brother who were morons and simpletons."

Yet, somewhere in the family makeup there was the possibility of greatness. Achsa's cousin William, for example, became governor of Rhode Island.

Though her own formal education was slight, Achsa's family valued learning. From an early age she demonstrated uncommon drive and inquisitiveness, so the remote possibility of fame was within Achsa's visible horizon.

In her youth she was something of a prodigy. Her meager school experience was supplemented at home by her parents, and, at the extraordinary age of twelve, Achsa began teaching at the village's one-room stone schoolhouse. Though she was a good and competent educator, a few eyebrows were raised at some of her slightly oddball pronouncements. For example, she told her schoolchildren that their dead pets would go to heaven, and she created a local sensation when, after a death in the tiny village, she marched her students over to the funeral and explained, "These are the remains—this is only the shell—he is with God."

Although schoolteaching was an excellent occupation for a young woman in those days, God apparently had other plans for Achsa. In spite of her promising career and early independence, a mysterious malady struck her down when she was about twenty. For several years it progressed in debilitating stages, turning this bright, enthusiastic young woman into a cranky, antisocial recluse. We are not completely sure what happened to her. Her affliction has been described as "a scrofulous disease of the joints." This suggested a type of tuberculosis, but modern historians have speculated that it must have been some form of arthritis.

Whatever it may have been, she fought it. She even taught for two years on crutches, but it was a losing battle. Eventually it got so bad that she was confined to her room and, ultimately, couldn't even hold a writing implement.

But other odd symptoms invalidate today's speculative retrospective diagnoses: She got so she couldn't bear light; heavy shades were used to cover her windows. And noise, even common household sounds, became torture for her. As Betsey C. (Pelton) Soule wrote in an 1872 article prepared especially for Boston's *Banner of Light*, "Achsa . . . was seized by a fever, which followed the taking of a slight cold. The fever left her a very cripple, with weakened nerves. She complained so of the light that they were forced to exclude it from her apartment. Noise she could not endure, so the sounds of the kitchen were muffled as much as possible, in order that she might be at peace."

It was as if she were involuntarily entering a phase of heightened sensitivity, but at the time neither Achsa nor anyone else could guess there might be a reason for it.

In 1849, after she had become completely bedridden, she began keeping a diary. Reading her disheartened entries, one cannot help but think depression was a major component of her lingering malady. She chronicled the deaths of those around her, even watching her brother Ephraim waste away with consumption and die in 1850.

In her very first entry—dated June 1, 1849—she wrote, "Once more I am unable to walk or do anything else; have not been a step without crutches since Sunday and see no prospect of being any better; see nothing before me but a life of miserable helplessness."

She had been transformed from an unusually independent young woman of great promise to a hopelessly dependent drain on the family's meager resources. Still, in spite of the defeated tone of much of her journal, the zeal and determination she possessed prior to her affliction did not immediately abandon her. She sought the aid of local physicians and even tried what today we would call alternative therapies, including wearing "galvanic bands" and getting "magnetized." But nothing seemed to work.

"Her physicians said there was no hope of her recovery," Betsey Soule wrote, "and on several occasions she was thought to be dying. All available human skill was exerted, but in vain."

Achsa came to think of her room, "[t]he three windows of (which) were curtained with thick material, which created midnight at noonday," as a "prison" and a "living tomb."

She fought to retain some fragment of hope by reading and writing poetry, but was often unable to manipulate a pen. In time she was all but ready to give in and let the mysterious affliction have its way with her. Her diary and her poems express the decline of her optimism. As Walter J. Coates wrote in 1927, "Nowhere among Vermont writings is this attitude of longing, for life, for opportunity, for accomplishment— this intense spiritual rebellion at the decrees of Fate or Providence, at the raw deal dealt out by Destiny—so trenchantly reflected as in Achsa

W. Sprague's verse—that part of it called forth while imprisoned in a living dungeon of flesh."

"I scorn so mean a thing as life," she wrote, "I scorn the Giver, too."

*

During the winter of 1850 the Sprague family first heard about the famous "Rochester Rappings." It caused much discussion in the house, as it did all across the nation. Achsa's uncle Thomas Moore became quite interested in Spiritualism, and his household, like many others in Vermont, began experimenting with contacting the dead.

Though Achsa's body was of little use to her, her mind remained active. Needless to say, the fascinating topic of spirit return captivated her. "'Tis a beautiful idea," she wrote, "that our departed friends are around us and with us, that they can come back to guard us from temptation, to soothe us in affliction and to win us from sin."

Then one night Achsa heard tiny raps in her sick room. She found the faint tapping irritating. Eventually it grew intolerable. She figured the sounds must be coming from flies so she called her mother to shoo them away. In an effort to appease the girl, her mother went through the motions. The fact is, there were no flies; and the tiny tappings continued. Achsa had no choice but to become accustomed to them.

She later came to believe that this was the first attempt by the spirits to contact her. She then began to understand that the only possibility of her health returning was through the intervention of these spirits.

Ms. Soule wrote, "The first sensation preceding her cure, which was produced by the same invisible source, was an almost imperceptible, yet peculiar thrill in the thumb of her left hand, which had for sometime been benumbed and useless; its action was completely restored. Then an arm or limb began to be thrilled and exercised; though for a time said member was capable of being moved only when influenced [by the spirits], yet after a greater period, it became subject to her own volition. Afterwards her whole body became exercised."

This mysterious process ended a great suffering of seven years, two of which were spent in total darkness. Her spirit friends gave her the strength to rise from her sickbed.

With Achsa's recovery came the realization that the spirits had a mission for her. She found that they had granted her certain powers that she had never experienced before. Suddenly she was capable of automatic writing: Via her own hand the spirits composed encouraging prophesies about the coming end to her suffering and signed themselves "Thy Guardians." Once she completed a 4,600-line composition in just 72 hours. She also discovered she could draw and paint while blindfolded. And she could conduct spirit seances there in her Plymouth, Vermont, home. Her circle of family and friends grew—and daily they became more amazed at the change that had come over Achsa.

The same spirits that animated her hand to write also began to "exercise" her voice. Achsa would fall into trances during which she would speak eloquently and at length about subjects she knew very little about. She sometimes paced the room for hours, entranced, dictating to a secretary. Her primary themes were the divine grandeur of nature, the meaning of patriotism, and the understanding and application of religion. Thematically she affirmed faith and hope while frequently appealing for economic justice, including social and sexual equality.

Achsa gave her first formal public discourse at the Union Church in nearby South Reading on July 6, 1854.

After that her formerly quiet life did a complete turnaround: She found herself in the divine spotlight. She accepted invitations from Burlington, then from Boston and beyond. As her popularity grew, she found herself lecturing from three to six times a week. She traveled alone throughout New England, then journeyed to Maryland, Illinois, Iowa, Wisconsin, Missouri, and into Canada.

People loved her. As Betsey Soule wrote, "Her intelligence interested, while her amiability won all hearts. . . . As a woman she was pure and true; as a thinker she was deep and philosophical; as an orator, she was earnest and eloquent; and as a poetess, her imaginings were chaste, rich and beautiful."

She visited prisons and gave lectures there, following them with campaigns for prison reform. She opposed slavery at every opportunity. She advocated for the equality of women, reminding her listeners to condemn the contemporary notion that a "woman must be either a slave or a butterfly."

She gave benefit lectures, the proceeds from which went to charity, and she donated much of her own meager earnings to the poor. Her compensation was always left to the desertion of her audience. "I should like it if I had money that I might do more good," she said; "yet I cannot make spiritualism a stepping-stone to wealth; it seems like debasing the most beautiful things."

A Mr. Maynard wrote and offered to represent her, suggesting his management would increase her revenues. Achsa refused. "If money were my object," she wrote, "I might get four times what I do. But money is not my object. I would be instrumental in imparting truth and doing good. If I cannot do this, I have no wish to do anything."

All the while she did what she could to lift some of the economic burden from her relatives back home in Plymouth. When her father passed away in 1857, his last wish was that the angels deliver a eulogy at his funeral. His wish was granted; they spoke through Achsa.

*

It is difficult, while peering through the hazy glass of history, to get a look at Achsa at the lectern and to visualize the magic of her particular style of mediumship. Apparently she had a strong, earnest personality and was invariably perceived as genteel and likable. A Boston paper wrote, "Personally, Miss S. is extremely modest and retiring, possessed of those attractive and amiable qualities of head and heart which at once secure the confidence, respect, and affection of all who come in contact with her. The idea of deception or pretense on her part could be tolerated by no one who enjoys her acquaintance."

Photographs suggest Achsa was not a beautiful woman. In fact, her hectic schedule often left her looking tired and in some cases haggard. Still, she was apparently physically attractive and, when she spoke, generated a unique charisma that won converts as well as suitors. More than a half dozen men eagerly proposed marriage, suggesting they hadn't listened to a word she had said on the subject.

Throughout her life, Achsa remained single by choice.

During lectures she dressed in colorful clothing and, just before rising to speak, would perform an odd ritual. She would act as if she were washing her hands in invisible water. Then she'd wring her hands and pass her palms slowly over her face in what appeared to be a kind of cleansing ceremony. Finally, eyes closed, she'd rise and begin her lecture.

She normally commenced with a beautiful song and concluded with a long poem, "possessing much poetical merit and eloquence." Both were original and impromptu, composed on the spot in trance state with the inspiration of the spirits. She was also able to improvise hymns from subjects selected at random.

But most impressive was the spirit discourse. A writer from the *Terre Haute Daily Evening Journal* in Indiana pondered, "It is surprising how a lady, with less than the educational advantages of the clergyman or the lawyer, can pour forth, for an hour and a half or more, such beautiful sentences with such eloquent and impressible elocution, as no clergyman or lawyer, of our acquaintance, can equal."

Her lectures were always "packed to suffocation" and the circle of her influence grew to include thousands.

*

It is also difficult to summarize Achsa's short but influential career as a mystic, medium, and miracle worker. Twentieth-century historians seem little interested in the reality of the supernatural aspects of her life. Though Achsa herself was a hundred percent convinced her worldly accomplishments were inspired by her otherworldly guardians, historians prefer alternate explanations. For example, *A Plymouth Album* (1983), a local history prepared by Plymouth townspeople, maintains she recovered "from a disease with which she was bedridden for seven years, by *almost supernatural powers* of self-help" [emphasis mine].

Leonard Twynham, who in 1941 tried to rescue her from obscurity with a couple of articles in the Vermont Historical Society's magazine, strove to establish her as an important (though formerly undiscovered) Vermont writer. Yet he does admit, "Her accomplishments in literature are notable, but not so significant as her lectures or her personality."

Most recently Achsa was discussed at some length by Ann Braude in her fascinating book *Radical Spirits* (1989). Ms. Braude tends to dismiss Achsa's "angels" as deception or delusion, a contrivance that enabled her to publicly articulate her feminist and reformist views. Ms. Braude writes, "[Achsa] provides an ideal case study of the role played by mediumship in empowering a woman to assume a public career." Achsa Sprague's collected writings, Ms. Braude says, "depict the inner struggle of a woman at odds with the social strictures of her age. For Sprague wrote the messages herself, while in trance. Both the doubts and the reassurance emerged from somewhere within herself."

*

Whether miraculous or mundane, Achsa's 1853 "cure" marked the beginning of a new life for this complicated small-town woman.

She toured the country for six years, traveling all by herself, enduring uncomfortable public transportation, often stopping at different towns every other day. Generally she'd stay at the home of an area's leading Spiritualist family. In so doing she made wonderful friends all over the country.

Her routine was to speak each Sunday at the major town by invitation. Then, during the week, she'd address gatherings in smaller settlements in the vicinity. Sometimes she spoke twice a day. Her life was extremely full and busy, and it is a mystery how the recovered invalid persevered so tirelessly for so long.

Achsa's death also poses a bit of a mystery. As some tell it, her old illness suddenly came back to finally claim her. But if that old illness were in fact rheumatoid arthritis, it should not have been fatal.

Others say she was afflicted with "a throat problem" that silenced, then killed her.

Perhaps Walter J. Coates was closest to the truth when he wrote, "She literally wore herself out with work."

During the summer of 1861, Achsa was in Oswego, New York, to speak at a convention. She was, as Coates says, "Attackt with brain fever after a lecture." For a while she convalesced at the home of Mr. and Mrs. J. H. Crawford, where she devoted all of her diminishing strength to completing poems. Yet, perhaps sensing what was coming, she longed to revisit the Green Mountains and the loved ones who waited for her there. She made the trip in spite of her friends' pleas that she should stay and rest.

But she was never to recover.

She continued to write at a rate of about 500 lines a day. Then, after a carriage ride to Rutland and back, the end came. Achsa W. Sprague passed into the Spirit World on July 6, 1862, at age thirty-four.

Her funeral at the church in Plymouth Notch was as crowded as her lectures had been.

But the grave seemed not to silence her.

"Again and again her utterances from spirit-life inspire mediums of the land," Betsey Soule wrote in 1872, "and from the demonstrations received, we know that her labors in behalf of humanity are not yet finished."

She made frequent appearances—in spirit form—at the Eddy seances in Chittenden. And on June 17, 1876, a letter from Achsa appeared in the *Banner of Light*. "Although it is some years since I passed away," she wrote, "I am still a worker in the spiritual realm, still holding my position as a medium. . . . True, my body lasted not many years, but my spirit was ever strong, and it is strong today."

From her new home in the next realm Achsa continued to write for various spirit newspapers. Then, in 1881, via a medium, she allegedly authored a book called *Achsa W. Sprague and Mary Clark's Experiences in the First Ten Spheres of Spirit Life*.

In retrospect, all we can conclude for sure is that Achsa W. Sprague's recovery, career, passing, and posthumous publications are mysterious indeed.

Perhaps the answer lies in the three words inscribed on Achsa's tombstone in the little cemetery near her mother's house in Plymouth Notch. It says simply, "I STILL LIVE."

Who knows, maybe it's true.

The Wicked Witch of Wall Street

Vermonters have always been known as a thrifty lot. But if tightfistedness were an Olympic event, the all-time champion would be Hetty Green, Bellows Falls' own Queen of cupidity.

For whatever it may be worth, Hetty was not a Vermonter by birth. She was born Henrietta Howland Robinson at New Bedford, Massachusetts, in 1835. Her family had made a fortune in the whaling industry and had become completely obsessed with money. The Robinsons passed their monetary monomania along to Hetty.

By the time she was six years old Hetty sat on her father's knee so they could read the financial papers together. At these times Daddy dispensed such wisdom as, "Never owe anyone anything, not even a kindness."

As a young woman she'd launch a bombast any time the Robinsons considered spending even a modest amount of money. She realized that every dime her parents spent was a dime she would fail to inherit later.

On her twenty-first birthday Hetty refused to light the candles on her cake, saying she didn't want to waste them. Next day she cleaned them up and returned them to the store for a refund.

This parsimonious performance seems especially odd, for on that same twenty-first birthday Hetty inherited seven and a half million dollars, beginning a trend that would eventually make her the richest woman in the world. And perhaps the most eccentric.

When her father finally passed away Hetty inherited another fortune, which she tried to compound by beating her aunt Sylvia out of her portion of the legacy.

Then Hetty upped her ante considerably when—shortly after the Civil War—she married the portly forty-six year-old merchant Edward H. Green, a native of Bellows Falls, Vermont. Though Green was also a millionaire, Hetty insisted that he sign a premarital agreement relinquishing all claim to her money.

Apparently Hetty was in a bit of a hurry to have children; if she didn't, and if she were to die childless, she was afraid her money would be passed along to her relatives, a notion she couldn't abide.

So Edward and Hetty had two children, Ned and Sylvia.

Through a series of shrewd but more conventional investments Hetty made their fortune grow, and won herself the title of "The Queen of Wall Street." However, rival investors, jealous of her repeated successes, preferred to call her "The Witch of Wall Street"— and that's the title she eventually took to her grave.

Not only was the witch preternaturally clever in managing her considerable funds, she also gave a whole new definition to the word wicked.

It seems she enjoyed destroying people. As she had already demonstrated with her aunt, Hetty wouldn't even spare the people closest to her. When she and her husband disagreed over the purchase of some railroad stock, she mercilessly railroaded him right into the poorhouse, where he died owning nothing but seven dollars and a watch.

After Edward's death Hetty's eccentricities grew unchecked. For a time maternal instincts seemed to override her niggardly nature. She placed her daughter in a convent—not because the girl was especially pious but because convents didn't charge room and board. And, in perhaps her most unselfish gesture, Hetty swore she'd make her son Ned the richest man in the world.

That is, if she didn't kill him first. One time in Bellows Falls, little Ned injured his leg in a sledding accident. Hetty tried treating him at home but his condition worsened. She knew if she took him to a local doctor they would charge her for the treatment. So she made Ned wait until their next trip to New York, where she could take him to a free clinic. Hetty dragged the suffering boy from clinic to clinic, looking for a doctor who'd treat him for free. By the time she checked him into a charity ward of a Manhattan hospital, gangrene had done its work. Sometime later Ned lost his leg to the surgeon's knife.

But Hetty got even by forcing one of the clinics out of business.

*

In Vermont, Hetty's neighbors remembered her as that eccentric rich woman in the big, square, yellow-brick house on Church Street: a mansion without the costly convenience of plumbing. She owned only two or three tattered secondhand dresses that were either black or so dirty they looked it. She never washed her underwear because, she said, washing would make it wear out faster. In winter she stuffed newspapers under her clothing to save buying an overcoat. Hetty never paid her bills unless she was forced to, and then she wrote checks on scraps of paper in order to avoid printing fees. When she traveled she rode around in a carriage that had last been used as a hen house. She always went to bed before dark so she wouldn't have to burn candles.

Sadly, these were the conditions under which Ned and Sylvia grew up.

*

Associates on Wall Street remembered a kooky old crone too frugal to rent an office. Instead, she set up operations on the floor of the Chemical and National Bank. Working from old crates and boxes, Hetty paused only long enough to eat a lunch of cold oatmeal from a pail, or to snack on raw onions, a delicacy she considered economical and highly nutritious. This miserly millionairess bought daily newspapers, read them, and resold them at a two-cent profit.

In later years her caution turned to paranoia. She moved from one cheap boarding house to the next, trying to avoid tax collectors, creditors, kidnappers, and fortune hunters—all the enemies she was sure were out to rob or poison her.

It was her practice never to take a direct route anywhere. Her evasion strategies included doubling back after pretending to leave, unpredictable dodges into alleyways, and concealing herself in the recesses of doorways. Strange at it may sound, such tactics actually helped her to avoid state and city tax collectors. Hetty had no intention of giving her money away. In fact, no one was ever quite sure just what Hetty intended to do with her fortune.

Surprisingly, in 1910 the elderly Hetty turned the bulk of management responsibilities over to Ned and went to live with a friend—rent free, of course. There, at the home of Annie Leary, a Papal Countess, Hetty confronted the cook about squandering her employer's money on whole milk when skimmed milk was far cheaper. It was one of many such disputes, but this time the cook answered back. Hetty had never experienced such insolence. Right in the middle of the argument, Hetty suffered the series of strokes that killed her. On July 3, 1916, Hetty Green died. She was eighty-one years old and worth over 100 million dollars.

Hetty's body was taken back to Bellows Falls to be buried in the family plot in the Immanuel Cemetery. But for years it was impossible to find her grave; you see, the "Richest Woman in the World" spared herself the expense of a headstone.

*

In her own perverse maternal way, Hetty had provided well for her children. She saw to it that Ned got a good education. Then she bought him the Texas Central Railroad and a branch of the Houston & Texas so he could hone his business skills.

And, she saw to it that her daughter Sylvia got plenty of on-the-job experience mending clothes, cooking, washing dishes, cleaning, shopping, and doing all the things necessary to marry her off in 1909 to the sixty-three-year-old Matthew Astor Wilks, the millionaire great-grandson of John Jacob Astor.

But in addition to life skills and a shared fortune, Hetty left her children something else as well—a wealth of eccentricities.

In a sense, you might say that Ned and Sylvia had grown up poor, in spite of their mother's fabulous wealth. When Hetty died, Ned began to overcompensate.

This six-foot-four-inch one-legged giant began squandering money at a rate of three million dollars a year in a kind of self-indulgent postponed adolescence. He acquired the largest stamp collection in the world and had a collection of jewels that wasn't far smaller. Ned liked to indulge his compulsion to acquire by collecting such fancy finery as bejeweled chamber pots and diamond-studded chastity belts. He also had one of the most complete libraries of erotica in the United States. Of the many high-priced call girls with whom he kept company, he finally married his favorite—a woman named Mable from Chicago.

He named his private Pullman after her, and acquired a fleet of other novel transportation vehicles, such as a collection of race cars and even a blimp.

Without getting into the symbolism of it all, Ned's goal was to have the longest private yacht in the world—bigger than Morgan's or Astor's. Unfortunately, because of the war, he wasn't permitted to build one. So instead he bought a 225-foot Great Lakes passenger boat, had it cut in half, and added 40 feet to the middle.

Always preoccupied with size, Ned had just started his collection of whale penises—commencing with a 14 footer—when death collected him in 1936.

*

Ned's sister Sylvia took more after their mother.

She showed up after Ned's death with four armored cars and armed guards to collect her brother's 20-million-dollar gem collection. Then she went back to the seclusion of her Fifth Avenue apartment where she lived like a hermit, using her mother's dilapidated furnishings and replicating her mother's spending habits.

To be fair, she was slightly more generous than Hetty. She did, after all, donate her father's old house to the town of Bellows Falls. She had it bulldozed in 1940 to make room for a park. But her civic-mindedness ended when some local ingrate asked, "Why didn't you leave it standing and donate it as a community house?"

"Why don't you donate yours," Sylvia said and stalked off back into seclusion.

Sylvia passed away on February 5, 1951. Because of her mother's careful family planning she was the last Green. And, because there were no close relatives to inherit it, Sylvia's 90-million-dollar estate was divided among sixty-three charities.

The Truman Show

In *Green Mountain Ghosts* I wrote about a wonderful human oddity from Cabot, an eight-year-old mathematical prodigy named Zerah Colburn. In addition to extra brains, Zerah had extra digits as well: he had six toes on each foot, but that probably does not explain his numerical prowess.

Nor does it explain why Vermont should produce a second similarly gifted child. The heir to Zerah's computational wizardry was a farm boy from Royalton named Truman H. Safford. Truman was born in 1836, just two years before Zerah passed away, which eliminates reincarnation as a possible explanation.

Anyway, Vermont's second youthful human calculator went on to become, arguably, the greatest mental prodigy this country has ever produced. The source of his peculiar genius remains a mystery; it was almost as if he *knew* things without first *learning* them. For example, at just twenty-two months old Truman could recite the alphabet. Apparently he'd taught himself from his set of toy wooden blocks.

One day when he was six he announced to his mother that if she would tell him the distance around their farm in *rods*, he would give her the same measurement computed in "barleycorns."

Mrs. Safford didn't know the perimeter of their farm. With a bit of research she found it was 1,040 rods. Her son concentrated, went through some peculiar facial contortions, and in less than a minute announced that 1,040 rods is equal to 617,760 barleycorns.

I should add that I have no way to verify this figure. Armed with a dictionary and a pocket calculator, it took me a good deal longer to determine that 1,040 rods equals 17,160 feet—a fair sized piece of property. I still have no idea what a "barleycorn" is.

But the calculations involved were a good deal easier for this simple farm boy who could solve complicated geometry, algebra, or trigonometry problems. In his head. In seconds. Without pencil and paper.

In 1846, before he was ten years old, Truman created an almanac for the town of Bradford. It was so successful that the next year the boy expanded his operation and created almanacs for Boston, Philadelphia, and Cincinnati.

Perhaps it was while compiling his almanacs that Truman discovered what was to become a lifelong interest in astronomy. In any event, his fame spread and pretty soon legions of skeptical inquisitors requested they be permitted to test him.

A Rev. Adams of the American Bible Society grilled him for three hours. Truman had always been a frail and nervous boy, so as the grueling interrogation continued he grew more and more exhausted. His obvious fatigue only encouraged the Grand Inquisitor to assail him with more difficult questions. Ultimately, Rev. Adams asked the boy to multiply a fifteen-digit number by itself.

Another minister witnessed the results of this debacle. His report gives us some insight into the visible signs of the boy's mysterious internal calculating processes. He wrote, "[Truman] flew around the room like a top, pulled his [trousers] over his boots, bit his hand, rolled his eyes in their sockets, and then [seemed] to be in agony, until, in not more than one minute. .. [he produced the correct answer]." It was the largest sum Truman Safford ever computed and it left him completely exhausted.

Perhaps recalling Zerah Colburn's sad end, Truman's parents put a stop to the torturous tests and all other exploitation.

Edward Everett [not the same Edward Everett we'll meet in a later chapter], then President of Harvard, recognized Truman's obvious potential. He persuaded the family to move to Cambridge, Massachusetts, so Truman could get a proper education.

Truman graduated from Harvard in 1854 but stayed on as an astronomer. Then, in 1866, he was made director of the Dearborn Observatory at the University of Chicago. Later he taught astronomy at Williams College, where he remained until his death in 1901 at age sixty-five.

If there had been some quantifiable method or technique to his lightning calculations, Truman never revealed it. Either it was a secret he refused share, or a problem he just couldn't solve.

Indeed, there was something almost supernatural about his amazing intellect. At Truman's funeral President Carter of Williams College said, "[Truman] came nearer to Goethe's claim that by reading one page of a book he could tell all that there was in it, than anyone I have ever known."

Perhaps Rev. George Denison of Kenyon College most effectively summed up the mystery and meaning of Truman H. Safford's life and career. He said, "I believe him to surpass anything on record in the history of man and to open a door by which we are permitted to see something of what our minds are, and what they can become, when the natural body shall have been exchanged for the spiritual."

Bristol's Forgotten Prophetess

There is an old, all but forgotten manuscript in the archives at the Sheldon Museum that—if events had unfolded differently—could have changed the world.

It is dated March 29, 1843, and it is written in the hand of a Congregationalist minister, the Reverend Calvin Butler of Bristol, Vermont.

Mr. Butler carefully describes events that had happened to one of his parishioners, Mrs. Melissa Warner, about two weeks earlier. He was careful not to interpret anything she said, so the modern reader is free to ponder the content of the text and to speculate about the meaning of the events described.

Today we must ask, as did Rev. Butler a century and a half ago, what in the world happened to Melissa?

As we approach the millennium, many social scientists speculate that human behavior will change: we'll witness a resurgence of mystical thinking, supernatural experiences, and end-of-the-world terrors.

But mystical visions and doomsday predictions have always been business-as-usual here in Vermont. For example, in *Green Mountain Ghosts* I wrote about William Miller, whose thrice-failed end-of-the-world prophesies nonetheless led to the Seventh-Day Adventist church. And there was John P. Weeks of North Danville, who died, visited Heaven and Hell in the company of his Guardian Angel, then came back to tell the story. And who can forget that venerable Vermont seer Joseph Smith, whose early mystical dabbling eventually evolved into the Mormon religion?

These Vermonters—right or wrong—have been immortalized as a result of their mysticism.

And then there's poor Melissa.

According to Rev. Butler's account, on the 13th or 14th of March, 1843, Melissa experienced a startling daytime revelation.

At around noon, while wide awake and working in her home, she chanced to look up at the sky. There, unbelievably, she saw two men suspended among the clouds. They descended "quick as lightning from heaven." The airborne pair did not come all the way to earth. Instead they hovered weightlessly near the top of her house.

The closer one seemed to radiate a golden glow as he sat, half-reclining in an invisible chair, suspended in midair. Melissa saw a wound or opening in his chest that somehow convinced her that she was looking at Jesus Christ.

The second form remained a little farther away, but Mrs. Warner clearly saw it was a luminous cloud. Again she somehow knew who it was: God the Father.

Instantly the vision expanded full-scale to include crowds of sinners. Mrs. Warner said they were "standing . . . speechless and . . . perfectly petrified with horror, agony, anguish, and unutterable despair . . . at the dreadful doom they saw hastening" toward them.

After Mrs. Warner had a moment to digest the terrifying scene before her, Jesus spoke directly to her, saying, "You see I am coming [and] have advanced almost to the earth and shall soon be there." He commanded Mrs. Warner to "warn the impenitent of their danger and instruct them to prepare for my coming. Tell all of my speedy approach for they are stupid and insensible of it.

"Make haste," he emphasized. "Make the greatest possible haste. Lose not a moment."

Then, as she stared directly at him, he disappeared. The shocked multitude vanished, too. When she looked around for God the Father, he had gone as well.

But Mrs. Warner was not alone.

And her ordeal was far from over.

At this point a dark cloud descended, "as if part of the Heavens were let down toward the earth."

This vaporous presence she recognized as the Holy Ghost. But, as God spoke directly through it, Mrs. Warner noted one peculiar detail: The central part of the cloud opened and closed like a mouth as God spoke, explaining how Mankind's stupidity and disbelief arose from human reason, vain philosophy, and worldly reasoning. And, it insisted, they *had better change their ways*!

With that the cloud vanished, leaving the startled Mrs. Warner alone and completely confident that the second coming of Christ was just a few days away.

*

Almost immediately afterward, as might be expected, doubt began to set in. What she had seen was impossible; who in the world would believe her? If she told such a story around town it could ruin her family's reputation. At the same time, the tortured woman feared that if she didn't speak up, the blood of souls would be on her hands.

She imagined a dialogue with "The Tempter," who told her what "a foolish thing" it was and "filled her mind with all sorts of temptations to prevent the public or private announcement of what she had seen and felt."

Satan reminded her that God *had* deceived Jonah and might well be deceiving her, too.

The poor woman was so wracked with doubt that she longed for yet another assurance that "Christ was really and truly to come." She dared not pray for further evidence because, as she well knew, the former display was "so clear and unequivocal."

Wrestling constantly with her uncertainty, Mrs. Warner waited, allowing several days to pass before she cautiously mentioned the event to her family. But she soft-pedaled it, saying only "that she had certain evidence" that the second coming was at hand.

On Sunday evening, March 19th, hoping for a quiet rest, she retired at midnight and fell asleep. A little before 2:00 A.M. she was awakened by something gently stroking her face. She opened her eyes to see an agitating cloud hovering above her bed. It was Jesus, sternly reprimanding her for her disbelief and for failing to spread the word about his arrival. Then he left, gathering up and vanishing into the wall as quickly as a bolt of lightning.

She was unable to sleep any more that night. The following day she was so upset that family members remarked on her trembling.

Screwing up her courage as much as she could, Melissa Warner spent time the following week writing several letters to distant friends, telling them to prepare for the second coming, "which she assured them was nigh at hand." Then, on March 29, 1843, determined to do her duty, Mrs. Warner sought out her clergyman, Rev. Calvin Butler, and told him everything. He wrote the description from which this chapter is taken.

*

The upshot, of course, is that Jesus failed to put in the promised appearance, so Mrs. Melissa Warner, Bristol's reluctant prophetess, faded into historical oblivion.

But perhaps her obscurity is undeserved. Perhaps the timid farm woman actually saved the world by failing to pass on fair warning that it would soon end. Maybe the angry God decided that if Melissa wouldn't hold up her end of the bargain, why should He hold up His?

In many ways Melissa's fantastic experience is typical of the religious fact or folly that was common among our Protestant ancestors at that time. But there is one detail about it that, at least in my mind, makes Mrs. Warner's vision extraordinary and worthy of closer study.

It is an odd bit of business in the earliest part of the manuscript when she describes her initial visual impression of the two mysterious visitors. Remember, she is talking about the two entities that arrive from the sky. This is an exact quote from Rev. Butler's account:

"In their appearance they were very similar. They were very large in stature and had very large heads and very long faces. Their faces were dark brown but like the mulatto. Their eyes were closed. Their hair of dark brown hung curling down upon their shoulders. They wore hats and were dressed in black clothing. She saw nothing white about them and when she saw them they retired a little into the heavens and changed their appearance."

And changed their appearance?

If the confused Mrs. Warner had made up or imagined the whole incident, one wonders why she would have included this odd shape-shifting episode? Why not say simply that a vision of Jesus and of God the Father manifested in all their celestial magnificence? Why depict long-haired, dark-skinned men in black who appear, notice that she is watching them, and only then zoom off and disguise themselves as recognizable religious icons?

As strange as the whole story must have sounded to Reverend Butler in 1874, it seems every bit as strange today. And today the odd events in Bristol are not nearly as easily explained.

TWICE HANGED

Sex. Murder. Courtroom theatrics. Madness. And a grisly death. Rarities in Vermont, perhaps, but nonetheless dear to the heart of every American. Yet long before the days of lethal au pairs, O. J. Simpson, or JonBenet Ramsay, there was that most sinister of all Vermonters, Mary Mable Rogers.

Mary Mable Rogers?

For more than eleven straight months she made page one headlines all over New England. Yet in spite of her fleeting fame, poor Miss Rogers was forgotten long before Windsor's Castle-on-the-Connecticut was transformed from prison to elder-housing.

Even her name is unmemorable, more readily evoking a prim spinster than a nubile femme fatale. But at the turn of the century, Malevolent Mary was the center of a media whirlwind rivaling anything from today's scandal sheets or tabloid TV.

For Mary was the last woman to be hanged in the state of Vermont.

And weirder still—she was hanged twice.

Rightly so, perhaps, for she perpetrated what one newspaper called "the most diabolical crime ever committed" in the Green Mountain state. That crime, of course, was murder. And it is likely she killed more than once.

Married at fifteen, she and her twenty-eight-year-old husband Marcus lived in Shaftsbury, Vermont. When their two-month-old daughter died suddenly, vigilant in-laws suspected foul play. Mary maintained the child had simply slipped from her lap and landed on its head.

However, the next time someone died at Mary's hands there was no ambiguity. In 1902, after three years of marriage, Mary deserted her husband and moved to Bennington. To bankroll her newfound independence she wanted to get her hands on a $500 life insurance policy. Trouble was, her husband was still alive. So, with the aid of a love-struck, though dim-witted, admirer, Mary feigned reconciliation. To prove she had seen the error of her ways, Mary took Marcus for a romantic stroll along the Walloomsac River. They sat down at a pleasant spot where she tied him up, smothered him to death with chloroform-soaked handkerchiefs, attached a fake suicide note to his hat, and dumped him into the water.

The inept crime was quickly solved; her moronic accomplice fessed up to save his own neck. After a three-week trial, Mary was sentenced to death by hanging. However, popular sentiment in Vermont dictated that women should never be hanged—not even for murder. Vermont's legislature disagreed. When they reviewed her case for clemency, Mary lost by forty votes.

The sheriff carted her from Rutland jail to Windsor prison. Along the way great masses of people waited at every train station get a look at her. Apparently she was an extremely attractive woman. One newspaper described her as "tall, well-built, with flashing black eyes and great masses of raven hair."

Media excitement brought the nation's women to her aid. One crusader from Ohio accumulated 36,000 signatures to save Mary from the gallows. A Connecticut woman rallied support through publicity, fund raising, and petitions. In prison Mary received an avalanche of letters and gifts. She also hosted a procession of visitors—including many state and prison officials—who apparently took a liking to her. She was given a sitting room with a window and all the books, games, and needlecraft she wanted.

Meanwhile the hangman, Sheriff Henry Peck of White River Junction, was building the gallows, sending out invitations to the execution, and supervising the setup of a "media room" at the local railroad station.

Opposing forces gathered strength, bombarding the attorney general, governor, and press with letters and petitions. Defense lawyers worked maniacally on inventive appeals. Three different well-wishers tried smuggling poison to Mary so she could beat the hangman.

At length Governor Bell granted the first of three eleventh-hour reprieves. During the investigation the prison itself came under scrutiny.

Though corruption was disclosed, the Vermont Supreme Court still rejected Mary's request for a new trial.

Before Sheriff Peck could assemble his gallows a second time, Governor Bell granted a second reprieve so lawyers could prepare a writ of error for the U.S. Supreme Court.

This too was refused. Peck went back to work on the gallows only to be interrupted again by another ingenious legal ploy. This time Mary's lawyers took her—and her growing entourage—to Brattleboro U.S. District Court for a writ of *habeas corpus*. The buggy she rode in was like a circus wagon, flanked by reporters and curiosity seekers from all over the country.

The Brattleboro judge sent the case along to the U.S. Supreme Court, while the ever-optimistic Sheriff Peck decided to leave the gallows standing.

Somewhere along, Mary did a little creative defense work on her own. Although she was constantly under observation or soundly secured in solitary confinement, she somehow managed to get pregnant. She was gambling that officials would not further tarnish their declining image by hanging a pregnant woman. But her success as a gambler was no better than as a murderess: the Supreme Court refused to hear Mary's appeal, and Governor Bell didn't buy the alleged pregnancy.

On December 7, 1905—at age twenty-two—Mary Mable Rogers was hanged for the first time at Windsor prison.

But remember, she was a tall woman. When the trap opened she landed safely on her tiptoes.

The second hanging occurred when the executioner and a physician rushed forth, grabbed the rope, and hauled Mary choking and thrashing into the air. Though all local newspapers said the execution went smoothly, it actually took Mary fourteen and a half minutes before she strangled to death.

Her legacy is a case with more twists than a Vermont backroad, littered with cherished public attention-getters like scandal, sex, corruption, and murder. There's a cast of colorful characters including a vamp, a victim, an entrepreneurial hangman, and a succession of guards with records soiled by drug dealing, suicide attempts, and more. There is the high drama of courtroom combat, legal gymnastics, and Supreme Court rulings. And of course there's the population of Vermont who, then as now, remain sharply divided on the subject of capital punishment.

Sounds like a movie of the week to me.

THE MEANEST MAN IN PEACHAM

On the morning of Friday, March 5, 1869, Ben Kimball and some men from Peacham woke to the aftermath of one of the worst snow storms in Vermont history. They dug their way through shoulder-high drifts, rounded up their oxen, and began the near-impossible task of breaking out the snow-covered roads.

But Ben's sled turned up some cloth, brightly colored against the virgin snow. Upon examination, he discovered the cloth was attached to the corpse of an old woman, frozen on the road.

Soon the crew made more gruesome discoveries. The body of a local woman, thirty-five-year-old Mary Davis, sat near a stone wall where she'd apparently frozen to death. They then found her son's body. Eight-year-old Willie was upright, poised as if he'd been fighting his way through the storm from Farrow's farmhouse back to his mother's side.

Authorities at the grim scene slowly pieced together a tragedy that says more about the cold heart of man than it does about the cruel Vermont winter.

The old woman was Mrs. Esther Emmons, an impoverished widow of seventy-four. She had been in Hardwick, taking care of her son, who'd recently become disabled. With no income, he'd applied to the town for assistance. The overseer of the poor—properly frugal with public funds—told Mrs. Emmons that *her* upkeep was not the town's responsibility; she would have to leave.

Her daughter Mary and eight-year-old Willie came from Peacham to fetch her. But they'd have to walk the twenty miles back home. So on a cold, clear Thursday morning they set out. Although Mrs. Emmons was hearty for her years, she still slowed them down.

By the time they reached Peacham Woods, a barrier of thick storm clouds had buried the sun. Light flakes drifted around them.

Rather than cross the little-traveled road through Peacham Woods during a storm, they decided to seek shelter at one of the few homes along the way. First they stopped at the Bean place. But Mr. Bean, with all the human warmth of Pontius Pilot at the wash basin, turned them away.

Trudging onward, the trio entered the woods. Snow was falling heavily now. Overhanging branches offered little protection. Flakes piled on their shoulders and hair. Wet clumps clung to their feet. A stinging wind drove icy crystals against their barely protected faces. They would stop, cling together for warmth, then move on a few more yards.

Between fierce blasts of wind they heard the unmistakable tinkling of sleighbells. A heavily bundled neighbor recognized them and stopped. It was a one-horse sleigh, not big enough for everyone. And the little horse was too exhausted to pull much additional weight. The driver could only take the old woman.

But Mrs. Emmons elected to stay with her family. All were confident of a night's lodging at the next house.

As the fury of wind and snow increased, the old woman could barely move her numb and exhausted legs. The younger people had to pull her along as the Stewart farmhouse came into sight.

Hope gave way to an appalling surprise. Without explanation, and in words more chilling than the raging storm, Stewart curtly dismissed them, saying, "I'm taking no one in."

The unbelieving family turned away, facing the storm at its worst. Their only hope was the next farmhouse, owned by the Farrow family. Known to all as kindly folks, the Farrows lived less than a mile down the road. But could they make it?

As we have already seen, they could not. The next day, tracks still visible in the snow told part of the story: Mrs. Emmons had fallen repeatedly; Willie and Mary had picked her up and helped her along. When she could no longer stand, Willie went for help. He had struggled toward the Farrows' farm, no doubt guided through the blinding snow by a lighted window. But the boy had become confused; he'd turned around within thirty feet of safety. Perhaps that was when the Farrows turned out their light to go to bed.

Later, during questioning, Mr. Farrow said that yes, he had heard faint calls amid the howling storm. But—in an incredibly gothic disclosure—he attributed the cries to his demented daughter who was locked away in a room upstairs.

As the local minister put it, "None who lay this side of the fatal spot is guilty."

The embarrassed townsfolk eventually erected a monument to atone for their collective sins. The epitaph in Peacham cemetery reads:

Erected by the Citizens of Peacham to the memory of Esther Emmons, aged 74, Mary Davis aged 35, and Willie aged 8, a mother, daughter, and grandchild who perished in the snow on the night of March 5 A.D. 1869 having traveled on foot nearly 15 miles during the day.

But in the minds of most, it was cold-hearted Mr. Stewart who was to blame. Reportedly, he suffered horrendous guilt for the rest of his life. Even on his deathbed he relived the horrifying events of 1869. Just before he died—so the story goes—his body shivered as if from terrible cold. He cried out that he was freezing. And, though it was mid July when he died, Mr. Stewart's corpse was as cold as ice.

The Mystery of Charles Mudgett

On a dark, blustery morning in July 1890, the people of Cambridge, Vermont, might have thought a Wild West show was coming to town.

When the train pulled into Cambridge Junction two masked men jumped off. Each carried two six-guns and looked very much like cowboys. They waited by the tracks, peering about ominously, holding people at bay with icy stares.

Soon two similarly attired individuals jumped out of the baggage car.

The first two stood guard as the second pair of masked men unloaded a big box. It didn't contain props for a cowboy show, however. Observers soon recognized that it was a casket. Two bodyguards remained with the coffin at all times as the other pair went into town to make arrangements for a burial.

The casket was guarded constantly. No one—not even the undertaker—was permitted to approach it.

As curious townsfolk looked on, the four masked strangers loaded the box onto a horse-drawn hearse and accompanied it over the bumpy gravel road to the cemetery in North Cambridge. They instructed the undertaker to be sure the grave was two feet deeper than normal. Though hired men dug the eight foot hole, the four masked men placed the coffin into the ground and remained to oversee the interment.

Comparing notes afterward, all the observers agreed that the mysterious pallbearers behaved as if the box were unusually heavy.

Until the casket was securely covered with earth it had been constantly under surveillance. No one was allowed to touch it or lift it or move it or open it.

The grave was then sealed with a huge slab of concrete.

An oversized gravestone weighing more than three tons topped the whole thing. It is a three-tiered monument that stands about eight feet tall. To this day it is the largest and most prominently placed stone in the remote little North Cambridge cemetery.

Finally, the whole cemetery plot—about fifteen feet by twenty feet—was framed with a stone curbing. It is interrupted only where two steps face the headstone, defining, in effect, an entrance to the bordered grave.

When all was done, the masked men disappeared as mysteriously as they had come.

During the whole ordeal, townsfolk were buzzing with questions and speculation. They had, of course, identified the dead man and had put together a possible scenario explaining what had just gone on in their little town.

The mysterious strangers had returned to them the body of a native son, Charles H. Mudgett.

Mudgett had been born in North Cambridge in the early 1860s. He was the oldest son in a family of nineteen children. Some remembered him as the "black sheep" of the Mudgett family. Though handsome and poised, Charles had always been a restless, sullen lad who rebelled against his father's authoritarian nature. He always seemed too confined in his own hometown, occasionally getting into trouble with the neighbors and storekeepers.

When he was old enough, he left home, heading west to seek his fortune. For a long while his family heard nothing from him.

Then word about him began to drift back into town. According to some accounts he had struck it rich out West. Others said he had bought a big ranch in Montana and was earning a fortune in cattle. Still others heard that he had turned to crime, robbing trains, banks, and Wells Fargo wagons.

But the fact is, no one knew for sure what had become of Charles Mudgett until the day he came home in a box. And then all they knew was that he was dead. Trouble is, they couldn't even be sure of that.

For over a century now the people of Cambridge have been puzzling about the fate of Charles Mudgett. His unconventional homecoming is only the tip of the mystery. His gravestone in the North Cambridge cemetery is a constant reminder that the mystery may never be solved.

At first sight, the headstone seems normal enough, but even a brief examination is guaranteed to leave the observer puzzled; the stone and gravesite definitely have certain peculiarities.

First, it is massive, the biggest in the graveyard, clearly visible from anywhere in the cemetery. It must have cost a great deal.

The front of the gravestone is inscribed as follows:

CHARLES H. MUDGETT
BORN AT CAMBRIDGE, VERMONT, ON THIS HOMESTEAD OF HIS FATHERS.
DROWNED IN EARLY MANHOOD IN THE
MISSOURI RIVER, AT FORT BENTON MONTANA.
JUNE 29th, 1890
IN THE EXECUTION OF HIS DUTY.
BROUGHT TO THE HOME OF HIS CHILDHOOD
BY HIS LOVING FRIEND, MILTON EVERETT MILNER.
HE WAS STRONG, HANDSOME, BRAVE, KIND, SINCERE,
A HERO AND A GENTLEMAN.

At first glance the story in stone might seem innocent and straightforward enough: Mudgett had found work on a Montana ranch belonging to Milton E. Milner. He had been drowned on the job, crossing a river. His employer, who had become fond of the young Vermonter, returned him to his hometown and oversaw his burial.

But let's look a little closer. The stone is also covered with odd words and puzzling symbols. Clues, perhaps?

Below the inscription there is a circle that encloses a backward L in which two reclining hearts are carved. Circling the hearts—between two more L's, are the Latin words "AVE ATQVE VALE" meaning "Hail and Farewell."

The back of the stone, in all capital letters, says:

A LITTLE SEASON OF LOVE AND LAUGHTER,
OF LIGHT AND LIFE, AND PLEASURE AND PAIN,
AND HORROR OF OUTER DARKNESS AFTER,
AND DUST RETURNETH TO DUST AGAIN,
THEN THE LESSER LIFE SHALL BE AS THE GREATER,
AND THE LOVER OF LIFE SHALL JOIN THE HATER,
AND THE ONE THING COMETH SOONER OR LATER,
AND NO ONE KNOWETH THE LOSS OR GAIN.

Strangely, both ends of the stone are engraved with identical odd symbols: two backward L's, one at top right, the other at bottom left. At bottom right there is a cross, the top and right arms of which are connected by a parabola to form what might be a hybrid of an "X" and a capital "P." At the very bottom, the name "MUDGETT" is carved. The left end of the stone is identical except at the bottom. Instead of saying MUDGETT, as one would expect, it says "MILNER."

Facing the grave from outside the stone border, one sees two steps. The bottom step is blank; the top says " MILNER."

In the grass, between the step and the stone itself, off to the right, a smaller stone says simply "Charlie." Though there is plenty of space for more caskets, apparently "Charlie" is the only one buried on the large plot.

I suspect that by now the mysteries of Charles Mudgett's tomb are becoming obvious. Over the century since his burial there has been a good deal of conjecture about what it all means. So much, in fact, that the grave has taken on a certain "atmosphere." Some local folks tend to avoid it; children won't set foot within the stone perimeter. Perhaps these simple superstitions are all that is left of the controversy that once surrounded the death and burial of Charles H. Mudgett.

But questions remain:

First, why all the pistoled pomp and circumstance? Why was it so important that none of the locals could open—or even touch—the casket?

Why did four men from "away" have to hide their faces? If they had transported "Charlie's" body all the way from Montana they would have been unrecognizable to the good people of Cambridge, even without masks. So what was the point?

Why is the grave two feet deeper than normal?

And why is there more than one name on the tomb? It is logical that Mudgett's should be there; it's his grave. But why should Milner's name appear three times? Once on the step and twice on the marker?

What is the significance of the odd, eerie poem? Is it a cipher of some kind? Is there some hidden meaning?

And what do the symbols mean? The backward L's? The strange looped P? The reclining hearts? The Latin? Is there a message waiting here for someone with the key of how to read it?

Local lore is full of conjecture, but no one knows for sure. No one has ever opened the grave to find out.

One theory that seems to connect most of the puzzling elements is that something other than Charles H. Mudgett lies below that monument and cement slab. Some people believe a treasure is buried there.

If so, that would explain the armed guard and the heavier-than-usual casket.

The same theorists argue that the men were all masked to screen the fact that one of them would have been recognizable without a disguise. That masked man was, in fact, Charles H. Mudgett himself. Maybe he had made a fortune in ill-gotten gains. Then, to escape jail or even hanging, he had used the death story to switch identities: Maybe Mudgett became Milner. The hometown burial would have two effects: it would stop local folks from coming West to find him, and it would give him a nest egg to return to, if at some point he were to come back to Vermont.

If there really was a Milton Everett Milner, not much, if anything, is known about him.

One local story holds that he was the owner of the Montana ranch where young Mudgett met his death by drowning. This bachelor rancher might have been Mudgett's employer. Supposedly he'd taken the young Vermonter under his wing and—because Charles had died "in the execution of his duty"—had borne the expense of returning him home to his family. The odd gravestone markings, then, might be nothing more than the brands associated with Milner's cattle ranch. But if that were simply the case, locals argue, why the masks, guns, and surveillance of the coffin?

And why would Milner want his name on the tomb?

And why wasn't "Charlie" buried with his family? He's all alone in the fifteen-by-twenty-foot plot. The rest of the Mudgetts lie elsewhere.

There are probably a hundred other scenarios to fit the odd assortment of details surrounding the mystery of Charles H. Mudgett. At this point the answer, if any, lies buried two feet deeper than usual, under several tons of granite, concrete, and earth.

WILD TALENTS

A Taxing Process

Many things in this book may be a little difficult to believe, but here's one that challenges even my credulity: the State of Vermont actually licensed clairvoyants.

At first, even state archivist Gregory Sanford found the notion a bit far-fetched. "As much as the idea appeals to me," he said, "I do not believe the state ever licensed clairvoyants. I got lost trying to imagine what the licensing exam must have been—applicants would not be told where the exam was but would have to use their powers to locate it; would there be a written exam or would applicants simply sense what the questions were?"

Mr. Sanford's own clairvoyant powers proved limited as he later found that for thirty years, from 1947 to 1977, practicing seers, palm readers, and fortune tellers had to be licensed by the state.

The law was originally passed in the 1930s, with the tax commissioner responsible for licensing. In 1962 the function was transferred to the secretary of state.

There was no test—perhaps because mind readers would find it too easy to cheat—but people did have to complete a formal application and pay an annual fee. They also had to have their fingerprints and photograph on file.

The practice was stopped in 1977, and I'm not sure why. Mr. Sanford speculated that the reason might have been to protect state economic forecasters from charges of professional incompetence.

Clara

One of Vermont's most noted seers escaped this taxing process because she passed away at about the same time the law went into effect.

She was Clara Jepson, and at least for a time she was the best known seer in Vermont. During the first half of the twentieth century she worked her magic in her big white house in downtown Pownal. It was on the opposite street corner from the town physician. People use to go to Clara to find out what was going to be wrong with them. Then they'd cross the street to the doctor's office for some preventative medicine.

Her wild talent was that she could somehow discern future events—as well as the location of lost and hidden objects—in the folds of a white, lacy handkerchief. The occult information would somehow be disclosed to her as she gathered the material into her fingers.

Ms. Jepson was consulted on some of the state's most famous mysteries, including the disappearances on Glastonbury Mountain (see *Green Mountain Ghosts*). She was even consulted on important national cases like the Lindbergh kidnapping.

In her later years Ms. Jepson made a number of rather grim predictions about the future, but, at least so far, they have not come true.

Clara Jepson, the seer of Pownal, died in 1948 at the age of eighty-seven.

Luvia

People in Marshfield still talk about the many miracles worked by their much-loved and properly licensed resident seer, Luvia Lafirira.

She lived in a neat, white, red-trimmed farmhouse beside a red barn where her husband, George, raised cattle.

Born in Plainfield just after the turn of the century, Luvia was a fifth-generation Vermonter. A tiny, bright-eyed woman in a cheerful, spotlessly clean home, she most certainly did not conform to anyone's mental picture of a soothsayer. She used no props—no crystals, tarot cards, or handkerchiefs. When asked a question she would simply ponder silently for a moment, as if trying to recall some long-forgotten name or face. Then she'd communicate a "psychic impression" that would, hopefully, prove helpful to the questioner.

Luvia often dealt with the simple routines of country life: finding a heifer that had wandered off, locating lost eyeglasses, or recovering a misplaced coat. But sometimes she'd apply her skill to locating missing relatives or guiding police to stolen goods or hidden corpses.

Born Luvia Page, she discovered her mysterious abilities during her high school years. Whenever her classmates lost something, she would somehow know where to find it.

Before she married George Lafirira in 1922, she asked him how he felt about her "gift." At first he had no real objections, but in time he grew to like it. He especially enjoyed meeting all the interesting people it brought to their home.

Early in her career—in the late 1920s—she was awakened at four in the morning by a distressed family from Walden. Their little boy had wandered off, and they'd been searching for him most of the night. The parents were beside themselves, afraid he might be hurt, trapped somewhere, or in danger of freezing to death. They'd made the trip all the way from Walden to ask for Luvia's help.

After a moment's thought, Luvia was able to point toward the west. He's in that direction from your home, she told them. And he's much further away that you'd expect. But he's found himself some shelter and he's perfectly all right.

That's what she told them and that's exactly what they found. The child was fine; he hadn't even caught a cold.

An East Montpelier woman's son vanished after twenty minutes of playing in the yard. His mother had been keeping an eye on him, but she'd looked away briefly. When she looked back he had disappeared.

Family and friends searched for hours before calling the state police. Finally the distraught mother sought Luvia's help by telephone. Without seeing the grounds or meeting any of the people involved, Luvia was able to say—over the phone—that she could see the boy clearly. Just go north from your watering trough, she said, and you'll find him sitting under something feathery-looking near lots of water. Again she was able to ease the parent's fears by assuring her that her son would be completely all right.

They found him just as she'd said—in a watery area with lots of beaver dams. He'd wandered off to go swimming, but had found it too cold. They discovered him sitting under a bushy little fir tree.

In her book *Summer Kitchen*, author Elizabeth Kent Gay tells of a meeting with Luvia. The author had recently made a series of moves, from Massachusetts to California to Calais, Vermont. Somewhere over those many thousands of miles, she had lost a chest of silver. She guessed it must have been misplaced or stolen somewhere en route. No doubt it would be impossible to recover—a lost cause, even for Luvia. But, after her characteristic moment of silent pondering, Luvia said she could see the silver. It was in a dark cluttered room, up against a brick wall.

Deciding to give it one last go, Ms. Gay returned to the house she had originally left near Boston. There she found the silver. The chest was in the attic, right up against a brick chimney. She'd simply forgotten to pack it.

Dr. Pare

Until it was torn down in the 1970s, there was an unassuming two-story farmhouse at the corner of Dorset Street and Kennedy Drive in South Burlington. Situated on what once had been farm land, it was surrounded by a white picket fence. For years it was obvious to passersby that the owner raised poultry.

There was one curious thing about this otherwise unremarkable residence: it was almost always surrounded by cars. Way too many cars. Sometimes a hundred at a time. A quick check of license plates would reveal that visitors were not just Vermonters. Vehicles came from all over New England, Canada, and sometimes from as far away as California.

But why? What was the big attraction?

They had all come to see the owner, Dr. Henri Napoleon Pare.

Dr. Pare was a very unusual doctor. In fact, he wasn't really a doctor at all; his title was honorary. Though he'd never studied medicine, he was a remarkably effective healer.

His mysterious healing gifts were his birthright, for Dr. Pare was one of a rare and vanishing breed—he was the seventh son of a seventh son.

Many cultures consider a seventh son to be especially lucky and to possess occult powers. They allegedly make excellent doctors because of their instinctive knowledge of magic and medicinal herbs. In Ireland, even the saliva of a seventh son is valued as potent medicine.

Generally a seventh son's gifts are not confined to healing. They're also considered clairvoyant. They can find lost or hidden objects; sometimes they can read thoughts.

In France, a seventh son is said to be "gifted with the lily"—the fleur-de-lis emblem of the former French royal family. Dr. Pare was descended from the French tradition. As the seventh son of a seventh son, his gifts were considered incredibly powerful.

A Vermonter by choice, Dr. Pare was born in Brigham, Quebec, in 1891. In 1930 he moved to his Dorset Street home, raised poultry, and remained until his death in 1967.

He was known as a modest, gentle, and generous man who charged no fees for his services, dispensed no medicine, and made no claims about his healing powers.

Nonetheless, his reputation as a healer grew. So many ailing people appeared at his door that eventually he gave up farming to devote all his time to the people who needed him.

Today, as families get smaller, seventh sons are becoming rare, maybe even an endangered species. It is likely that most of us have never been treated by a mystical healer. We might wonder what the experience is like. Though each practitioner probably has his or her own style and technique, a visit to Dr. Pare—according to people who knew him—went something like this:

A Shelburne woman said, "What I remember of Dr. Pare was that he always had a line of cars outside of his house, starting at six in the morning."

His sister would take down names and time of arrival, so people could be seen in order.

Next, according to a Burlington woman, "You'd go into his house and he'd have several people lined up. There was a waiting room there. We'd wait in the waiting room, and then he'd take us in this other room, and that's all there was, no prayers, no nothing. He didn't say anything special to us. When we'd go in, he'd ask us where we hurt and that was it.

". . . The treatment took ten to fifteen minutes," she continued, "not long, but there was always a waiting line. But he wouldn't work on Sundays. You couldn't go to him on a Sunday."

The one thing most people remarked about was the healer's hands. A typical description: "His hands were just as hot as a hot pad."

Though no money was charged, there was always a price to pay. A woman explains: "Anyone who was cured by him would have a terrific headache for 24 hours after they saw him and he told them this before he would treat them."

But the amazing thing is that Dr. Pare's puzzling treatments were often successful.

In one case a woman had a recurring pain in her shoulder. She had been to several medical doctors who could find nothing wrong with her. But the pain just wouldn't go away. At her father's suggestion she visited Dr. Pare. When he lifted her arm, she could feel the extraordinary heat from his hands. He told her that by nightfall she would feel nauseated but after she vomited she would feel better—and the pain in her shoulder would be gone.

And that is exactly what happened. The pain never bothered her again.

A Proctor woman had a sore on her leg that wouldn't heal. After one visit to Dr. Pare, the sore vanished completely.

A lifelong asthma sufferer had his asthma cured after just one visit.

Another man endured months of suffering with back pain. Conventional doctors and their medicine did no good. At his wife's insistence he visited Dr. Pare. Not only did the treatment give him relief, it also made him a believer.

Sometimes curious or skeptical people would try to test the doctor's powers. According to one lady, "A few times he'd get people in who wouldn't really be sick. But he knew; he could feel whether something was wrong with you or not."

The pattern was often repeated: doubters became believers.

In time Dr. Pare became Vermont's best known healer. When he passed away his death was reported in newspapers, and on radio and TV.

But, in spite of his excellent reputation, certain doubts remain. As one woman put it, "It's strange . . . they say he could cure anyone . . . but his wife was always sickly for as long as I can remember. I'm not sure if he wanted . . . it that way or not."

Lyse

It has never been satisfactorily explained how these mysterious seers acquire their wild talents. In some cases it may be a birthright—as with Dr. Pare. In other cases, like Luvia's, it may be inherited or divinely bestowed.

But in at least one odd instance, it seems to have been the result of an accident.

In the mid-1960s a dump truck, owned by Cody Chevrolet of Montpelier, was traveling down a steep hill in Barre. It went out of control and crashed into a house owned by Mr. and Mrs. Ludger Savard.

Their sixteen-year-old daughter Lyse was with them inside the house when the collision occurred. It caused severe structural damage to the building, but there was no direct impact between Lyse and the vehicle. She was showered with light debris but sustained no physical injuries.

Soon, however, she found she was not all right.

Within two weeks she went to see their family doctor, Ernest Reynolds. Dr. Reynolds found she was excessively nervous, under great emotional distress, troubled by faintness and periods of trembling. At night she was routinely plagued by sleeplessness. And even when she slept, nightmares disturbed her rest. Additionally, she suffered from diminished appetite resulting in weight loss.

After seeing her a few times, Dr. Reynolds referred her to Dr. P. L. R. Forrest, a psychiatrist. Medical and psychiatric care continued for approximately two years.

In 1967, on Lyse's behalf, her parents brought suit against Cody Chevrolet, Inc., in Washington County Court in Montpelier.

In court the truck driver, Albert Smith, foreman for the defendant, described the odd accident. He said at about 4:40 P.M. he was bringing the vehicle to the Cody Garage for repairs. While heading downhill he heard a peculiar noise and discovered that his vehicle was freewheeling. Later, an investigation showed the truck's drive shaft had dropped off.

All Al Smith's efforts to control the vehicle by braking and gear-shifting failed. Even his emergency brake wouldn't stop the truck. The result was the impact with the Savard house upon which the lawsuit for negligence was founded.

Lyse Savard, a high school senior at the time, gave her version of the story under oath in the Montpelier courtroom. She said that after the three-ton truck crashed into her home, her life changed radically.

The accident, she felt, made it possible for her to see and communicate with dead persons. She told the court that she once saw four caskets with people sitting in them. She identified one of the people as a Mr. Paul Constant, who reportedly had killed himself, his wife, and their two children. In her vision, Mr. Constant was holding a gun.

Lyse's mother told the court that following the accident the family had taken a trip to Canada. While there, Lyse said she could see people rising from the ground around gravestones. She told her father to stop the car because "Mr. Constant wanted her to go and get him."

Lyse Savard had no affection for her newfound psychic ability. She wanted it stopped and hoped the suit against Cody Chevrolet would cover her medical expenses.

The case went all the way to the Vermont Supreme Court, but the court's findings were based on severe mental and emotional trauma resulting from the accident. If her visions were acknowledged at all, they were considered a symptom rather than an injury.

While the court did uphold her case for damages, it did not insist that she apply to the state treasurer's office as a practicing clairvoyant.

PLACES

Mostly haunted. Some historic. Exotic. Or just plain strange. Not the sort of places guidebooks call to your attention.

As we tour Vermont in this section we'll encounter ghosts who reside in the oddest of spots. A few linger after hours in office buildings. Others lurk in educational edifices. Still others enjoy the haunted hospitality of inns and hotels—where their stays are never brief.

Some venerable phantoms reside in the state's most historic buildings; others prefer more modest surroundings.

All the sites in this section can be viewed or visited. But their occupants are fickle phantoms; try not to be disappointed if the ghosts don't visit you.

HOUSE OF THE FEASTING DEAD

People sometimes ask me why I'm so interested in all this scary stuff? Ghosts, murders, disasters, that sort of thing?

In the old days I'd scratch my head, searching for some earnest psychoanalytical response. But the truth is, I can't figure it out. It's in my hardwiring, I guess, right along with an appetite for pasta and an affection for hummingbirds.

At the same time, if I were to try to reconstruct where the dark interests began, I'd have to return to the mid-1950s and to Cuttingsville, Vermont. It was there that I first encountered Mr. John P. Bowman.

Mr. Bowman was long dead, of course, but I encountered him just the same. I saw him whenever my father took the family on a trip along Route 103 to Rutland.

As we passed through Cuttingsville, we couldn't help but see Mr. Bowman's deserted Victorian mansion, the sinister-looking Laurel Hall.

It was a spooky old place, dark, faded, scary enough to give me nightmares. I eagerly imagined myriad frail phantoms lurking amid the darkness within.

But the mansion wasn't the weird thing. Something far weirder stood directly across the road on the border of a cemetery. It was a somber granite mausoleum.

And something weirder still was almost always visible on the steps of that tomb. A figure. Life-sized. Dressed in a nineteenth-century mourning cloak and holding a wreath and a key.

It was Mr. John P. Bowman.

To scores of uninitiated travelers, Bowman must have looked exactly like a ghost as he knelt there, completely white, absolutely motionless, silent and forlorn. But, as I learned long ago, it wasn't a ghost; it wasn't even alive. It was a marble statue. And it's still there, halfway up the steps, just exactly as it was when I was a boy.

My father told me the story several times. I'm not sure if my persistent questions ever inspired him to embellish, but I remember many of the details to this day.

Though he said Mr. Bowman "musta been kind of a peculiar fella," I think my father nonetheless saw him as a tragic figure. Dad told me Bowman had been a rich industrialist from some faraway state who had moved to Vermont with his family. Then, following a tragedy the details of which no one seemed to remember, Mr. Bowman's happy home life vanished when his wife and daughter died, leaving the grieving millionaire alone in his spooky old house. There he remained, an eccentric recluse, pondering the mysteries of death, studying occult sciences, and performing odd rituals. As Dad told it, the grief-shattered Bowman was convinced that somehow, through reincarnation, or by employing some arcane alchemical formula, he was going to find the key that would bring his family, and eventually himself, back from the dead.

Eventually the research, the solitude, and the years took their toll on the aging isolationist. He became ill. Following a period of suffering and decline, he passed away. Then his body was moved for safekeeping to the vault across the street.

According to local lore, Mr. Bowman left a rather unusual will. It provided that the remainder of his substantial fortune would be used for upkeep on the house and mausoleum. Professional caretakers maintained the grounds. Servants cleaned the rooms and regularly changed the bed linens. Every night, so the story went, the cook and butler prepared and served a full formal meal in the candlelit dining room.

Mr. Bowman wanted everything to be ready if he should arrive home unannounced. And if he were to show up at mealtime, supper would be waiting.

*

Because my father had told me the story, I believed it. For years I passed it along as if it were true. Over time certain enticing additions came to my attention. I heard there was a treasure buried somewhere on the grounds, or sealed securely in some secret compartment deep within the mansion's nooks and crannies. And of course there were ghost stories, spectral presences encountered fleetingly by unsuspecting tradesmen working alone within the seemingly abandoned house. Another told of the faint sad sobbing of an infant who could never be located among the confusion of empty rooms.

Some folks even claimed Bowman's heavy marble statue occasionally came to life, creaked itself erect, and, like a sentient golem, surveyed the grounds its creator had abandoned so very long ago.

While I was in high school, some of us would make occasional ghost-hunting expeditions to Cuttingsville. On warm summer evenings when the moon was right, we'd sneak up to the door of the mausoleum. Looking through the barred entrance revealed an unearthly and vast interior, far larger than the outside dimensions would suggest. What seemed like magic was done with mirrors, an ingenious illusion. But all the time we knew that the real Bowman bodies were in those creepy catacombs, each resting forever on "A Couch of Dreamless Sleep." In the foreground, statues detailed exactly how everyone had looked during the brief bloom of life.

Sometimes, on a dare, one of us would stand on the steps and peer directly into the kneeling Bowman's marble eyes. Then we'd dash across the road and peek through the windows of his home. To this day one friend swears he saw a white and faintly luminous shape drifting through the darkened interior.

*

Recently, in preparation for this book, I decided to get the real scoop on Mr. Bowman, his eerie estate, and his eccentric ideas about the afterlife.

I was happy to discover that John Porter Bowman was not an out-of-stater at all. He was a native Vermonter, born in 1816 at his grandfather's tavern in Clarendon; you might say his exposure to spirits came very early.

Though educational opportunities were limited, he was an ambitious young man so he ventured to Rutland to learn the tanning trade.

Eventually he set up his own tanning business. In the early 1850s he ran for, and won, a seat in the Vermont legislature.

Apparently he preferred business to politics, so in 1852 he moved to Stony Creek, in New York's Adirondack region. There he started a more ambitious tannery operation on 6,000 acres of hemlock forest.

The enterprising Vermonter's business took off. The American Civil War proved especially good fortune for Bowman. Business boomed as he manufactured the boots, saddles, soles, and the other leather products that were in such great demand by the Army.

He hired dozens of people, erected a small town, and married Miss Jennie Gates of Warren, New York. The couple's vision of an idyllic future included raising a family and building a grand summer home in his beloved Vermont.

But while he prospered professionally, he was personally plagued by great misfortune. The couple's first child, Addie, died an infant in 1854. Their second daughter, Ella, survived longer, but in 1879 she succumbed to illness at age 22. The next year, 1880, Mrs. Bowman followed her daughters to the grave.

Shortly afterward, Bowman dispatched crews to Vermont to begin work on the summer home his family had long dreamed about but would never see. His Cuttingsville complex, a monument to his loved ones, consists of the mansion, Laurel Hall, and his Neo-Egyptian "Laurel Glen Mausoleum."

The incredible crypt was a colossal undertaking, involving over a year's work by 125 sculptors, stone cutters, masons, and laborers. The total cost exceeded $75,000, a staggering amount that today would equal about one-and-a-quarter million dollars.

Construction included 750 tons of granite, 50 tons of marble, over 20,000 bricks, and more than 100 loads of sand.

But they built it right; it has been there more than one hundred years. No doubt it will stand, virtually unchanged, for a thousand more. And all the while, kneeling outside on the steps, never quite getting a look inside, is the ghostly statue of Bowman himself, dressed in mourning cloak, holding gloves, a funeral wreath, and that mysterious key.

In 1887 the flesh-and-blood John Bowman, shattered and alone, sold everything in New York and came home to Vermont to stay. Each morning he'd look out the front windows of his mansion and see the eerie white apparition of himself, frozen in stone, forever kneeling at the door to the mausoleum.

He saw this tableau daily until 1891, when, after eleven years alone, John P. Bowman died.

It is true that he had no heirs, and that he used his will to establish a trust to take care of the house and the mausoleum. He also stipulated that nothing could be sold. But the fascinating details about changing bedclothes and cooking meals are, as far as I can tell, creative embellishment.

Before his death Bowman supposedly talked a good deal about reincarnation and resurrection. There was nothing unusual about such speculation for a nineteenth-century gentleman with a Christian background and a curiosity about alternative belief systems, like Spiritualism.

We don't know to what degree Bowman's thought may have been influenced by Spiritualism. Even if he believed in the Summerland, there is no evidence he experimented with any sort of thaumaturgy or necromancy. But solely within a Christian context, it would not have been too great a leap for locals to have assumed that after the Resurrection, Bowman planned to rejoin his family in the summer home he'd made for them.

Then there are the weird stories: What about the apparitions, hidden money, and ghostly babies crying?

Well, we know that no child of Bowman's ever lived in Laurel Hall. And the money, hidden or not, depleted rapidly as the cost of upkeep, labor, and materials increased.

In fact, back in 1950 the trustees had to sell off the art and the elegant furnishings to add dollars to the trust.

Maybe that's when the supernatural legends began, too. In a July 27, 1950, article in the *Rutland Herald*, the wife of longtime caretaker George Jones stated that her husband had become so sick and tired of newspapers plaguing him for scary stories about the house that he decided, "If they wanted a story, I'd give them one."

Maybe he did.

*

Unlike its builder, the old Bowman place has been reincarnated several times. For a while it was the "Haunted Mansion Book Shop" (which, the owners allegedly swore, wasn't haunted at all). Then its many rooms housed a collection of antique shops, the rent from which helped support the trust.

Today it is newly painted and undergoing extensive restoration. The goal is to return Laurel Hall to its original splendor. The books and antiques are gone now and the building is used only occasionally, for special events.

When I recently revisited the old mansion, I didn't find it nearly as scary as I did when I was ten. To these jaded adult eyes, even the statue across the street no longer resembled a ghost.

But, at least for me, something unsettling about the place remains. It took a while to figure out what was bothering me, but in time I realized it was Bowman's position on the stairs of his tomb. He's frozen midway, eternally caught, eternally suggesting the questions all adults ask about the afterlife.

Will we remain as earth and stone? Or will we ascend, pass the gate, and join our loved ones once again?

What Dwells on Depot Street?

There is nothing odd looking about the house itself. The lawn is well kept and large. Flowers decorate the yard. A tall maple tree provides shade on hot summer days.

Even the house's proximity to the Catholic Church and rectory suggests it should be immune to any sort of occult disturbance. But, during the 1940s and early 1950s, this ordinary-looking duplex on Depot Street was home to something other than the Wyatt family who had just bought it.

Of the various hauntings chronicled in this book, the events on Depot Street in Ludlow are among the best documented. They were recorded by Hattie Gray, who had lived there and experienced the strangeness. The Wyatts, Hattie's grandparents, bought the place for the most unselfish of reasons: they wanted to share it with Hattie's parents and their five children. The house was designed for two families, constructed with two nearly identical apartments. Hattie's grandparents took the upstairs apartment. Hattie's parents lived below.

She recalls how easily her grandparents acquired the place; no one else seemed to want it. There was something dismal about it, she says, in spite of the lofty maple trees and the cheery syringa, lilac, and currant bushes that lightened the yard. She wrote, "In the evenings the brightness of the street light on the corner served only to give the house a more dark and gloomy appearance as the black shadows seemed to move and sway."

Because the families had relocated to Ludlow from Woodstock, they hadn't been privy to the various local stories about their new home. But at school, and around the neighborhood, Hattie and her siblings quickly tuned in to the tales and brought stories home. Supposedly two elderly ladies had lived there. It had been their practice to rent rooms to young women who attended Black River Academy nearby. One young lady, so the story went, discouraged by poor exam scores or depressed by more serious problems, had hanged herself in an upstairs room.

Perhaps it was her spectral presence that began to make itself known to the family right from the start. An unexplainable sensation of uneasiness overtook anyone who happened to be alone at night. Strange sounds echoed in the quiet interior, but could never be traced or identified. Footsteps resounded in unoccupied rooms or marched invisibly along the halls or down the empty stairways.

But it was all low-level spiritual activity; nothing truly remarkable happened. At least at first.

Then Grandmother became ill with pneumonia.

Eva, Hattie's mother, sent the children to stay with a neighbor and remained in the house to provide nursing services. One night, as Eva entered the dark kitchen for medicine, she saw "a white ghostlike shape" rise like smoke from the floor in front of her. She wasn't able to identify it, but that was the first time anyone had seen anything otherworldly in the house.

Within hours after the shape appeared, Grandmother passed away. In retrospect, we can only speculate about what Hattie's mother saw. Was it the ghost of the hanged girl? The Angel of Death making his rounds? Or perhaps Grandmother's departing spirit?

In any event, after that Grandfather was left alone in the upstairs apartment with only his little black terrier, Mickey, to keep him company.

Understandably disturbed by the loss, Grandfather slept poorly in the nights to come. Then one night his fitful slumber was disturbed by a presence in the room. He felt a trembling sensation.

Coming immediately awake, he discovered his little dog—who normally slept at the foot of his bed—crawling into his arms and shaking as if it were terribly frightened. Grandfather looked around the dark room.

There, beyond the foot of his bed, rising from the floor, he saw a wispy transparent form. As it grew it seemed to take on a familiar shape. It looked like his wife; he recognized her easily as she hovered in their bedroom, gazing sorrowfully at him.

After that Mickey and Grandfather moved downstairs to stay with his son's family. This relocation left the upstairs front bedroom empty and set the scene for the most puzzling incident recorded in Hattie Gray's account.

"A few nights later," Hattie wrote, "everyone was asleep in the small hours of the morning. Suddenly *Clatter! Crash! Bang! Thump!* The girls were awakened with a start and clung together terrified.

"'What was that?' they whispered.

"They clung and listened and shook."

Hattie and her terrified sisters were in the front bedroom, directly below the one in which Grandfather had seen the apparition. The persistent banging they were hearing came from a room they knew to be empty. Yet the sounds were loud enough to suggest heavy furniture being moved around.

"Then a new sound split the darkness," Hattie wrote. "The shrill ki-yi-yi-ing of a frightened dog. [We] recognized Mickey's scared yelping. Meanwhile the thumping continued as before."

In near panic the terrified girls called out to their father, "Dad! Dad! Something's happening to Mickey!"

Father awoke, heard the racket, and glanced through Grandpa's door only to find him sound asleep. But the foot of the bed was empty.

Father hurried up the stairs, opening doors and turning on lights as he went. Though it sounded as if the place had been trashed, he noted that everything seemed pretty much in order as he made his way toward the noisy bedroom.

Upon his entering the upstairs dining room, the crashing stopped. His heart must have been pounding as he slowly opened the sliding doors to the front bedroom. There, on the middle of the abandoned bed, he saw Mickey cowering, crying pitifully, his hair standing straight up. When the terrified animal saw the open door he leapt through it and "ran like a streak through those rooms and down the stairs as though pursued by demons."

Father quickly noted all else was normal within the room. In spite of the incredible racket, none of the furniture was out of place.

Hattie Gray describes her father as "a common-sensical sort of man, no superstitious nonsense about him. He had laughed and scoffed and made light of other odd happenings [in the house]." But this time, as he came slowly down the stairs, Hattie noticed that he had "a very queer look on his face."

"That's a very strange thing," he said. "How did Mickey get up there with all those doors closed?"

It was a question that puzzled the family for many years to come.

*

Hattie's account recalls other odd events, like the loud persistent knocking at the kitchen door while she and her sisters were preparing a noon meal. Again the dog took cover as hair bristled on the back of its neck. When the rapping didn't stop, one of the girls called pleasantly, "Just a moment!"

Still the rapping continued.

The girl made her way to the door and opened it between knocks. No one was there. After much searching and puzzled head-scratching, the sisters were unable to determine the source of the knocking.

On another occasion, sometime after she was married, Hattie slept with her husband in the upstairs bedroom. It was still dark when he got up to leave for work. Admittedly Hattie could have been still partly asleep when she heard her long-dead grandmother's familiar hacking cough in the nearby living room.

Then Hattie heard the shuffling sound of her Grandmother's bedroom slippers approaching the door. She says that for a moment, in her half-sleep, she thought it was the old days and Grandma was coming to awaken her.

Then she remembered.

Fear seized her; she could not move. And the shuffling footsteps kept coming.

Just before the footsteps reached the door Hattie regained control of her muscles, flung herself out of bed, bolted through the other door, and ran down the front stairs to the apartment below.

After a while the family got used to their invisible roommates, but odd occurrences continued. Hattie noted that footsteps were often heard overhead. They'd cross a room, then head down the front stairs. They'd pause for a moment, then continue. No one, she says, ever heard the footsteps going *up* the stairs.

The family saw doorknobs tuning apparently by themselves. Water faucets turned on and off unassisted. Locked doors to the outside would be found wide open, as if to let something out. Or in.

Sometime in the early 1950s Hattie's family sold the house. After she moved out she kept an eye on the place for a while. "Various families have lived in that upstairs apartment," she wrote, "but none has stayed very long."

*

The house is still there, of course, but it is changed. I visited it recently with Hattie's daughter, Marcia Manner. Marcia originally brought the place to my attention and showed me her mother's account of the odd events there.

I saw nothing about it that would suggest the strange parts of its history. Like many old Vermont houses, it telescopes back from the street in six segments. Two so-called "witch windows" are visible from front and back. Somewhere along it got converted from two to seven apartments.

Are there still stories about it?

While visiting Ludlow I asked an number of people if they knew of any haunted houses on Depot Street. No one did.

I even talked to some of the tenants, asked if it was a comfortable place to live. No one said anything about ghosts, odd noises, or peculiar occurrences.

Perhaps a seven-apartment house is simply too crowded for ghosts. Or perhaps ghosts too, like their human counterparts, eventually shuffle off this mortal coil. Apparently some of them do it wearing bedroom slippers.

Who Haunts Redstone?

Though it may look like the set for Shirley Jackson's *The Haunting of Hill House*, that mysterious mansion high on Terrace Street overlooking Montpelier is in reality a state office building. But, as anyone who has ever worked there will tell you, it is no ordinary state office.

Known as "Redstone," this brick and sandstone mansion was unique in its day and remains a one-of-a-kind oddity in Vermont's historic and architecturally diversified capitol city. It eludes easy description. Sometimes it's compared to a Bavarian hunting lodge, sometimes to a French chateau, or even to a German nobleman's estate. Whatever its prototype, it was erected in 1891 with only one intention: to impress.

Redstone was commissioned by Professor John W. Burgess, founder of America's first school of political science at Columbia University. He had visited Vermont after his wife's death in 1884. While passing time with his friend, famed Vermont artist Thomas Waterman Wood, Professor Burgess met and married a lovely local woman, Ruth Payne Jewett. She was highly intelligent, well educated, and an accomplished musician. She had studied painting in New York and had been tutored locally by Mr. Wood himself.

Redstone was to be the couple's "summer home," built on land that Ruth's father Colonel Jewett had given them as a wedding present.

But almost from the start, things went wrong.

Locals didn't take to the couple. Perhaps it was because the New York college professor was perceived as some high-falutin outsider. Or maybe it was the "unseemly" age difference: Professor Burgess was forty years old at the time of their marriage; Ruth was but nineteen.

Whatever the motive, Redstone became a focal point of local contempt. Though community pride in the new landmark was aggressively encouraged by a gushing 1891 article in the *Vermont Watchman and Journal*, townsfolk refused to be impressed. Even as landscapers adorned the treeless building site with white pine and Norwegian spruce in an attempt to replicate a "Black Forest" environment, normally taciturn observers were heard to mutter, "Cripes, if they wanted a house in the woods, why didn't they build it in the woods?"

Nor did the neighbors appreciate Redstone's pretentious architectural eccentricities, with its balconies, grand corner tower, asymmetrical roof, ostentatiously oversized windows, and regal view of the Winooski Valley. Montpelierites dismissed it, calling it *"that Redstone buildin'"* as if to distinguish it from the more humble dwellings it looked down upon.

Professor Burgess won permanent scorn by publicly taking the wrong side on Mr. and Mrs. Martin Kellogg's will. He openly argued that their money should go, not to family heirs, but rather to the town. That was precisely their wish, of course, but, through his outspoken support of the Kelloggs, Professor Burgess alienated most of the community. The resulting discord, he wrote, "robbed me very largely of my peace of mind."

Townspeople were also outraged when Professor Burgess invited Confederate President Jefferson Davis's grandly obese widow, Varina, to visit Montpelier for a whole summer. Memories of Civil War loss and cruelty were still vivid in Vermonters' minds, so Burgess's hospitality seemed somehow insulting, nearly treasonous.

And nobody was too pleased about the professor's ongoing friendship with German Kaiser Wilhelm—especially after the outbreak of World War I.

Perhaps the most damaging gossip soared whenever Professor Burgess returned to New York, leaving Ruth alone at Redstone. Word got out that her friendship with elderly artist Thomas Waterman Wood was a bit too friendly. Their homes were visible to each other across the valley and the alleged lovers supposedly signaled each other, sometimes using lamps, to arrange illicit rendezvous.

The Burgesses' ne'er-do-well son Jewett's marriage to a lowly local lass did little to improve public opinion. Needless to say, it occurred against his parents' wishes—there were the class and educational differences, you know. As might be expected, Jewett soon deserted his youthful wife and their baby daughter. Professor and Mrs. Burgess continued to support Jewett, but ignored the abandoned pair. Predictably, young Jewett then went on to leave a trail of broken hearts and abandoned children as he blissfully squandered the family fortune.

In short, during their time in Vermont, the Burgesses were amazingly unpopular. There is little evidence of their personal happiness and plenty that their elevated ways consistently antagonized and alienated the townspeople.

They sold Redstone in 1911 and moved away.

In 1938—the year of her death—Ruth Payne Burgess suffered her final indignity. During her funeral procession along Fifth Avenue in New York City the whole cortege was officially forced to a halt so that her son Jewett could be arrested for nonsupport of his second wife.

And so it was . . .

*

Redstone continued to hold its aloof, solitary vigilance over the city of Montpelier, though its history after the Burgesses is in most ways unremarkable. Although occasionally occupied between 1911 and 1941, it was in steady decline. From 1941 until 1947 it stood vacant. Local children threw stones through the windows and dared each other to venture inside. Inevitably, "stories" arose.

Then, in 1949, the vandalism—but not the stories—ended when Vermont's newly formed State Police purchased the building for $25,000 and began renovations. It has remained with the state ever since. Today it houses the Secretary of State's office and the Vermont State Archives.

But, as we shall see, state employees may not be its only occupants.

*

Long after the Burgesses sold Redstone and later, following Professor Burgess's death, Ruth seemed drawn to Montpelier. For years she summered at the Pavilion Hotel and was a familiar sight in local shops and along Main Street.

And, many say, her presence is still very much a part of the house on Terrace Street. Perhaps they are only referring to the portrait of Ruth that still hangs on the wall. No one entering Redstone today can fail to notice it there by the central stairway near the entrance. Lovingly executed by Thomas Waterman Wood, it shows her to have been a striking young woman, serene and lovely in an aristocratic—almost mystical—sort of way.

This painting, like the unique building the Burgesses built and abandoned, remains a reminder of fundamental balances that were apparently never struck: the balance of a middle-aged man and his teenaged bride; of a dysfunctional family and the community with which it never found harmony; and the balance of a grand house's facade in contrast with its inner workings.

Paul Gillies, for twelve years Deputy Secretary of State, recalls discovering some of Redstone's deception when his office moved there in 1984. "It was clear a lot of money had been spent fixing it up to *look* nice. . . . [But] the rafters sometimes didn't meet the studs. We nearly lost the whole first floor when we . . . put in a large photocopier. It started creaking; everything was shaking. It was [in danger of] going down because the floor boards didn't meet the joists."

One suspects these misalignments and imbalances may in part account for the mysterious "something" that occasionally makes itself known in that strange old house.

A ghost, perhaps?

Most people suspect it is the tenacious spirit of Mrs. Burgess herself, who just never seemed to want to leave.

Mr. Gillies suspects he has personally encountered Mrs. Burgess's spirit. "I don't normally go for this sort of thing," he cautioned me, "but my experience teaches me differently."

He often worked long hours in the building. Sometimes, especially during election season, he had to stay all night. All by himself. "Frequently," he said, "I would have these . . . hair-raising sensations that I was not alone."

Generally they occurred in the vicinity of the big central staircase. "At first it was really unnerving. I never left, but I always thought, *I don't need to be around here.*"

Computer equipment mysteriously fails in the same vicinity.

Rita Knapp, a Unit Administrator, describes the time they moved a computer printer from the hall by the stairs to a former bedroom. "[The printer] was never disconnected," she told me. "The box was physically dragged around the corner and [placed] in that room."

But no matter what they did, the printer wouldn't work at its new location. "The letters would start to print out okay, then all of a sudden it would print garbage. Then it would go back to printing the letter. Or leave big spaces and jump around on the page."

Simply stated, they could not solve the problem: "We changed plugs; we changed cables; we tried everything we could think of. We even had the state come in and do testing for radiowave frequencies, because [of the] old state police tower outside."

State technicians tested but found absolutely nothing wrong. Yet no one could get the printer to work properly in that room. "So one day we picked it up and moved it around the corner and back into the hall. Never a problem since."

It may be important to repeat that the printer was never disconnected. The printer—with all cables connected—was simply moved from one location to another. It failed to work in one spot; in the other it worked fine.

Ms. Knapp also reports another common communications tool behaving uncommonly.

"People will hear their phones clicking. Like somebody's picked up an extension, except there aren't any extensions on any of these phones; they're all private lines. And there isn't any way that we know of that people can tap into it. But they'll hear that distinctive click. Then they'll notice that it'll click again."

And then there are the lights.

Like Paul Gillies, Peggy Atkins of the Professional Regulations Division has experienced after-hours weirdness. She recalls, "There are about four of us who work here late at night. After we get through, before we go out, we shut off all the lights.

"Once we looked back and the lights were all back on. We came back in thinking somebody just forgot to shut them off, so we did it all over again: shut everything off. When we got back out to the car the lights were back on. By that time we said, *Let's get out of here!*"

Lights? Letters? Phones? Could it be that someone is making unsuccessful attempts to communicate?

If so, who? And from where?

As we have said, the common wisdom is that it is the spirit of Mrs. Burgess. But in the light of other odd experiences, one has to consider other suspects.

For example, what are we to make of the single visual encounter?

Kathy White, a staff member at State Archives, told me, "I had one spiritual experience here at Redstone where I walked into the vault one morning and I saw a long black skirt swoosh around the corner at the other end. I checked it out and there was nothing there."

If there had been a live, three-dimensional person attached to that skirt, she would have had to pass Kathy to get out of the vault. Granted, it could have been the spirit of Mrs. Burgess, but—strictly speaking—what would she have been doing in the basement vault? Remember, in the Burgesses' time, Redstone was a Victorian household; they had servants. The lady of the house would never need to descend to the basement.

So possibly what Kathy saw was the shade of some still-loyal servant whose name has been long forgotten.

And isn't it also likely that a spectral servant might be responsible for another peculiar happening at Redstone? Occasionally strange, out-of-place aromas waft through the ancient rooms. The odors are so vivid, real, and easily identifiable that, according to numerous witnesses, it is just as if someone were cooking dinner.

"You could smell things like pot roast," Peggy Atkins recalled, "nice meals that made you real hungry. Sometimes it would be chicken. Most of the time it was roast beef or pork roast. It smelled so good. We used to think maybe somebody was using the microwave, but we'd go around and we'd check—nobody had used the microwave."

Of course, Redstone's kitchen facilities are long gone. As yet no one has been able to determine where the odors were coming from.

Because Ms. Atkins works in the part of the building that used to contain the kitchen and house the servants, one's suspicion is reinforced that a spirit, other than Mrs. Burgess's, may be hard at work preparing a meal that will never be ready.

But whoever or whatever that spirit might be, no one has reported an unpleasant experience at Redstone. In fact, everyone agrees that if a ghost resides there, it is benign, maybe friendly. And if it turns out to be the spirit of Mrs. Burgess, her new neighbors seem to enjoy her a lot more than did those of a century ago.

As Paul Gillies said, "I finally got to a point where . . . I had spent more hours in the building than Mrs. Burgess. And I said, 'Hey I'll haunt you from now on.' After that, when I heard it or felt it, it was kind of friendly. I'd made my peace with the thing."

TENURED TERRORS

In early 1997 the University of Vermont contracted with me to do an article for the fall issue of their magazine, *Vermont Quarterly*. It was to be the first-ever census of the ghosts that occupy UVM's many historic buildings.

After several weeks of work, my conclusion was this: when it comes to school spirit, UVM deserves some kind of award. In fact, it might be the most spirited school in Vermont. Ghosts have been reported in no fewer than eleven of its buildings, and there are enticing rumors about another three or four.

Perhaps UVM's best known spirit is the venerable Henry, whom generations of students have met in Converse Hall.

The massive, brooding, ivy-cloaked structure was built as a men's dormitory in 1895. Henry showed up in the 1920s.

Said to be a reclusive, overburdened, and highly stressed medical student, Henry was failing academically and socially. Profoundly melancholic, he hanged himself in the attic.

Today he's dead but apparently not gone. Since Henry's demise strange things have happened in the ancient rooms and corridors of Converse. Doors mysteriously open and shut. Possessions vanish. Bewildered students discover their locked rooms have been rearranged. And a certain rocking chair is seen to rock . . . all by itself.

A young woman told me about the time she went alone to a study room, turned on the lights, and began working at one of the carrels. Suddenly she heard the tattoo of typing several desks over. The room had been dark when she entered; she'd seen no one come in, yet the typing continued. Puzzled, she got up and followed the sound to the desk where the noise seemed to originate. No one was there.

One night another Converse resident was disturbed by the sensation of someone stroking her nose. Frightened, she woke her husband, who groggily insisted it was just a dream. When they were almost asleep again, a crash jolted them fully awake. The wall mirror lay shattered on the floor. The frightened couple couldn't understand why the heavy mirror had fallen; it had been bolted to the wall. The mystery deepened when they saw its four bolts were still securely in place.

An oddly poignant story involves a female student whose mother passed away. Following the funeral the young woman returned to Converse. Upon entering her locked room she found everything soaking wet: furniture, clothing, even the walls themselves. The janitor couldn't find any leaks, broken pipes, or open windows. There was simply no explanation. Someone said it was as if the walls themselves had been weeping for the girl's loss.

Henry seems to plague women more than men, perhaps predictable behavior from an eternally adolescent male. Today he's considered a prankster; when anything odd happens at Converse, folks say, "Oh well, it must be Henry."

*

Henry sets the example for most UVM haunts. Like him, other school spirits are heard but not seen. Such is the case at Booth House at 86 South Williams Street, the home of Public Relations.

The Booth family occupied it from 1913 to 1967. But one of them, apparently, has been slow to leave.

Though the ghost has never been identified, one suspect is John E. Booth, an eccentric horticulturist who brought a special kind of life to the premises by growing beautiful botanical rarities. Somewhere along, tellers of ghostly tales awarded him the title "Doctor."

Like Henry, the eccentric doctor's ghost is blamed for any peculiar incident on the premises. His reported antics include noises, flickering lights, and weird air currents that make it difficult to open certain doors. Admittedly Dr. Booth's spirit has never been very spirited: his ghostly neighbors are more aggressive.

*

Grasse Mount, the elegant, two-story federal mansion at 411 Main Street, houses University Advancement. Built in 1804 by Thaddeus Tuttle, this Burlington landmark was a private home, changing hands several times before UVM bought it in 1895.

Many people agree that someone, or something, benign but excitable, lurks within its walls.

When Continuing Education was there during the 1980s, most of the ghostly goings-on occurred upstairs. Susan Greenhalgh, the financial manager, was working alone one evening in 1984. Doors were locked, windows closed and secured for the night. Susan was the only living soul in the building—or so she thought.

Between eight and nine o'clock something happened. Susan said, "The windows in the window jams just started to go back and forth—a huge rattling. I could see the motion, but there was nothing there."

Wind might be the immediate explanation, but Susan says no. "It was still light outside; I could see there was no wind. I'm a windsurfer, so I'm always looking for that."

Over the next couple of hours the commotion escalated. The heating system began clanking and banging—the familiar cacophony of ancient plumbing. Trouble is, it was summer and the heat was turned off.

"I stayed there an hour and a half, maybe two," Susan told me. "I walked out of the room when the windows were beating themselves back and forth. I said, Okay, you can have the building. I can't concentrate any longer."

Lynne Ballard, former interim director of Continuing Education, recalls a similar evening. Around midnight the silence was broken by loud noises upstairs: doors slamming, drawers banging, footsteps pounding. Fearing vandals—but secretly suspecting the ghost—she phoned her husband, Bill, a senior campus administrator. Though skeptical about ghostly noisemakers, Bill arrived to find the commotion so active, loud, and unsettling that he summoned security guards. The officers arrived, searched, and left, finding nothing. Though embarrassed, Bill was far less skeptical about the invisible realm.

Grasse Mount has been relatively quiet since renovations began in 1985. Perhaps the ongoing disruption drove its unseen residents away. Sometimes, however, just the opposite occurs: long-quiet spirits can become agitated during construction projects.

*

Because the historic Old Mill is the university's oldest building, one would expect a whole volume of ghost stories. Surprisingly, there are few.

However, massive renovations concluded in 1997 may have provoked a veritable carnival of spirit activity. Will Old Mill residents discover they are sharing their new offices with spectral colleagues? We'll have to wait and see. But during the changeover, at least one construction worker—a young man named Todd—had a curious encounter.

Late one afternoon while moving furniture, Todd decided to explore the top floor of the Old Mill. It was a mysterious area that had been closed off and inaccessible for years. Todd found its abandoned classrooms eerily frozen in time, with student desks in place, and chalkboards—complete with writing—still on the walls.

While alone among the dust and shadows, Todd experienced an odd sensation. "Something sort of jumped into my mind," he told me. "It felt like somebody was there . . . watching me. The hair stood up on the back of my neck."

Though he wasn't frightened, the sudden and inexplicable intuition surprised him. He left immediately.

Reflecting recently, Todd said it was as if he'd been suddenly transported into the midst of an operating classroom. He experienced a vague sense of invisible activity, but the strongest impression was of a little girl, "maybe five to seven years old, in one of those puffy Sunday dresses. She's the one that stood out, but there were others, too."

A ghostly visitation? A strong psychic impression? A spirit uprising? Todd doesn't know what occurred in the Old Mill. All he knows is that he didn't like the unfamiliar feeling at all. Yet, to this day, he can't get it out of his mind.

*

Number 481 Main Street houses two departments, Classics and Religion. Their phantom emeritus belonged to the latter, confining its activities to a single room: Professor Robert Gussner's office.

Colleagues had been complaining of inexplicable "bumps in the night" coming from a closet. In May 1973, a fearless graduate student borrowed the "haunted office" to work on a paper.

"At about two in the morning she called up terrified," Professor Gussner told me. "She'd been hearing noises in the office. So I got out of bed and drove the two miles in."

He found the student almost speechless with fear. "She was practically in a state of collapse," Professor Gussner recalled. "She was so white, I thought *she* was the ghost."

They searched the office, especially around the closet, but, predictably, found nothing.

Perhaps fearful of losing more sleep, not to mention graduate students, Professor Gussner took action. "I did a Hindu exorcism," he said. "There's a certain Sanskrit chant that you do to the four corners of the room asking the person kindly to depart."

Apparently the ritual worked. The noises stopped and have never started up again.

*

The spirits in the Continuing Education building at 322 South Prospect Street seem to have attempted an exorcism of their own. First, they subjected a woman to routine ghostly disturbances: pounding, flickering lights, switching computers off and on. When the woman failed to react, the haunting escalated. "When the floor started to vibrate," she said, "I knew it was time to get out!"

No one knows who the ghosts are or why they picked the Continuing Education building. I've heard fragments of a story involving a schoolgirl who was killed in a gas explosion. Perhaps she stayed on, continuing her education in the spirit world.

*

There is another haunted room in the Lambda Iota fraternity at 440 Pearl Street. The resident ghost, or at least the resident ghost story, involves the esteemed alumnus Lyman Rowell, once UVM President.

According to sketchy details passed along by the L. I. brothers, it all began in the 1920s during Prohibition. Rowell, like his fraternity brothers, found that enforced temperance cramped everyone's style. So he covertly set up a still in his room.

One day—so the story goes—the still exploded. Fire damaged the attic and roof before it was brought under control. Then firemen discovered a body in Rowell's room; a brother had been killed in the blast.

Douglas Reed, who recorded the story for UVM's Folklore Archives, wrote, "The damage has been repaired, and Prohibition is long over, but for many years after that, some of the brothers who lived on that floor . . . would claim that the ghost of the dead brother still lurked in that room."

*

The Admissions Building at 194 South Prospect has a fairly run-of-the mill haunting. The indications are unremarkable: footsteps, doors opening and closing, noises from nowhere. This haunting, like Converse Hall's, is attributed to a suicide: someone supposedly shot himself in an upstairs room around the turn of the century.

One admissions counselor swears she clearly heard papers rustling in an empty room. In an unsettling encounter, a UVM security guard reported feeling something invisible brush by him on the stairs. Whatever that presence may have been, it most definitely was not on its way out.

*

It seems only fitting that the history department at Wheeler House should have a ghost. Reverend John Wheeler, UVM's sixth president, guided the school through especially troubled times, possibly leaving some of his extraordinary energy behind. Later, the building was used as UVM's infirmary, so who can say what psychic residue remains? All we know was recently recalled by an anonymous Wheeler resident: "A number of years ago there was quite a bit of talk about a presence. I've been here twelve years and I've never witnessed it, but others have. And the presence was going by the name of Lydia. . . . People were referring to hearing Lydia walking the halls late at night."

I have not been able to find any Lydia in connection with Wheeler House. But there was a "Lucia"—Reverend Wheeler's daughter—who died of tuberculosis in 1871.

Whether it was Lydia or Lucia, she seems to have moved on. Today the Wheeler House ghost is nothing but . . . history.

*

The most dramatic of UVM spirits have not only been sensed, and heard . . . but seen.

On the corner of South Prospect and Main Streets stands "The Bittersweet," built in 1809, and named for the fruit-bearing vine. It houses the Environmental Program.

One wintry night in 1984 Madonna Gordon, an administrative assistant, and her 15-year-old daughter Tish were passing the house. They saw a light in an upstairs window and went in to investigate.

Madonna called out as they moved down the shadowy hall. An unfamiliar woman stopped them in their tracks! She looked about forty, with odd upswept hair. She wore a long, bell-shaped skirt and a high-collared blouse—the style worn around 1900.

Tish said, "It was like a shadow of a person, but it was a three-dimensional shadow."

Madonna saw the apparition several more times, but never as clearly. Others witnessed saw only a gray, filmy shape.

Some theorize that the Bittersweet ghost is Margaret L. H. Smith, who lived there for many years. Blind, poor, and without family, Mrs. Smith died in 1961 at age 94. Her twilight years were especially lonely after the tragic death of her husband. Her sadness may live on.

*

For the last stop on our ghost tour we visit UVM's spectral superstar, who resides at the Counseling Center, an old brick mansion on the corner of South Williams and Main. For years a private residence, it became UVM's Neumann Center and later the home of Counseling and Testing.

Many people tell of mysterious after-hours experiences. In the mid-1970s secretary Louise Gulla was working alone on a Saturday afternoon. Around four she heard the front door open and close. Footsteps climbed the stairs. She called, "Hello," but no one responded.

Later Ms. Gulla asked a visiting student to go upstairs and see who was there. He checked thoroughly but found no one.

A janitor mopping floors one dark morning was startled when something unseen knocked his bucket over, sloshing dirty water everywhere. As he tried to determine what had happened, overhead lights began flashing. He actually saw the light switch flipping up and down. Immediately he put in for a transfer.

Richard Does, former director of Counseling and Testing, had the most unsettling encounter. One evening while alone in his office, he saw "a spectral image gliding down the stairway."

He observed it clearly; it was "an elderly man with distinct facial features and a bulbous nose." A receding hairline and thick sideburns framed the apparition's angry expression. No hands or feet were visible at the ends of his old-fashioned jacket and trousers.

Dr. Does said the entire figure was "kind of translucent and shimmering like a jellyfish."

Before drifting away, the specter glowered directly at Dr. Does as if to ask, Just what are you doing here, mister?

Dr. Does asked himself the same question and left.

Other people working alone in the building have heard the conventional sounds of a ghost: footsteps, doors, and the like. But this building offers something else: sneezes and coughs, suggesting the spirit world is not free of ghostly contagions.

Who haunts the Counseling Center? Perhaps it's the spirit of Capt. John Nabb, a colorful seafarer who lived there in the nineteenth century. Or maybe it's Prof. Eldridge Jacobs, a UVM geologist who died in 1957. For some reason folks have taken to calling the ghost "Captain Jacobs," adding more confusion to this already perplexing subject.

*

It is difficult to imagine UVM without its ghosts, yet today many of its classic haunts are quiet. Perhaps they have earned their diplomas and moved on to haunt other schools and homes around the country.

As we continue our tour of Vermont's haunted houses, I can't help but wonder how many of our resident ghosts are UVM graduates.

Green Mountain Seminary

If you're driving north on Route 100 and passing through Waterbury Center, a peculiar three-and-a-half-story, rust-colored building is likely to catch your eye. I guarantee it will hold your attention, but you may not be able to explain why.

Perhaps it's the vigilance implied by its elevated position. Perhaps it's the subliminal suggestions implicit in the nearby graveyard. Or maybe it's the blood-red hue of its clapboarding or that the fact that night seems to fill its interior, visible through the darkened windows. But whatever the reason, there is something stark about the building, something eerie and fascinating.

In preparation for a painting, noted Vermont artist Francis Colburn took a series of photographs that emphasized its New England Gothic allure. In my frequent trips up and down Route 100, I often stop to stare at the building and let my imagination run wild.

It appears to be deserted, but it isn't—the town library is inside. There are also two apartments and a mail-order business. Yet, for some reason, it still appears disused and vacant.

In its heyday it was—and is still—known as the Green Mountain Seminary.

Incorporated in 1862 by the Freewill Baptist Society, its stated goal was to promote "literature, science, the useful arts, morality and the doctrines and duties of evangelical religion." Perhaps such a lofty mission is enough to have given this austere edifice some kind of spiritual jump start.

Anyway, the seminary was dedicated on September 1, 1869, offering

"College Preparatory, Academical, Commercial, and Ladies' Full Course of Study." The first class consisted of 106 men, 104 women, overseen by four teachers and a principal. But all too soon the coming of Vermont's community high schools made the seminary's tenure rather brief. In 1906 it closed permanently.

In 1913 the town bought the building and operated it as a grade school. Part of its appeal was that the seminary had originally used the second floor as a chapel. Its ceiling, and the third floor above, had to span a forty-four-foot space with no support from below. Clever builders solved this architectural puzzle by constructing the roof using massive king-post trusses set ten feet apart. They actually "hung" the third floor from these trusses, using wrought-iron rods one inch thick. This ingeniously designed interior chapel was easily converted into the grade school's combination gymnasium and theater. But in 1969 this incarnation also ended when school districts consolidated.

From then on the Seminary was underutilized and occasionally vacant.

Or was it?

The current owner is Eric Chittenden, who also owns the Cold Hollow Cider Mill nearby. Eric is a member of a venerable Vermont family whose roots go back to the state's first governor, Thomas Chittenden. In a recent conversation, Eric confirmed what I had always suspected: the Green Mountain Seminary might be haunted.

He told me that his cider mill used to sponsor a basketball team that practiced in the gym. The team had been organized by Cold Hollow's general manager, who had attended UVM on a basketball scholarship.

One fall evening in 1979 or 1980, just prior to Hallowe'en, a few members of the team were practicing in the gym. When Eric went over to join them, he was surprised to find all the men standing at the top of the stairs. They were agitated and obviously nervous. Clearly something was wrong.

One man asked Eric, "Is this place spooked, or what?"

Eric said, "Why do you ask?"

"Well," the man said, "we took a break after we finished the game and we heard footsteps upstairs, on the third floor. We thought it was you, so we went up and looked, but there was nobody up there. But as soon as we got back down, the footsteps started again."

Apparently this process was repeated a couple of times. The footsteps were loud enough, and the third floor was empty enough, that the men had become frightened. So frightened they wouldn't continue the game. In fact, for a while they decided they were never going to play there again.

Though Eric finds it somewhat amusing that a group of macho athletes became frightened in a spooky old building, he refuses to dismiss their story.

"These were grown men," he said, "adults. I thought they were pulling my leg at first. But they were dead serious. . . . That's what lends a lot of credibility: None of these people are people who embellish."

If there is a ghost in the Green Mountain Seminary, Eric isn't sure who it might be. He told me, "Somebody said [it was] a teacher who used to draw up on the top floor and the teacher died."

Though Eric himself has had no direct experience with the haunting, he says, "I've heard every creak the building can emit. But I haven't heard the footsteps."

So how does he explain the apparent haunting?

"It's a big building," he says, "and it's an eerie building. There is a lot of history, so it just lends itself to those sorts of tales."

And, as he's quick to add, "The stories persist. Especially with people who work over there late at night."

The Bennington Bottle Monument

On the first page of Southern Vermont College's full color catalog they say, "anything is possible here." They go on to talk about "spirited learning" and their "spirit of accessibility and cooperation."

What do you suppose they're hinting at?

A visit to the campus can only reinforce the impression that there is more to SVC than meets the eye. The school, housed in the former Edward Everett mansion in Bennington, has the air of a haunted fourteenth-century British castle.

And, if it's ghosts we're looking for, we'd better start with Edward Everett himself.

Born May 18, 1851, Everett moved to Bennington after his mother married Henry W. Putnam, Sr. He stayed long enough to graduate from Bennington High School in 1869, then moved to Ohio to seek his fortune.

He seemed especially adept at making money in this pre–income tax era. First, he bought a share in the American Bottle Company. Then he bought the whole company. Eventually it became largest bottle manufacturer in the world.

In order to seek a less expensive way to keep the glass fires burning, Everett prospected for oil and gas in Ohio, and found them. As his fortunes increased he invested in real estate, cattle, oil, orchards . . . and more glass. Everything he touched turned to gold.

In 1886, after buying Oren Granger King's Newark, Ohio, glassworks, he married King's daughter, the aristocratic Amy. Together they had three daughters: Mary, Amy, and Ann.

Everett returned to Bennington in 1910 as one of the richest men in the country—and the richest man in Vermont. There he bought up 1,220 acres. In 1911 he began building his grand summer house on the eastern slope of Mt. Anthony. While the house went up, he began planting his orchard—the largest in the world: 75,000 apple trees, 3,000 plum, 2,000 quince, and hundreds of pear. It extended ten miles south into Pownal.

The two million dollar house was equally ambitious, if not more so. He hired thirty-two stone masons, who traveled from Italy to quarry, trim, and place 32,000 cubic feet of granite. Neighbors watched an endless chain of wagons pulling block after block of stone up the steep one-mile driveway.

Crews worked seven days a week, ten hours a day, to complete the mansion's exterior within the six months before winter. The mansion itself took two years to finish. The opulent interior contains twenty-seven rooms, with marble for the fireplaces and stairways imported from Italy. The silver door handles, lamps, and crystal chandeliers came from England. Cuba supplied mahogany for the dining room.

All the rooms were furnished in high-Victorian splendor. Lush tapestries and original oil paintings covered the walls. The floors are "parqueted" with intricate designs framed by rooms paneled with oak on the first floor, maple on the second, and fir on the third.

Looking outside, it is difficult to determine which is more splendid, the mansion itself, or the panorama that contains it.

Edward Everett's home was a veritable castle, grand, imposing, elegant, and regal with its cobbled courtyard, "porte cochere," one hundred–plus pagan statues, and thirteen-tiered cascade fountain. There was a seven-room gate house, a barn and stable, carriage house, two greenhouses, and various other buildings. Its lawns and gardens required forty-five full-time groundskeepers.

Edward, his wife Amy, and the three girls moved into "Orchard House" in 1915. But their time together was to be short-lived. Amy died in 1917 when Edward was sixty-five years old.

But the mustachioed millionaire wasn't one to pine away in solitude. Abnormally vigorous for a man of his years, he quickly started a scandalous flirtation with Grace Burnap, a singer who was thirty years his junior. Mindless of public outrage, they began traveling together. In 1920 they became man and wife. In his early seventies, Edward became the father of two more daughters.

In April 1929 Edward Everett died at age seventy-seven, thus touching off what might be called "The Second Battle of Bennington."

This battle was fought in Vermont courts over the dispensation of the Everett estate. His three daughters from the first marriage sued when they found they were to inherit only one tenth of their father's wealth. They argued that Everett was not in his right mind when he signed his will. Grace, they maintained, had unfairly influenced the failing old man, compelling him to leave nine tenths of his substantial fortune to her alone.

Lasting from January to late March of 1930, it was the longest, most gossip-inspiring trial in Vermont history. Testimony left the magnificent Glass and Bottle Baron of the American Industrial Revolution looking like a pitiable weakling, utterly dominated by his Lady Macbeth of a wife.

The community had never taken to Grace the way they had to Everett's first wife. They and the court sided with the daughters. At length the will was overturned. The daughters each got one-fifth of estate. Grace and her two daughters were awarded the remaining two-fifths. But Grace got to keep the mansion, where she occasionally lived until 1952.

Such passion and high melodrama could easily provoke a TV mini-series.

Or a haunting.

In 1952 Grace sold the house for $65,000 to the Order of the Holy Cross. Perhaps the old place took on an additional level of spiritual energy during its two decades as a monastery.

In 1974, when Southern Vermont College took up residence there, students and staff quickly realized they were not alone.

Many ghost stories have to do with people working security. One oft-repeated scenario has a solo security guard patrolling the Everett House. Suddenly doorknobs begin turning back and forth in rooms known to be empty.

A variation involves discovering an open door that should be closed and locked. As the guard reaches out to close it, the door slams shut by itself.

Perhaps Judy Corbett, Director of Campus Life, strayed from her area of expertise when—while all alone in the mansion at night—she heard weird noises and footsteps.

Occasionally people smell perfume. Someone mentioned sniffing cooking odors—beef stew, to be exact—on the third floor where the servants used to live.

Jim Marsden, SVC Director of Facilities, recalls a late fall night in 1982 when he was summoned to the Everett House by college security staff. The officer on duty reported strange noises coming from the upper floors of the building; their origin could not be precisely located. He suspected students might be in the building attempting a prank on Security.

When Mr. Marsden and the officer determined the disturbance was on the third floor, they set off to investigate. Finally they traced the noise to room 315, a faculty office, formerly a servant's quarters.

The room was locked, but sounds were definitely coming from inside. Mr. Marsden attempted to enter using his master pass keys. The lock disengaged but the door itself could not be pushed open; there appeared to be an object holding it closed. Puzzled, Mr. Marsden pushed against the door with his shoulder and body weight. He was able to move it back far enough to peer inside.

A large office desk and chair had been placed tightly against the door from the inside. But no one was in the room. The only other way in or out was via the window. But it was closed and locked and over forty feet above the ground!

One thing that lends distinction to the Everett haunting is that apparitions are frequently seen. Dark shapes lurk in the haunted halls. A mysterious "Woman in White," believed to be the ghost of the first Mrs. Everett, is occasionally spotted within the house or prowling the grounds.

Two other shapes—perhaps the Everetts' daughters?—were spotted close to Hallowe'en, 1994. The school was producing a "Haunted Hay Ride" along a dirt road that leads to the campus. Various scary skits were staged along the way.

Two students, Scott and Gwen, were in charge of the graveyard stop. Between truckloads of "victims" they noticed two girls—apparently in costume—walking from the back woods, crossing the road, and heading toward the front woods. They seemed to be barefoot and there was something odd about their faces.

Scott didn't recognize them, nor could he figure out why they should be out there to begin with. So he called to them.

They stopped and turned. Their faces were alarming. Scott and

Gwen agree the two girls were wearing something that distorted their features.

Masks maybe?

The frightened students thought not. They swear they were cauls.

The two mysterious girls continued on their silent way across the road and up to the woods where they disappeared.

Thinking about it later, Scott and Gwen realized how very odd the whole thing had been. First, it was odd they could even see the unfamiliar figures in the profound darkness where the incident occurred. Second, why should they be so sure cauls had masked the facial features? Gwen was so unnerved by the incident that she wanted to return to her room.

Whether this encounter was natural or supernatural, the irony is fun: as Scott and Gwen were preparing to scare other people, they got scared themselves.

A far less frightening tale involves a woman who used to play piano in the theater. Sometimes when she was practicing there by herself, she'd see little "wisps of smoke" dancing around on the stage in time with her music.

Student Christi Yates and a friend saw a peculiar shadow late one night after a play rehearsal. She says, "At the end of the hallway we could definitely see a form. I could see enough to tell it was a male or a manly form. The nose was sharp; I couldn't make out the rest of the face. We went partly down the hallway until I couldn't go any further because it scared me. And I don't scare easily."

Christi struggled not to turn away, tried to open herself to the experience.

"He was standing there but I also saw him running toward me and moving back, then running toward me and moving back. Like a movie—it's hard to explain."

This "pulsing ghost," as I have come to call it, is unique in my experience.

So are the three-dimensional shadow entities perceived by Evan Pringle and his friend Brandy Dillensneider. Stranger still, they had their mysterious encounter outside, in broad daylight.

Evan, a senior, is editor and chief of the school newspaper. Currently, he is a stringer for the *Bennington Banner*. He has had an active interest in campus ghosts since this experience in 1995.

Evan and Brandy were enjoying a short hike to a small pond on the Everett property, known as Upper Pond. As they looked across the water, Brandy noticed—and pointed out—two shadows on the opposite side.

She says, "Once I realized those could not possibly be our shadows, could not possibly be from trees or anything, I asked Evan if he was seeing it."

Evan saw them too, but they were unlike any shadows he'd ever seen before.

"What I saw basically was two lines of shadow—they looked to be two-dimensional—lying on the ground. At first they looked like they might have been a shadow cast by a tree or something, but there was nothing to cast the shadow. Then they focused in a little, and they just kind of popped up into three dimensions, standing upright.

"One was taller than the other one. I got the impression one was an adult and the other a child, but other than that I really couldn't see any features."

Evan and Brandy watched the shadows for about two minutes. "While we were looking at them it was pretty easy to tell that they were looking at us, too."

After a while he saw something else. To corroborate what he was seeing, Evan asked Brandy, "Did one of them just move?"

"Yes," Brandy said, "the taller one leaned over toward the shorter one."

"So," Evan told me, "I knew that we were definitely seeing the same thing at the same time. It was very interesting."

Brandy and Evan wanted to get a little closer. As they made their way around the pond, they had to look down to avoid bushes and rocks. When they looked back, the shadows had disappeared.

Brandy's recollection is almost identical to Evan's, but she adds this fascinating detail: "The shadows weren't *on* anything. I could see the heads *over* the edge of the hill. I could see right away that they were not shadows on the ground."

In other words, part of the shadow seemed to be suspended in the air, hovering above the crest of the hill.

Apparently Brandy saw them more clearly than her companion. "I could tell easily that it was a woman and a little boy. And that the clothing was not modern. I couldn't see the facial features that well, but I could see the shapes of the bodies: it was a woman and little boy."

Evan's research suggests one might have been the shade of Edward Everett's first wife, Amy. The child, he suspects, was a friend of the family who had been deaf in life. He further believes there may be as many as seven ghosts in residence.

Could be. In the short time I spent on the Southern Vermont College campus, I came to realize there are hundreds more stories like these. The only conclusion I can draw is that there is occasionally truth in advertising. As the SVC catalogue says, "Anything is possible here."

Ghost Academy

The Vermont Police Academy in Pittsford seems perfect for a haunting. Built in 1907, it was used as a tuberculosis sanatorium until it closed in 1960. The sprawling complex of old brick buildings remained empty for a decade, until reincarnated by the State of Vermont as a training facility.

I spoke with Captain David Schmoll of the UVM Police and with Brian Searles, Chief of the South Burlington police Department. Both have worked at the Academy, Captain Schmoll as a firearms instructor, Chief Searles as Executive Director of the Vermont Criminal Justice Training Council. Both agree there has been a lot of talk about ghosts.

As is so often the case, building renovations seem to provoke ghostly activity. During 1985, Chief Searles's first year at the academy, restoration was being done on the third floor. There an unrenovated room was used for storing old medical equipment, gowns, religious items, and hospital china. There were also patient records—big books listing all the patients between 1907 and 1960.

A good friend of Chief Searles's was on the faculty at the time. One very hot day he went up to check records regarding an acquaintance who'd been there as a patient. The storage room was hot and muggy. Its one small window was always closed so no air moved.

Suddenly, unaccountably, the officer felt a cold wind that seemed to come from nowhere. As if animated by unseen forces, the pages of the book he was reading began to turn by themselves. And the officer quickly left the premises.

A Fish and Wildlife Department officer received a similar scare. He'd made an early morning visit—around 5 A.M.—to pick up training materials stored in the basement. As he opened the door to the storage area he heard shuffling footsteps overhead. Then the door slammed shut. He opened it again and checked the area around it. The door slammed a second time and the Fish and Wildlife officer took his leave in a hurry.

Occasionally people actually catch a glimpse of something. Around 1989 two male students on the second floor opened the door to their room and saw an orange glow. As they watched dumbfounded, the orange haze began to move. And so did the trainees. When they returned with prospective witnesses, the glow had vanished.

About a year later another of Chief Searles's friends ran a summer substance abuse project for teenagers.

Two or more kids were exploring the old building when they peeked through the door of an upstairs room. What they saw left them genuinely terrified. Boxes were moving around all by themselves. The officer didn't see this firsthand, but says he believes the kids—they were really scared.

One story involves a talking ghost. Back in the late 1970s and early 1980s it was unusual for women to be in law enforcement. The few female trainees had separate quarters above the kitchen.

At this particular time there was only one woman trainee on the premises. When she came down with a serious flu one afternoon, her instructor sent her to her quarters to rest. At some point she had a visitor. Someone pushed open the spring-loaded door and entered the room. Then a female voice clearly asked, "Are you all right?"

Later, the trainee found someone had left her a glass of water and some aspirin.

When she was finally feeling better the trainee tried to find her concerned visitor to thank her. Trouble was, there were no other women in the class. And the few women employees—clerical and kitchen staff—were all accounted for. No living soul had entered her room.

That a ghost walks those ancient halls was an accepted fact back in the days when the place was a hospital. Today, many current occupants believe it as well.

The few who claim to have seen her clearly describe a woman dressed in white—a woman who looks remarkably like a nurse. But no one knows for sure who the ghost might be.

The common wisdom is that her name is Mary. Supposedly she came from South Barre and died from TB contracted while employed at the hospital. I've heard her medical records are still on the premises, but I have not examined them.

She is sometimes spotted in the halls and rooms or occasionally in the enclosed glass-paneled walkways that connect the main building with two outbuildings.

Once David Schmoll was walking in this area when he ran into a former nurse and her daughter. They chatted about how things had changed. She asked if David had heard the ghost stories. The woman explained how the place had been a TB sanatorium and that many people had seen the ghost nurse.

She told David how she and some other employees had been out walking when they saw a woman standing inside, looking out from the windowed walkway. They went in, but no one was there.

The ghost nurse is consistently perceived as friendly, like a guardian overseeing the place. A helpful, peaceful, benevolent caretaker who just wants to be sure things are running smoothly.

*

However, I spoke with one former employee—a young man named Tim—whose experience at the Academy did not convince him of the spirit's benevolence.

In the summer of 1990 Tim was helping to run the Green Mountain Teen Institute, a drug and alcohol prevention program for high school kids. Before the seminar began, the entire staff assembled for training.

Almost at once people started talking about their minor run-ins with the ghost. Some heard toilets flushing. Others heard shuffling feet as if in paper slippers. One woman walking alone down a hallway heard footsteps directly behind her. When she turned around, the corridor was empty. Several trainers complained that the doors to their rooms repeatedly opened on their own.

After listening with interest, Tim suggested that no one mention these unsettling incidents to the incoming students. "The last thing we needed was a group of fifty frightened high schoolers. It would undermine what we were trying to do and generally make our jobs much harder."

But weird things kept happening. And pretty soon things started happening to Tim.

Once he was alone in the gymnasium practicing his guitar. When he finished his song he heard clapping. He looked around but no one was there. Oddly, he told me, the clapping did not echo as it should in the huge, empty building.

The following day he was delivering something to another staff member's room. No one was around, so he went into the room to leave the package. Then he heard a knock on the closet door. He said, "It was one of the stand-up wardrobes, and the door was already open. There was no one inside, nor was there anyone else in any of the nearby rooms."

When the knock came again—louder this time—Tim left hurriedly, never looking behind him.

Later that day an event occurred that seemed to change the nature of these benign encounters.

Several trainers were in the gym setting up a volleyball net. Its posts had flat, heavy metal bases that had to be screwed into plates in the floor. One staff member was having trouble with the screws; for some reason they wouldn't turn.

Suddenly, almost magically, the screw dropped directly into its hole, trapping the young man's thumb between the heavy metal plates. He cried out as mounting pressure squeezed his flesh.

Tim ran to help, but found he couldn't release the screw. It had apparently screwed itself into its hole without being turned. They had to drop the net and pull on the pole to release enough pressure to remove the hand.

Tim said, "[W]e have no idea what could have made [the screw] drop into place. The bolt was not stripped in any way; [neither] was the hole."

Yet the injury was severe enough to warrant a hospital visit.

"I can't say this was a deliberate attack by [the ghost]," Tim told me, "But we have no [other] explanation for what happened."

Should we perceive this event as a show of spectral hostility? Or, was it helpful hospitality gone awry? Then again, the whole incident could have been nothing more than a remarkable accident. Such ambiguity, I'm afraid, is often the nature of super-nature.

I asked Captain David Schmoll what he believed about the haunting at the Vermont Police Academy. He said, "My job and outlook on life prevent me from being a believer in these kinds of tales."

Chief Brain Searles reminds us, "It's a very old building; it's full of noises."

And each year new classes of recruits quickly learn the ghostly history of their school. Wild imaginations, and wilder pranks, can be common.

So the stories, like the ghosts, live on.

A Ghost at Long Last?

The more I talk to people about haunted houses, the more I realize just how many there are. I used to imagine every Vermont town had at least one; now I believe it's impossible to find a village with so few.

And I repeatedly learn that ghosts materialize in the most unexpected places, places one would swear could not be haunted at all. For example, the most conspicuous building in the town where I grew up: the inn in Chester, Vermont.

This grand, three-story structure stands right on the green at the center of town. It has been there since 1923, when it was built on the site of another inn that had burned down in 1920. So in one form or another, the Chester Inn has held a prominent spot in town for well over a century.

As a child I walked past it every day without the slightest inkling something mysterious might be going on inside. As a young man I spent a bit of social time there, at the bar, restaurant, or at some amiable gathering or community function. Over the years I knew three different owners, and once—in the early seventies—I even worked there for a couple of weeks during leaf-peeping season. My main responsibility was to stand at the desk and act folksy. My uniform was a flannel shirt, blue jeans, and corncob pipe. I'd answer the phone, take reservations, and tell colorful stories about the area while directing tourists to local spots of interest.

What I *didn't* tell anyone was that the inn was haunted. Because I didn't know it. Possibly the various innkeepers thought conjuring "those sorts of spirits" would be bad for business. Or maybe the specter just never encountered anyone sufficiently psychic to interact with it. Then again, perhaps the ghost was perfectly content and had no reason to make itself known . . . until recently.

Since I moved away from Chester the inn changed hands again. In 1986 Jack Coleman bought it and set about an ambitious renovation program that has contributed to, and greatly changed, the place's character.

A retired university president and man of many talents, Jack had always wanted to be an innkeeper, so when he bought the Chester Inn he renamed it The Inn at Long Last.

Maybe the name change was what the ghost was reacting to. Perhaps dead Vermonters, like their living counterparts, just don't like change. But . . . well, I'm getting a little ahead of myself.

A Big Change

Jack Coleman set about redecorating all the rooms. He gave each a specific name rather than a number, and created for each a theme and unique character. Two or three months into the renovation process, he discovered that one of the rooms—room number 16—came complete with a unique character nobody bargained for.

Jack's partner was his son Paul, a giant of a man, six foot four, with an authoritative voice and a commanding presence. During the renovation, Paul's dog was always at his side as he moved from room to room in the old building. The animal obeyed him faithfully—except when he commanded it to go into room 16; it wouldn't even approach the threshold. Puzzled, Paul finally tried dragging the protesting animal into the room. But as soon as he released its collar the dog fired back into the hall like a ball from a cannon. That may have been the first time the topic of ghosts came up.

As the years passed, Jack, a rational man and a skeptic, became more and more convinced there was an unpaying and invisible guest in room 16. To him, the most persuasive piece of evidence was one in which he was directly involved: It had to do with a telephone. He'd had phone jacks installed in rooms 16, 18, 20, 22. But the only *telephone* was in room 16.

It is important to note that Jack doesn't live at the inn. He lives alone in the building next door. But his home phone is tied in directly to the hotel switchboard. Nobody can reach him by phone except through that switchboard. If no one is at the switchboard, Jack cannot receive any calls. But, for the first four and a half years—every night—his phone would ring between 1:30 and 2 in the morning.

At first he would jump up to answer it, but no one would ever be there. It would ring just once, then remain silent until the next night. After a while, Jack says, he got used to the single ring and learned to sleep through it. But he remained puzzled because it would happen when nobody was in the inn. That is, when the inn was closed and completely vacant. No one could explain why, and no one was able to fix the problem.

But the problem was finally solved when they moved the telephone out of room 16. After that, Jack's midnight calls stopped forever.

Jack later told the story to a guest at the inn, a psychic woman who claimed to be a ghost expert. She said she wasn't surprised by the mysterious calls; ghosts love telephones, she explained, and that's exactly the way they use them.

She also said that on two occasions during previous visits as she was walking past the door to room 16, she felt as if something unseen had reached out and grabbed her around the throat. Both times she distinctly heard a name—it was "Roger."

She said Roger is the ghost of a man who burned to death in the fire of 1920.

One member of the inn's staff claims to have actually seen the ghost. The woman worked as a waitress and sometimes as a housekeeper. Once, while cleaning the bathroom mirror in room 16, she says she saw the reflection of a white ghostly figure over her shoulder. Her companion did not see the ghost, but saw the woman's face turn absolutely white almost instantly.

Jack told me about the incident that to him seemed the most unpleasant. Michael, the inn's chef, lived with his wife in an apartment two floors above the kitchen. Both were devout Catholics who loved to read; their apartment was lined with bookshelves. Michael's tastes were eclectic but his wife's interest was in self-help programs and do-it-yourself psychology.

One night when they were in bed they heard strange noises in the living room. When Michael investigated he found their books scattered all over the floor, maybe three or four from each of the different bookshelves around the room. But none of Michael's books were in the pile. Just his wife's books, all dealing with pop psychology and New Age–type themes.

The unpleasant part of the story is this: Among the fallen books was a smashed statue of the Madonna, its pieces spread all over the floor like a jigsaw puzzle.

Is there a connection? Is there some meaning in this senseless act? Jack can't say for sure.

Although this episode has sinister overtones, most of the ghostly activity centered around room 16 is pretty benign. Guests definitely complain of strange noises, but admittedly those could be the buiness-as-usual sounds of an old building.

Other events seem to have the tone of good natured pranks. For example, women's lingerie will sometimes disappear from room 16, only to reappear elsewhere, sometimes surprising—maybe even embarrassing—guests in other rooms.

Some Detective Work

So, if there is a ghost haunting The Inn at Long Last, whose could it be? And why does it seem to use room 16 as its headquarters?

Perhaps after naming room 16 "The Lord Peter Wimsey Room," Jack was inspired to do a little detective work. He knew that the former inn had burned down in 1920, and had been rebuilt on the old foundation in 1923. Had anyone died in the fire—possibly someone named Roger—like the ghost expert had told him?

Jack says, "That story has to be wrong, because when I was new to the village and working on the renovations outside, people would come by and introduce themselves. Some were very elderly and they had been here the night of the fire. . . . They told how bitterly cold it was and how the fire company hosed down the two buildings beside the inn to keep them from going and never mentioned anybody burning to death."

And I agree with Jack: witnessing a death by fire would be memorable.

However, he did uncover a story about a married couple from Bellows Falls who came to the Chester Inn for their honeymoon. Supposedly the groom died at the inn the night of their arrival.

Jack's check of town records bears this out. But did he die in room 16? There simply is no way to tell. And could his name have been Roger? Memory, and town records, just aren't that complete.

When I interviewed him, Jack had owned the inn for over a decade. I asked him if he had come to believe one of his permanent guests is something supernatural.

His says his bottom-line belief is that something *is* there. Otherwise there's no way to explain how his phone could ring when the inn was closed and nobody at all was in the building. And there's no way to explain why his son's dog would go anywhere but into room 16.

Ghost Hunting

Although I am endlessly fascinated by the paranormal, I had never experienced it. I'd never witnessed a UFO. I'd had no contact with angels or demons. I'd never had a premonition or a near-death experience. In short, I had never had any kind of personal encounters with the unknown, the psychic, or the supernatural.

But I thought returning to my hometown might give me a chance to see a ghost.

On November 17, 1994, I was in Chester to do a reading from a recently published book, *Green Mountain Ghosts*. I had arranged to spend that night at The Inn at Long Last, hoping for an opportunity to do a bit of investigating.

I checked in after the reading, at roughly 10 P.M. The inn was officially closed—everyone was on vacation between foliage season and ski season—but, as a trusted hometown boy, I was permitted to stay there alone.

The point is, I was staying all by myself. All resident staff members were away and the owner lived elsewhere.

Feeling brave at the time, I asked if I could stay in the haunted room. The owner said, "No." Though I can make that sound ominous for dramatic effect, the reason was simple and straightforward: he wasn't keeping that part of the inn heated.

Instead, he gave me what he calls "The Dickens Room," one of the biggest and most beautiful in the place.

My plan was to read for a while, then go out and ramble around the narrow, dimly lighted corridors of the old building. I had even brought along a flashlight for the occasion. If I couldn't spend the night in room 16, at least I could check it out sometime after the witching hour.

For close to an hour I lay stretched out on the comfortable bed, flipping through one of the books that came with the room. I think it was a copy of *Great Expectations*. All the while, my ears were tuned to the familiar sounds of an old building: the creaks and groans of hundred-year-old timbers expanding and contracting as the temperature changed, the rattle and clunk of the ancient heating system, and the faint traffic sounds admitted by the less-than-soundproof windows.

Sometime around midnight I began to get a bit drowsy. I figured I'd better get up and get on with my ghost hunting.

But I snapped to full attention when I heard the first sound. It came from the floor above me, a slow scraping noise. Distinct. Unmistakable. Of sufficient duration to be absolutely sure I was hearing . . . something.

And it was nothing like any "old building" sounds I'd ever heard.

It wasn't water in pipes. It wasn't mice. It wasn't even squirrels in the attic.

There it was a second time!

Yes, I had it: it sounded exactly as if a large, heavy cardboard box were being pulled—or pushed—across a gritty wooden floor.

What could be making such a sound? The rooms are carpeted, I recalled. And so are the hallways. So what could be scraping?

I hate to use this chapter to make a public confession, but I have to admit that I didn't go out to check. Instead I got up and locked the doors to my room as all the stories about the inn's haunted halls came crashing back at me. Suddenly all the stories of ghostly confrontations I'd heard and written about were ultra-vivid in my imagination.

And here I was, completely alone in the inn. With something upstairs.

Fear of the unknown was very real at that moment. Although the doors were secured, it was impossible to sleep. Nor could I read. My mind raced. My gaze flashed from corner to corner. My heart pounded. Every sound was thunder. Though the inn was not hot, I felt myself sweating.

Then—wide awake, hypervigilant—I heard the sound a third time. There could be no mistake. It was not the product of my imagination. Not the trickery of a sleepy brain. Animals? Not unless the were rearranging sizable boxes. My pal Rick Bates playing a joke? No way. It was the middle of the night and he had to work in Brattleboro the next morning.

The noise was real. It was a lengthy, dull, gritty scrape, and it was coming from overhead and to my left. There is no question that I heard it. No question that I checked my doors to be sure I was locked in.

I suppose this story would have a more dramatic ending if, like some

Lovecraftian antihero, I went screaming into the night to be discovered the next day cowering under a park bench on the green, shaking and babbling, my hair turned white as a Vermont snowfall. Or if I had grabbed my flashlight and gone stomping up to the third floor to confront whatever it was that was rearranging the furniture up there.

In my own defense I can at least say that I did stay put. I held my ground in the locked room and remained there for the rest of the night. I even slept a bit.

The next morning I mentioned the sounds to Carolyn Stacy, a hotel employee who arrived to go through the "check out" ritual with her hotel's only guest.

She said she couldn't imagine what I had heard. "Let's go have a look," she said.

I followed Carolyn up the stairs. We eventually figured out where on the third floor the sounds must have been coming from. There I was surprised to find, not a guest room, not a hallway, but a linen closet.

She opened the door. Nothing on the closet's tiny floor could have caused the disturbance, but we did find something slightly strange. At the rear of the narrow closet we saw a small door about three or so feet high.

"Where's that go?" I asked.

"I don't know," she said. "I've never seen it before. Let's have a look."

I followed her through into a large storage area. This was clearly where the sounds must have been coming from. The floors were wooden and adequately gritty. And the room was full of cardboard boxes. They were placed helter-skelter so it was impossible to determine if any of them had been moving, much less what might have moved it.

A ghost? I hardly think so. More likely "an undigested bit of beef, a blot of mustard, a crumb of cheese, a fragment of an underdone potato," as Dickens's Scrooge described Marley's specter. But the fright was real. There's no question about that. And it made me understand better the terror so many of the people I interview describe when they tell me about their face-to-face confrontations with the unknown.

EQUINOX

Since colonial times the Equinox Hotel has been linked with every phase of Manchester, Vermont, history. It began as a humble tavern where local rebels plotted revolutionary escapades. It expanded and prospered, tempting tourists to sample its scenic surroundings, bathers to bask in its healing waters, and eventually presidents, whose patronage elevated its reputation to one of New England's finest resorts.

In one form or another, the Equinox has been in operation since 1769. Since then it has been variously known as Thaddeus Munson's Inn, Widow Black's Inn, Vanderlip's Hotel, The Taconic, Orvis Hotel, and finally the Equinox, after the 3,800-foot mountain, its one local rival for size.

It is without question the centerpiece of the town.

I remember it during the late 1960s and early 1970s when I lived in nearby Chester. By then it had fallen onto hard times. Trends in tourism had changed. Its hotel facilities, once state-of-the-art, had become old-fashioned. Upkeep was expensive, improvement unaffordable. Decline was inevitable and obvious.

We'd occasionally drive by and I'd gawk at its peeling and pale remains. Its pillared porch and marble walkways were relics of a vanished age. It reminded me of some giant Jurassic roadkill sprawled there by the side of Route 7. I was sure this nearly extinct behemoth, flattened by the great depression of the 1930s and left to die, would probably never recover.

In 1973 it took its last breath. Just one year after it was awarded a long-deserved place on the National Register of Historic Places, it closed.

And the shadow of the wrecking ball swung closer with each passing season.

But unlike the dinosaurs, the Equinox came back from the dead a decade later. And thus began the multi-million-dollar restoration that would return it to its former splendor.

But perhaps the attempts at resuscitation brought something else back to life as well.

I am uncertain when Vermont's grandest hotel picked up its reputation for being haunted. Employee accounts uniformly suggest reconstruction and resurrection went hand in hand within the newly papered, freshly carpeted hallways of Vermont's answer to "The Overlook."

I first heard about the ghosts back in 1996 from a former Equinox public relations person. When I visited the hotel in 1998 I thought the whole thing might have been a put-on when head concierge Linda Malachuk and historian Wendell Coleman took me on a tour of the place. We started with an old poster-sized photograph of the hotel in which the "ghosts" were clearly visible. They were obviously the hazy female forms of a double exposure. But as the stories unfolded, it was clear that some of the guests had never deserted the old place.

Linda Malachuk has worked there for eleven years. As head concierge this pleasant, intelligent woman is in an ideal position to be privy to all reports from employees as well as guests.

When her tenure began she quickly discovered that housekeepers were afraid to enter certain rooms because of unaccountable noises, rapid changes in air temperature, or things that vanish and appear elsewhere.

"There're a lot of disturbances up on the third and fourth floors," Linda told me. "At night, when the security men go around and do room checks, they'll find a door will be open. They'll look in and for no reason at all the shade has flown up and is wiggling, or the rocker is rocking."

Another source told me that housekeepers and security staff have witnessed peculiar goings-on in a certain room on the second floor north. Ice chests, chairs, and things that just suddenly appeared in the room were discovered piled up like a pyramid, stacked one on top of another. There was no explanation for it. The people I talked to found the event impossible to interpret—what could it possibly mean?

Linda suspects the problems started at the time of the hotel's renovation. "During 1989 to 1991 we revitalized all the rooms—every single room. Carpeting was taken out, but the window shades were left up. It was up in room 440—they seem to like that room—the shade was all cut in pieces just like a jigsaw puzzle. There was only a handful of employees who were working at that time. And they kept running into this all the time—the shades being cut up."

She also recalled a hotel guest who worked for Guinness Corporation. He went into his room, put his keys on the table, then stepped out for a moment. When he came back his keys had been separated from the chain and thrown all over the room. "No explanation for it," Linda said. "No one had been in that room. So we just figured it was the ghosts again."

To Linda, the funniest story is the one about a lady who came down to the bar and said to the bartender, "Tonight I want the whole bottle of wine, because I gotta get some sleep. I can't have these ghosts keeping me up again."

The scariest story involved a hotel security guard who was summoned to the room of four panic-stricken guests. The guard, Linda told me, "is a very strong Vietnam vet; he's seen it all." But when he saw what was happening in room 329 he turned around and walked out.

Luckily he is still working there, though now he's been promoted to engineering. I was able to track him down and get the strange tale directly from him.

Robert Cullinan started working a the Equinox as a security guard in 1985. Since then he has had a number of strange experiences, culminating with the encounter in room 329.

For example, he and several other guards experienced an odd multi-sensual phenomenon on the third floor of the south wing. He says, "You can be walking through there in the middle of the night and you can hear somebody approaching you. You can hear the footsteps. And you can feel the air around you getting colder and colder. At a certain point it feels like a freezer passes right through you. Then you can hear the footsteps continue on behind you. There have been several instances when that's happened. I just stood back by the wall and said, 'Go ahead.'"

He experienced this frequently enough so that he almost refused to return to that particular hallway after two o'clock in the morning.

"There've also been voices," he says, "people talking to you, tapping you on the shoulder. You turn around and there's absolutely nothing there."

I ask if he can understand what the voices are saying.

"It's not distinct. It's kinda like a mumbling. It's far away but it's very close to your ear. . . . It's very unusual. It's like it's coming from somewhere else but it's almost right next to your ear. It'll make you spin in a circle real quick. This has happened in instances when there's been absolutely nobody in the hotel at all."

Finally he told me about the weirdest experience, and it was exactly as Linda Malachuk had described.

"It was your typical night," Robert Cullinan began, "thunder and lightning, just like you read about.

"A gentleman and his wife called up and said they were experiencing some very disturbing things in their room and could we please come up and fix them. So I knocked on the door. They said, 'Come in.' I used my passkey and I opened the door.

"Just the initial walking in I was dumbstruck. The rocking chairs were going. The shades on the lights were spinning—not fast. But they were going around in a circle. And by God the bed was walking across the floor!

"Now this man and his wife were over in the corner with eyes about the size of garbage can lids. And I can understand that. His two kids were just totally freaked. They were scared to death, they were crying.

"So I walked in the middle of the room. And I asked them, 'Are you seeing the same thing that I'm seeing?' I didn't believe my own senses. And he said, 'Yes.'

"About that same time I'm in the middle of the room. There's nothing else around me. I'm not particularly a lightweight, I go about 220. It felt like somebody had their hand underneath my feet and just gave me a shove. And I came darn close to a foot up in the air and came back down.

"That's when I told this gentleman, 'I'd be happy to move you to another room, sir, but I'm out of here.' At that point I left. I think I looked like a porcupine coming out of there!"

As the unusual night progressed, Robert was not the only hotel employee to witness the strangeness. "There are six other written reports on it. I wouldn't tell anybody until I found out that other people had experienced the same thing."

*

It is difficult to guess who the Equinox ghosts might be, but Linda Malachuk says she believes they are friendly.

She says that occasionally, on the third floor, guests and employees hear the sounds of a mother trying to comfort a whining child. Linda is one of several who suspect it might be the shade of Mary Todd Lincoln. Mrs. Lincoln loved the Equinox and enjoyed returning year after year. She had made a reservation to bring Abraham with her in 1865, but it wasn't to happen. Although the hotel made renovations in preparation for the president's visit, fate had other plans for Mr. Lincoln. Perhaps Mary and her son Tad returned anyway and remain among the hotel's permanent residents.

Another could be William Marsh, who owned the original tavern on the Equinox's site. His land was taken away from him when he turned Tory. Maybe he feels it should be properly returned, and in his own way has repossessed it.

An additional phantom suspect is a member of the Orvis family. In 1866 owner Franklin Orvis named the hotel the Equinox. His son George later took control of the business. One day in 1918 George went up to the pond to go fishing or swimming.

He never returned.

Or maybe he did. Maybe he's still there.

A small contingent of individuals have a slightly more grisly explanation for the ghosts. In the old days there was a jail contained within the hotel. Local rumor has it that during the recent renovations parts of a human skeleton were discovered there. As my informant said, "Instead of turning them in—because it would cause disruption to the construction—they tossed them into the dumpster."

Maybe so, maybe not. But the files of ghostlore are full of phantoms whose activities are provoked by misplaced bones.

*

In a building as haunted as the Equinox, it is odd that apparitions are rarely if ever seen. I found only one case of a materialization. Caroline DeNatale recalled a gentleman who checked into his room one evening about eight years ago. Almost immediately he was back at the desk complaining that "two ghosts"—he said ghosts, not guests—"in white robes had rushed past him in his room."

Ms. DeNatale says, "He was real excited."

And it was his next remark that may give us the most succinct summary of the whole spectrum of events at the haunted Equinox hotel. According to Ms. DeNatale, the man said, "This is no story. This is true."

Rendezvous with a Ghost

It was a perfect night for ghosts.

June 25, 1998. On this date a series of storms began, storms that would turn much of Vermont into a disaster area.

I had driven to the Maplewood Inn in Fair Haven, Vermont, through one of those storms. Rain came so fast and dense that cars along Route 4 slowed to a crawl. Hailstones the size of my fingertip pelted my car. The black sky strobed an unearthly white. And thunder crashed, close by and ominous.

Oddly, the Fair Haven area was where, in the last century, William Miller had three times predicted the end of the world. This night it almost seemed as if his prediction were about to come true.

By ten o'clock I was tucked snugly in bed. The Hospitality Suite at the Maplewood was beautiful with its step-up, four-post bed and antique furniture. But I wasn't entirely comfortable; as the storm raged my mind riffled through all the stories innkeeper Cindy Baird had told me earlier that day. Ghost stories.

Surely the Hospitality Suite was the most haunted room in the place. And I was—at least so far—alone in that room, wondering if spending a night in this haunted chamber would provoke a face-to-face rendezvous with a ghost.

As I waited for the witching hour to come, I read through some of the historical documents Cindy had loaned me.

The house I was staying in was one of the most historic in the area. During the mid nineteenth century it had been part of the largest farm in Vermont. The owner, Asahel Kidder, had herded sheep, manufactured maple syrup, and raised dairy cows.

In 1880 Asahel's son-in-law Isaac Wood took over, enlarged the dairy, and started a creamery. The Wood family operated the same dairy until 1979. Over the years the farm was apportioned out and pieces got sold off. But it remained in the Wood family until Cindy Baird and her husband purchased it in June 1986.

Since then they have turned it into a romantic, antique-filled haven for travelers. The lovely Greek Revival style home, built in 1843, is on the Vermont State Register of Historic Places, and has been awarded National Register status.

But the house—like so many Vermont homes—is a hybrid. Part of it—dating back to 1795—had been across the street and may have originally been used as a tenant house, "tenement house," or tavern. It was moved and joined to the main house around 1870.

I knew my bedroom was in the oldest part of the house. As Cindy had said while showing me the room, "We don't even know what history may have transpired in this section."

Thunder crashed again. I knew if the storm didn't let up I would never get any sleep that night.

I put the reading material down on the bedside table. In the dim light of the reading lamp, I peered into the lumpy shadows of the room. I listened for sounds not attributable to the storm. In my memory, my conversations with Cindy echoed loud and clear.

"Over the years there've been a lot of strange sounds. . . . One evening I was sitting right here [in the room beneath my bedroom]. It was late; my husband was sound asleep. And I heard this bouncing sound right above my head. It sounded like a child playing with a ball. So I went running upstairs thinking there must be a mouse in here. I couldn't see anything. I didn't hear anything else."

I squinted into the dark. Saw nothing. Heard nothing. Recalled Cindy saying, "A couple of times I'd be sitting at my desk in my living quarters—which is in the newer section of the house—and I'd hear this squeaky board in the front hallway. Well, when somebody's walking through that hallway, you know it; you hear their steps because the boards squeak at regular intervals. I called out to my husband, 'Doug, is that you?' Nobody answered. I could still hear the footsteps, so I went out and there was nobody there."

Other people, including Cindy's father, have heard that same invisible pacer. I didn't hear it, though—just the rain and an occasional clap of thunder.

Cindy had also told me about feeling cold drafts and smelling cigar smoke in her home. But nobody here smokes cigars. In fact, cigars are forbidden on the premises. "I have a keen nose," Cindy had told me, "and I can't stand the smell of cigars."

Hearing knocks, feeling drafts, and smelling cigars are what you might call "Ghost Encounters of the First Kind."

Actually *seeing* evidence of ghosts is another thing. And there have been "Ghost Encounters of the Second Kind" at Maplewood.

"Once I had a lady and her son staying here," Cindy told me, "They were the only guests here at the time. And as far as I know they never went into the parlor. But when I went into the parlor that night I swore I smelled cigar smoke and the chess pieces were all moved around."

On another occasion Cindy discovered the glass guard on the shower in the Hospitality Suite had been unaccountably smashed. It was especially odd because the thousands of broken pieces were not in the bathroom, where they should have fallen. Rather, they were in the next room. The bedroom. The room where I was staying.

"The glass incident was in the summer of 1993. It's kind of scary. It was right on that pathway where a stairway used to be. Maybe what [the ghosts] were doing was walking up the stairway of the original entrance to the room. And out crashed that glass. . . . That's the only time I was a little afraid."

But I wasn't feeling afraid. At least not yet. Maybe just a little apprehensive, for the thing that had brought me to Maplewood that night was its reputation for "Ghost Encounters of the Third Kind." It is a rare phenomenon, but people have actually seen ghosts at Maplewood. Cindy Baird had shown me their written statements.

Kathy Jackson and her husband from Powell, Ohio, visited the Maplewood in September 1994. They stayed in the Oak Suite.

"I got up around two or three o'clock in the morning to use the bathroom," Kathy Jackson writes. "I then got back in bed and was settled when, at the foot of the bed, rising from the trunk placed there, I saw a man-sized and shaped 'white form.' It was not very clear, but I could see eyes and the vague shape of a man. He was about six feet tall. He seemed to come from the trunk. . . . I closed my eyes and thought 'this can't really be happening.' I did not look again and I assume the apparition left."

Her husband slept through the whole encounter.

"Kathy Jackson was really adamant about it," Cindy had told me.

"The funny thing about it was that we had found antique clothing in that trunk. There was a man's black overcoat, a woman's outfit, and a few jackets. Some of them are still hanging upstairs.

"My brother-in-law took some photographs on the stairs outside the Oak Room. But this was weird: Every time he took a photograph anywhere in the vicinity of those jackets, there were these white things. One of the photographs had a bizarre black shadow like somebody was standing, blocking a window. Several of the photographs had white things, like streaks or smoke. The strangest of all was he took a photograph of the staircase going up. When the pictures were developed, there was a white thing, like steam, coming down the entire stairway. It ended in kind of a form at the bottom."

But the most vivid Ghost Encounter at the Maplewood Inn occurred in the very room where I was trying to sleep. I couldn't help but recall the details, visualizing what had happened and anticipating what might happen next.

Saturday, February 13, 1993.

Between 11:00 and 11:30 at night.

Lillian Simcox of Oradell, New Jersey, was visiting with seven friends. "Our whole group was reading scripture and praying by candlelight and soft music. Most of the women had their eyes closed. I happened to have my eyes open and suddenly a young couple with a little girl walked from the bedroom entrance into the living room of the suite where we were all seated, continued to quietly walk through the living room, then headed down the stairs as if going to the first floor. It was extremely vivid.

"The man was wearing a black suit and was carrying a carpetbag. The woman was wearing a long blue dress, with a shawl and was carrying her hat in one hand. She was holding her little girl's hand in her other hand.

"They were dressed in 1800s dress."

*

So there I waited. For what? I wasn't sure.

I read a novel for awhile, waiting for something to happen. Finally I turned the light off.

Flashes of lightning occasionally lit the room. From the bathroom a tiny night light provided faint illumination.

I was tired but not sleepy.

After a while the dramatic atmospheric conditions tapered off. And in time—even with these strange stories swimming in my head—I drifted off to sleep. I had had no company that night, human or supernatural. I couldn't decide whether to be disappointed or relieved.

I remembered one thing that Cindy had told me the day before. "It has been pretty quiet since the ladies saw what they saw."

Yes, it was quiet.

All in all, my experience at the Maplewood Inn was comfortable and without incident. My theory about the haunting is that the ghosts have packed their carpetbags and moved away. Or they could be touring Vermont, moving from one haunted hotel to the next.

Then again, maybe they were simply determined to let me have a good night's sleep.

Perhaps the ghosts of Maplewood are every bit as hospitable as the landlords.

WHAT'S IN A NAME?

Ghost Hollow

As I am reluctant traveler, expeditions like my trip to the Maplewood Inn are rare. Generally, I prefer the sedentary amusement of pouring over Vermont maps. I enjoy the fanciful place names. Towns like Adamant and Goshen come to mind. Or Jamaica and Peru—oddly out-of-place designations that suggest incongruously exotic locales.

Closer scrutiny reveals more evocative names. There's Brimstone Corner near West Fairlee. Sodom—but no Gomorrah—by North Bennington. And I'm especially fond of Popple Dungeon, in my hometown of Chester.

But recently, when I was planning my trip to Fair Haven, I noticed another spot on the map that really fired my imagination. Just west of Fair Haven, on the New York border, is the town of West Haven. Within its perimeter I spotted the area in question—an area called Ghost Hollow.

West Haven, on the extreme southern tip of Lake Champlain, is oddly shaped: a droopy, pendulous peninsula, outlined by water. It sort of dangles into New York State. From parts of town you can drive directly east across New York before reentering Vermont at Fair Haven.

Anyway, West Haven's Ghost Hollow is—as far as I know—the only place in Vermont named after a ghost.

But whose ghost? And why was the ghost important enough to be commemorated in such a way?

I visited UVM's special collections to find out. There I discovered an article published in 1941 by Clara Gardner, who'd asked herself the same questions. She recorded the story as her father had told it many years earlier.

Before the railroads came to Vermont, Lake Champlain was a major transportation link between Canada and New York City. Here and there along the shore a number of settlements sprang up that were populated by boaters.

Such a community—made up of about a half dozen log cabins—was situated a couple miles inland at West Haven. To get there from the wharf, one had to travel along a narrow, rutted road. It passed a cliff where timber rattlers basked on sunny days, then entered a wooded hollow, where—day or night—it was always dark.

One cold March night more than two centuries ago, a young man hurried along this inhospitable path. His boat had been delayed and he was late for an important occasion. Nearly frantic, he rushed toward home to be at the side of his young wife, who was about to give birth.

Though it would be the couple's first child, it was, in many ways, a dreaded event. In those days home births could be frightening ordeals, generally attended only by inexperienced family members or ill-prepared midwives.

The young man traveled as quickly as he could in the utter darkness. Suddenly, just when he was feeling uncertain about his directions, the thick clouds parted overhead. In a moment of radiant moonlight, the young man was surprised to see someone coming toward him from the direction of the cabins. The figure, dressed in a flowing white garment that appeared almost luminous in the moonlight, seemed to be running. Yet she ran oddly; her arms and legs seemed not to be moving.

Within a few seconds the young man recognized the approaching figure—it was his wife. As always, she was coming to meet him.

But wait! As he started to wave, a half-formed smile froze on his face. He realized she should not be out and about. She should be at home in bed.

He watched the radiant figure stop near a little brook. It was as if she couldn't cross the water. Then, just before the sky went dark again, she vanished.

The young man's momentary joy turned to terror. Like all country people, he knew about signs and portents. Surely this had been a vision; he knew he was being forewarned about . . . something.

Filled with foreboding, he raced through the darkness to his cabin.

When he arrived home he was greeted by a familiar tragedy of frontier life: his young wife had died in childbirth. The young man quickly discovered that she had passed away at roughly the same moment he had stepped into the hollow where he'd had his last look at her.

Ever since then the place has been known as Ghost Hollow. And that is how it appears on maps to this day.

Cloak Island

Having more than a slightly elevated gothic level in my bloodstream, I have always been curious about another mysterious Vermont place name. You can find it on your map within Lake Champlain. Just let your eye travel north from Ghost Hollow in West Haven. Look for a tiny spot off the southeastern shore of Isle LaMotte, called, Cloak Island.

"Why," I wondered, "would anyone name anything *Cloak Island*?" There must be a mystery here.

I began my quest with a pamphlet from the Isle LaMotte Historical Society. It cites an old legend involving Icabod Ebenezer Fisk, a local selectman, lister, and father of nine. Though a practicing Quaker, he was renowned for bouts of terrible wrath. His wife Eleanor was often the target of his tantrums.

One foul, stormy night she decided she'd had enough. She took a horse and sleigh and lit out across the ice on Lake Champlain. But as far as her husband, her family, and the townspeople knew, she had simply vanished.

Come spring, when the ice went out on the lake, someone found her cloak washed up on the little offshore island. It has been known as Cloak Island ever since.

It's a good story and is apparently the one endorsed by the island's historical society. But a little research discloses that it is not the only explanation for the name of Cloak Island.

The *Vermont Historical Society Quarterly* offers a slight variation. In this version an old woman known as Granny Fisk vanished from her home on Isle LaMotte. Neighbors began to suspect that Granny had drowned. They employed an ancient bit of folk wisdom to locate her sunken corpse. You take a cloak belonging to the missing woman and float it on the surface of the lake. Supposedly it will come to rest over the body of its drowned owner.

In this case it floated away and drifted out to the tiny island, where it got snagged in some bushes. No trace of Granny Fisk was found there, but from then on the little scrap of land was called Cloak Island.

In a third explanation, the disappearing lady was not named Fisk at all, but Ellsworth, Grace Ellsworth. Following the death of her husband, Mrs. Ellsworth vanished one stormy night from the farm she shared with her three sons and their wives.

She had been unhappy at home, feeling unloved and unwanted.

While her husband had been alive, a prosperous lumberman—a widower—had been a frequent visitor in their home. Supposedly he dropped by again after Mrs. Ellsworth became a widow and suggested that the two of them would be much happier as a team.

Since she wasn't very happy anyway, she agreed.

They contrived an arrangement that would keep tongues from wagging while it insured the Ellsworth property would be divided fairly among the three sons.

One night the widower met the widow in a boat at water's edge. As the couple rowed away to start their new life, they cast Mrs. Ellsworth's bright red cloak into the lake, thus planting the "evidence."

Later during the search, the cloak was found tangled in the bushes of what would forever after be known as Cloak Island. The islanders concluded the unhappy woman had committed suicide.

According to some people, Mrs. Ellsworth returned to Isle La-Motte after her second husband's death. This is a slightly happier ending than what supposedly happened to Granny Fisk. The *Quarterly* said that some years after her disappearance Granny showed up in Champlain, New York, where her sons had swapped her for a work horse and a sawmill.

An alternate version of the story, buried deep in the archives of the Vermont Folklore Society, holds that things worked just the opposite, that the individual whose cloak inspired the island's name was not leaving Isle LaMotte, but approaching it.

In this rendition Isle LaMotte's tiny neighbor was once occupied by a sole tenant, an elderly lady who lived there much as a hermit.

She remained in her self-imposed seclusion all year round. The only time she would cross to the "mainland" of Isle LaMotte was during the winter, after the lake froze over. She'd bundle up in her heavy black cloak, cross the ice, and trudge up to the general store for supplies.

One winter the old lady did not make her annual trek for provisions—but no one noticed her absence. Gradually it dawned on the storekeeper that she had never come. That spring a small group of volunteers crossed to her little island. The searchers looked everywhere, but no a trace of the island's sole inhabitant could be found.

Finally one man spotted something among the litter of driftwood on the rocky shore. It was her black cloak, easily recognized by all.

The solemn searchers theorized that she had made her crossing too soon. She must have fallen through the ice before it was safely thick, meeting her death in the frigid waters of Lake Champlain.

No other trace of the woman was ever found.

And we have yet another version of how the island got its name.

The lack of harmony in these accounts demonstrates that how Cloak Island got its name is a multiple choice question.

At the same time, the slightly dissimilar narratives demonstrate something of the nature of folk tales: the "real facts"—more often than not—will be darkly cloaked in mystery.

A Nice Place to Visit

A visit to any of the haunted spots I have discussed so far doesn't guarantee a rendezvous with a Vermont ghost. Nor can a cruise on Lake Champlain be certain to provide a glimpse of Champ. And a hike up Mount Mansfield doesn't mean you'll spot any of the Weird Woods Walkers we'll meet in the next section.

But a field trip in the Green Mountain State can take you pretty far afield. And there are a few places you can count on to produce marvels.

Big Footprint

In *Green Mountain Ghosts* I wrote about a fascinating fossil that was discovered a long time ago in Bellows Falls. This natural curiosity, embedded in a rock near the Connecticut River, caused quite a stir in the scientific community at the beginning of the nineteenth century. It also captured the attention of students, travelers, and journalists from all over the country. The proud locals delighted in showing it off.

In his *History Of Rockingham*, L. S. Hayes describes the fossil as "a clearly defined footprint of a huge bird of some unknown species. It [looked like] an exact reproduction of an exaggerated hen's track and measured five feet in length."

Clearly this gigantic fossil was an important scientific find. One wonders, what could have made a footprint that big?

Well, thanks to a bunch of local jokers, we'll never know. Hayes tells us the faculty of Dartmouth College had arranged to move the curiosity to their museum in Hanover where it could be preserved and studied. But before the scientists could remove the stone, word got out. Rather than have their precious specimen relocated to New Hampshire, an unappreciative band of louts dynamited the thing to kingdom come.

But that occurred about two centuries ago. Hopefully nothing so irresponsible, short-sighted, and selfish could ever happen to Vermont's other two irreplaceable prehistoric relics. But you never know, so it's best to visit them while we can.

A Water Monster?

First, there's the wonderful specimen discovered in 1849 by a crew of workers who labored in the hot August sun, digging out the bed of what would become the first railroad line between Rutland and Burlington.

About twelve miles south of Burlington, digging near what is now Ferry Road in Charlotte, two Irish workmen found something extraordinary about ten feet below the surface of the ground. When they saw it, all work came to a halt: They had dug up a shovelful of broken bones.

For some time the puzzled laborers continued to pry pieces of bone from the blue clay of their widening trench. At first they tried to dismiss what they'd unearthed as the skeleton of a horse or cow, but soon they realized they had something far more unusual on their hands, quite possibly something completely unknown.

A local man, John G. Thorp, happened by and took a look at the bones. He reaffirmed how peculiar they were and convinced on-site engineers not to destroy any more of the mysterious skeleton.

But what was it?

Unfortunately, digging had shattered the unknown animal's skull; many bone fragments had already been carted off with the excavated earth. All they had left to study was the back portion of the skeleton.

Some observers were convinced that the bones were unlike those of any animal ever discovered in the Green Mountain State. And they were right.

Someone summoned naturalist Zadock Thompson from the University of Vermont to examine the creature. He was careful to retrieve what he could of the damaged skull along with a few teeth and some other missing bones. The more he looked and verified, the more inescapable his conclusion became. But it was most vexing: the skeleton had been unearthed more than a mile east of Lake Champlain—not to mention over 150 miles from the nearest ocean. Zadock Thompson and the railroad men found it difficult to believe they were looking at what could only be the remains of some large aquatic animal.

Dr. Thompson eventually determined they were the bones of an animal that normally inhabits arctic and subarctic marine waters: a white whale.

Weird. Why should a whale be buried in a Vermont field?

How did it come to be there? How could anyone explain it? All this was a major puzzle for early naturalists.

Since then the evolution of Vermont geography has become better understood. We now know that this whole area was once under water. Referred to as the Champlain Sea, it was a part of the ocean that extended into the Champlain Valley for 2,500 years following the retreat of the glaciers 12,500 years ago. The Charlotte whale was preserved in its sediments.

Although the whale has never been precisely identified, Dr. Thompson's conclusion seems right: it is most likely some variety of "beluga" or "white" whale (*Delphinapterus leucas*), measuring approximately twelve feet in length. Today it can be seen at the Perkins Geology Museum at the University of Vermont. It has been designated our official state fossil.

So far it is the only fossilized whale to appear in Vermont. But more than twenty specimens of beluga whales have been discovered in sediments from the Champlain Sea in present day New York and Canada.

I'm sure there are more whales out there to find.

And who can say what else lies waiting to be unearthed by a farmer's plow or turned up by the blade of construction equipment?

Isle LaMotte's Reef

Vermont's second prehistoric treasure is far older and even more important because it is unique. And it is definitely something no one would expect to find among the occasionally arctic acres of northwestern Vermont.

On tiny Isle La Motte, in the northern part of Lake Champlain, we have what most experts consider the oldest exposed fossilized coral reef in the *world*—some 480 million years old. The entire southern third of the island, more than one thousand acres, is made up of this spectacular natural resource.

On a recent visit I had the opportunity to view several outcroppings of that gigantic reef. Walking among the contoured black stones in a field near the historical society, it was easy to imagine myself on the floor of some pre-Paleozoic sea. The ancient stone protuberance was pitted with little scoop-like cavities in which I could almost visualize the big-eyed ghosts of tiny prehistoric fishes peering out at me.

Then, not far away, I visited the Fisk Quarry. "Quarry," however, is something of a misnomer because nothing has been quarried there for almost a century. Since "black marble" production ceased, nature has reclaimed the site, transforming it into a wetland and wildlife habitat, busy with birds, fish, and a profusion of colorful wildflowers. It is a timeless place. Tranquil. Quietly awe-inspiring. A fitting vantage point from which to observe the ancient reef with its unique fossilized population.

It is a mystery why coral, which normally grows in warm tropical seas, can be found in these northern climes. But it's a mystery easily solved. In the remote past—some 480 million years ago—the land that is now Vermont was beneath a tropical sea some twenty degrees south of the equator. Over the millennia the earth's crust shifted, spurred by earthquakes, volcanic eruptions, and the persistent pull of the tides. Eventually limestone formed, preserving a snapshot of ancient life just as Vesuvius's lava preserved the city of Pompeii.

Although the vast limestone band that preserves the prehistoric remains stretches from Virginia all the way north into Canada, the real geological mystery is, why do the oldest fossils reside at Isle La Motte? No one can say.

Scientists venture from all over the world to study the Vermont reef and its spectacular array of fragile fossils, which exist nowhere else in the world.

By studying that rock frieze of frozen life, experts get a picture of what our world was like half a billion years ago. Amazing critters like stromatoporoids (extinct sponges), solitary tube coral, and crinoids (ancestors of starfish) once thrived there and can still be seen like primitive statuary in bas-relief.

Mother Nature has left them in place to instruct us. But, of course, we may have failed to learn the lesson taught by the giant footprint in Bellows Falls. Today a marble company from Proctor wants to start grinding the one-of-a-kind reef into road fill. Depending on what course the future takes, the ancient creatures of Isle La Motte may take their place in memory and, under jackhammers and stone crushing equipment, may become, in irreversible reality, forever extinct.

The Isle of Magic Castles

It is only within the last couple of decades that the Champlain Islands have come into their own as a tourist destination. Topographically, the islands are of interest because they are very different from the rest of the state. The growing season is longer and the temperature, influenced by the surrounding water, is more constant.

But more important, it is an area rich in history. Samuel de Champlain saw the islands when he sailed down the lake in 1609. In 1666 Sainte Anne became the first settlement in what was to become Vermont. Built on the tip of Isle La Motte, its sturdy wooden fortifications proved ineffective against the onslaught of that first grueling Green Mountain winter. Forty out of sixty occupants became ill with scurvy; many died in agony.

This tragic beginning is a remarkable contrast to the wonderland the islands have become. One especially magical attribute may not be readily noticeable to the casual tourist.

Castles.

Lots of castles, some of which can be spied as you drive or bike around the islands. But they are not easy to spot, and that's part of what makes them magical.

Admittedly, though unlikely, there are castles elsewhere in Vermont. There's the so-called Wilson Castle in Proctor. Built in the mid-nineteenth century, this grand mansion is, in reality, a castle in name only. And the Castle Inn in Proctorsville may be fit for a king, but the designation "castle" seems a bit of an exaggeration.

However, in the town of Irasburg unsuspecting visitors have frequently been flabbergasted to see the turrets of a fifteenth-century fortress poking through the greenery. It is not a vision of Brigadoon, nor is it really medieval. This unusual structure has been there less than a decade and is the home of Harv and Sara Gregoire, who constructed it themselves, entirely by hand. These Vermonters just wanted to live in a castle.

But the Champlain Island castles are more the fairy-tale variety. Part of the fun is not knowing exactly how many there are or precisely where they are situated.

But to discover just one is a delightful experience.

You see, they are tiny, hardly bigger than a conventional doll house. You can spy them here and there, on lawns, in gardens, or directly on the shore, placed according to no particular design.

They are so perfectly rendered that one expects to see the wee folk flitting about, or to encounter a minuscule monarch like Bavaria's Mad Ludwig locked in combat with a rabbit-sized dragon.

The castles are created with such detail and intricacy that they cannot fail to ignite a sense of wonder and whimsy. Each small stone is positioned with precision, creating peaked facades and tiny towers with conical roofs. Some castles have moats, windows with wooden frames, tiny flower pots, and miniature window curtains. In the old days, some were equipped with electricity and Swiss watches mounted like clocks in the belfries.

Just looking at these unusual works of art suggests their builder had a highly developed sense of fantasy. But the magic they create is not without its mystery. We wonder, who made these tiny masterpieces? Why did he do it? How many are there and where, precisely, can we find them?

Most are on South Hero and Providence Island, because those are the spots where their builder lived.

His name was Harry Barber. He was born in Neuchatel, Switzerland, in 1900, the son of a stonemason. Harry lost a finger sawing wood, and with the insurance money he came to New York at the age of twenty-one. From there he made his way to Vermont and ended up in South Hero. There he worked at various caretaking and handyman jobs, picking up English along the way. Eventually he married a woman from Grand Isle and they started a family.

Harry was known as a hard and careful worker. He loved gardening and landscaping and often enhanced the property he worked on with imaginative stone artistry. During his eighteen years as caretaker on Providence Island, he built, among other things, a fanciful stone wall. Water dripped from a lion's face on the wall, on to a beautifully maintained rose garden.

Though Harry never mastered the English language, he was well liked and appreciated for his good humor, and his accordion playing, singing, and yodeling.

He built the castles as a hobby, designing them in his imagination and building them without plans or blueprints. Apparently he constructed them in sections in his basement and moved them on pipes.

There is no record of whether he sold the castles, and if so, for how much. But regardless of how they changed hands, they were created as labors of love.

In spite of how Harry may have appeared outwardly, there was a hidden element of tragedy about him. Though his motivations may not be clear, Harry Barber committed suicide in 1966 at age sixty-six.

Luckily for us, he left behind a magical legacy that has helped turn certain corners of Vermont into islands of make-believe.

Fort Wait

There are other mysterious structures in Vermont whose builders remain a mystery.

For example, on June 4, 1997, I accompanied my friend Tom Davis along with his cousin Bob Davis and Neil Sherman into the wilds of Corinth, Vermont. We were trying to discover something about the area's remote past—and at the same time trying to solve a local mystery.

Because of his ancestral roots, Tom has always been extremely interested in Corinth. While reading a town history he discovered references to two "Revolutionary era forts." One of them—known as Fort Wait—is apparently still standing. And we wanted to find it.

To say the area is off the beaten track would be an understatement. Tom's car bumped to the end of a barely passable road. Then we walked a good deal farther than I'm used to, finally entering woods that concealed a steep uphill climb. Tom led the way like a modern Natty Bumppo.

Strange place for a fort, I thought. And, as if reading my mind, Tom explained that the hillside would have been cleared back in the 1780s when the fort was supposedly built. It would have offered a panoramic and protective view of the surrounding valley.

Fighting fatigue and gravity, we pushed on, eyes peeled, eager for our first glimpse of the ancient ruin.

The climb got easier when we found what was left of a disused road. It had been built up and leveled with masonry walls that still looked solid enough to drive a tank over. Someone, sometime, had taken great pains to make this road permanent.

I'm not sure exactly what I expected to see up there on Hurricane Ridge. My most vivid mental images of "forts" were of the stockade variety in old western movies and, of course, the grand memory of Fort Ticonderoga, which I have visited frequently since I was a child.

But what I saw that day didn't conform to any expectation: big, dark, crumbling stone walls, so inaccessible and well hidden that they have eluded graffiti artists and developers.

Yes, the structure could have been a fort, or blockhouse. Its quarried stone walls stood five feet high in places. Buttressed against outcroppings, they stretched a good twenty feet or more. They were nearly a meter thick—too sturdy, I thought, for them to be a simple foundation.

Our sense of mystery grew because—in spite of what it says in the town history—many historians believe no Revolutionary-era forts have been identified in eastern Vermont. Of course, there were good reasons to have built defensive structures. In the 1700s settlers needed protection against frontier raids provoked by the English in Canada and generally carried out by Native Americans.

This "fort," however, wasn't on the top of the hill as I had expected. Its mid-hill location would make it vulnerable to attacks from above.

So maybe it wasn't a fort after all. And if it wasn't a fort—what was it?

First we discussed whether it might be associated with Corinth's once-active copper-mining business. There were many excavations nearby, but they were most likely the source of stones for the walls and road. The total absence of copper tailings suggested the copper mines were elsewhere.

And if it were something completely prosaic—say, an inconveniently positioned house or barn—it might have been constructed from logs that would have vanished long ago, leaving only its oversized foundation.

Finally, like the dirt road that brought us here, our discussion deadended. The four of us stood there silently studying the crumbling walls, each in his private reverie.

I felt frustrated and challenged at the same time. We definitely had a puzzle on our hands: an odd stone structure in a remote location. What was it? Who built it? When? And why? And what could have been the rationale for undertaking the monumental effort required to quarry stones and build walls so strong, solid, and enduring?

Corinth's "whatever-it-is" may never have repelled any frontier invaders, but surely its walls have withstood the assault of time, presenting us with a modern mystery. All we can say for sure is that there is something up there among the trees on Hurricane Ridge in Corinth, Vermont, and nobody seems to know exactly what it is.

Richford's Mystery Spot

To fully enjoy this last stop on our Mystery Tour of Vermont places, you're going to have to try to violate the law.

I don't mean to sound as if I'm promoting revolution or even civil disobedience. The specific law I have in mind is the law of gravity.

Folly, you say?

Perhaps so, but several years ago I started hearing about places where gravitational forces occasionally behave in extraordinary ways. Trouble was, such spots were all out of state.

Without testing any of them, I complacently came to believe that gravitational mandates are pretty inflexible. In fact, as I get older, its pull seems stronger each year. But, at least so far, my experience and learning had always corroborated Sir Isaac Newton's theory: objects tend to fall. Period.

But maybe not always.

According to the late Dolph Dewing of Franklin, there is a bit of contrary country up around East Richford where gravity can play by its own rules. Cars, for example, are said to roll uphill!

So, on September 8, 1996, off I went off in search of the magic spot. I drove from Burlington toward the Vermont-Quebec border, then headed east to that small cluster of buildings known as East Richford. From there I followed a five-mile stretch of gravel road that connects with Route 105.

This is real country. Farms more than a century old, tiny cemeteries, sagging fence lines, and waves of pastureland compose a timeless panorama. A slice in the greenery of a nearby mountain defines the United States–Canada boundary.

Although there are no visible clues to tip you off, the road winds in and out of Canada. As one slips unknowingly from country to country, perhaps there is some confusion about which laws apply. Anyway, it was along this rural no-man's-land that Dolph Dewing made his odd discovery.

At first he shared it with a few friends. Later, he took a busload of observers from the Franklin Senior Center. Then, on October 11, 1985, he brought the odd phenomenon to the media.

Reporter Nat Worman of the *County Courier* described how Dolph stopped his 1979 Dodge at his special spot. He stomped the accelerator, racing the engine to prove that the vehicle was in neutral. Then he waited. Within sixty seconds the car was moving forward at about 10 miles an hour. Half a minute later, it reached 15 miles per hour. Apparently the two-ton Dodge and its four passengers were moving uphill.

It may have been an optical illusion; it might have been antigravity. But whatever it was—magic or magnetism—Dolph Dewing was convinced it was a real mystery.

The topography hadn't changed much in the ten years since Nat Worman's article. Using his newspaper photo for reference, I quickly rediscovered the Mysterious Site.

There I parked my car and waited. Nothing happened.

So I moved along to the base of another little hill and tried the same routine. Still, nothing. After several relocations and several more unsuccessful tries, I gave up, ending my career as a lawbreaker. Sadly, I had discovered even I am not above the Law of Gravity.

Before heading home I drove into Richford for lunch. In one of the local restaurants I struck up a conversation with a man in his sixties who had grown up in the area. Needless to say, I asked him about East Richford's Magnetic Hill and told him about my failures there.

"What kind of car you driving?" he asked.

I told him it was a 1996 Honda Civic.

"There's your problem," he said. "Not enough metal in them things to work on any magnet."

Of course, I hadn't thought of that.

THINGS

Travelers' tales.

They return from away, full of conversation about the people they've met, the places they've been, the things that they've seen.

But when they return from Vermont, what sorts of things might they have encountered here?

Ghosts and witches and devils?

Monsters in the woods?

Chests of pirate gold?

Radiant cities in the sky?

A traveler might learn the secret that Vermonters have known for years: with so much to see right at home, what's the point of leaving?

Weighing the Dead

In *Green Mountain Ghosts* I wrote about an odd occurrence in Cavendish, Vermont. A young man named Sam Connor encountered his own ghost. For poor Sam the meeting was a portent of doom.

But Sam is not the only live Vermonter to view himself in an altered state. There is a similarly puzzling episode from Burlington. But the unconventional details are such that we are forced to ask, just what sort of thing are we dealing with? An out-of-body experience? A premature ghost? Astral projection? Psychic travel? Or something completely different?

The whole question seems to have something to do with the grandest of all debates: can human beings, under certain circumstances, actually leave their bodies and move around Earth in an ethereal state? And if the answer is yes, then what does it tell us about the moment of death? Does the spirit separate from the body and travel on to some unknown, nonearthly realm?

Only the dead know for sure. But for centuries certain of the living—shamans, psychics, and all manner of magicians, ministers, and mystics—have insisted body and spirit can be separated. That the intangible mind can leave the physical brain and then travel invisibly along psychic pathways.

An interesting example of this puzzling phenomenon is recorded in a little book I found in the special collections at the University of Vermont Library. Called *My Travels in the Spirit World*, it is an autobiographical account written by Caroline D. Larsen of Burlington. It appeared back in 1927, published in Rutland by the Tuttle Publishing

Company. Its lukewarm cover endorsement was provided by noted author and Spiritualist Arthur Conan Doyle.

Mrs. Larsen, a Spiritualist herself, claimed to have had many out-of-body experiences. Of those, the following example poses some interesting questions about astral travel and the phenomenon of ghosts.

In 1918 Caroline Larsen lived with her husband Alfred at 87 South Willard Street in Burlington. Alfred was a musician and teacher who specialized in the violin. On that particular evening, he and some friends were rehearsing at the Larsen home.

It was a gloomy fall night, so Caroline decided to go to bed early. She said good night to the musicians, then climbed the stairs to her room. Soon she was stretched out on the bed, listening to the musicians playing the adagio from Beethoven's Opus 127 Quartet.

She says she wasn't aware of having fallen asleep, so she was surprised to suddenly find herself standing beside the bed. Stranger still, she realized she was looking down upon her own unconscious form. Mrs. Larsen recalls that her body looked deathly pale, but everything else about it appeared perfectly normal.

Understandably bewildered, she started moving around. She left the bedroom, crossed a landing, and entered the bathroom.

Although she *knew* she was in spirit form, she nonetheless wanted to look into the bathroom mirror. Would her spirit be visible or invisible?

What she saw there left her completely dumbfounded. She *did not* see the reflection of the middle-aged woman who normally looked back at her. Instead, she saw herself as she had been years ago, when she was an eighteen-year-old girl.

Wondering if she could be dreaming, yet delighted all the same, she decided to present her new—or should I say old?—self to her husband and his friends downstairs.

But just as she stepped from the bathroom, another figure appeared before her. Mrs. Larsen described it as a female dressed in shiny clothing. The specter's obvious intent was to stop Caroline from going downstairs.

"Where are you going?" the figure admonished like a scolding mother. She then pointed dramatically to the bedroom door and commanded, "Go back to your body!"

Obediently, Mrs. Larsen returned to the bedroom. She wrote that she somehow sensed it would be wrong to argue with this luminous phantom.

There, in the darkened bedroom, Caroline Larsen once again confronted her seemingly lifeless body. With a feeling of profound regret, she returned to her recumbent middle-aged form, and, presumably, drifted off to sleep.

*

So what are we to make of this fascinating tale? Is it simply the fantasy of a middle-aged woman who laments the passing of her youth? Is it a reminder that no matter where we go, there's always someone who wants to boss us around?

Or is it anecdotal evidence that astral travel is a reality? And if so, what—if anything—does that suggest about life after death?

If our spirits return looking as we did at our most youthful and beautiful, why are so many ghosts described as grizzled old sea captains, one-legged phantoms, headless maidens, or small angelic children?

It is fascinating to speculate that Mrs. Larsen's experience gives us partial insight into what happens at the moment of death and maybe even a little peek at the afterlife. Could it be that, just as the Spiritualists believed, our form and personality remain intact? Did Carolyn Larsen gaze into the mirror and see how she would appear in the afterlife?

Of course, what Mrs. Larsen's narrative fails to include is what we might call "the moment of passing." What exactly happens during that instant when the metaphorical candle goes out? What is the transition going to be like? What occurs at the instant the "spirit" vacates the body?

*

Admittedly, I am not the first to ponder such questions. They have been investigated by people far more scientifically minded than I—for example, Dr. Duncan McDougal of Boston. Back in 1907, Dr. McDougal was trying to determine whether the human soul is corporeal, or completely intangible. He contrived a method of weighing human beings in the process of dying. Surprisingly, he discovered that, exactly at the moment of death, there would be a minor weight loss, measurable in ounces.

It was an interesting phenomenon, but I tended to dismiss it, thinking the weight loss had to be air expelled from the lungs or something equally prosaic.

Later, in conversation with my friend John Coon, I mentioned McDougal's research. John teaches English and drama at Colchester High School and, until that very moment, I had suspected him of leading a life as mundane as my own. But when he heard about Dr. McDougal, John came back with a personal tale of high strangeness: He told me about the odd circumstances surrounding the death of his father. Circumstances John himself personally witnessed.

At age sixty-five John's dad contracted some form of multiple sclerosis that very quickly became debilitating. In about two years the formerly vigorous man was pretty much confined to the house he had built. There his wife and children cared for him.

Although John was living with his parents at the time, he had to leave every day to teach. And because he was directing the school play, *Dracula*, he had to remain away until late into the evening.

Saturday, before the final theatrical performance, John was getting ready to leave home. On the way out he stopped in the living room to say good-bye to his dad. His dad looked up, obviously startled, and said, "That was a very pretty woman I was dancing with."

He had been dreaming, of course. John knew his father hadn't walked, much less danced, for several months. Still, it gave John an eerie feeling.

That evening, after the play, John stayed for the customary cast party. His students presented him with several gifts, including a framed poster for a French production of *Dracula*.

John arrived home in the wee hours, but his dad was still up, waiting for him. They talked for a while. John showed him the presents and told him about the play and the party. Then they watched the late show together. Today, John recalls the irony of the movie's title: *Death Wish*.

When the film ended, John put his father to bed and then went to his own room. He recalls it was very late but doesn't remember the hour.

Early the next morning, Sunday, John's mother rushed in. She was unable to wake John's father. He was unconscious, apparently in a coma. John phoned the family doctor and called an ambulance.

At the hospital John's Dad's condition degenerated.

That night he took a major turn for the worse. John and his mother remained with him most of the day and went home exhausted.

Early Monday morning, they got the dreaded phone call.

John and his mother rushed to the hospital. Luckily, they arrived in time.

John's mother went into the room first. When she came out, John and his nephew went in. It was about 5:30 in the morning. Almost at once John's dad experienced a massive convulsion. Then he relaxed. John says he could hear his dad's last breath, sort of a "death rattle." He knew his father had passed away right in front of him.

All John could do was stare at the body. But something moved! John swears he saw long strands of a peculiar white, fibrous filament streaming from his dad's mouth, ears, and nose. Directly in front of the two observers, this strange weightless substance seemed to gather into a ball above the corpse's head. Then whatever it was shot straight up toward the ceiling and vanished.

The two young men stood there in a bewildered silence. After several seconds John's nephew whispered, "What was that, Uncle John?"

John said, "I don't know."

And to this day he isn't sure just exactly what he saw that morning. He doesn't know, but he *believes* that strange fibrous substance was his father's essence leaving his lifeless body.

Maybe it was spirit. Maybe it was some kind of electrostatic charge. But whatever it was, John is convinced he saw the thing that gives the spark of life to human beings. He told me, "I really believe I saw what people call the soul."

And from my friend John's description, I'd judge that if Dr. McDougal had put that mysterious wispy substance on his scale, it could have weighted no more than a couple of ounces.

The Stone-Throwing Devil

Ever wonder where stones come from? Well, a certain Vermont farmer may have come to believe they drop from the heavens. And as amusing as that notion may sound, for the people involved it was absolutely terrifying.

The events began in the mid-1870s, during the heyday of American Spiritualism. Many local and out-of-state newspapers reported some highly strange goings on in the Vermont town of North Pownal.

It seems that Thomas Paddock, described by the Burlington *Free Press and Times* as "a respectable farmer, of excellent character," suddenly found his property under supernatural assault.

Sometime during October 1874, a mysterious shower of stones began to rain down on his house and outbuildings. They fell, the paper reported, "intermittently . . . and . . . apparently from the blue-arched heavens . . . without any visible mortal aid."

Fearing spirits, demons, or, worse, public contempt, Mr. Paddock and his family tried to keep the strange events a secret. But even in those pre-TV, radio, and telephone days, word got out fast enough.

And the stones continued to fall.

The farmer reported they rained night and day.

Upon examination he determined that the stones varied in size from tiny pebbles to four or five inches in diameter. In late November, a veritable boulder weighing more than twenty pounds dropped out of nowhere. It landed with sufficient velocity to make a three-inch impression in the frozen ground.

Amazed visitors to the farm tried to duplicate the phenomenon by hurling similarly sized rocks at the earth, but no one could create more than a slight impression in the solid soil.

The *Troy Press* reported other oddities in the behavior of the stones. For one thing, when they touched down they did not skip or bounce, as they would if they'd been thrown. Instead, they tended to "roll along as if propelled by some unseen power."

Stranger still, when examined, the landed stones were found to be hot, even in the chill winter nights.

Troy also reported what is perhaps the strangest behavior of a rock on record: "Sometimes they strike the roof near the eaves, and then slowly climb up the roof, over the peak, and roll off the other side."

Puzzled Farmer Paddock sought help from trusted local sages. He even offered a small reward to anyone who would "rise and explain" the mystery satisfactorily.

But no one rose.

And no one explained.

And the stones continued to fall.

The Investigation

Today we would probably refer to these strange events as "poltergeist phenomena," but back then frightened folks around Pownal took to saying these "ways of the dark" were the work of a "stone-throwing devil."

Still, we must wonder now, as people wondered then, whether it really was a devil. A poltergeist? The work of prankster spirits or spirited pranksters?

The Burlington newspaper maintained that Thomas Paddock's house was situated in such a way that no human being could hide and throw stones without being detected.

And local sages, after careful consideration, were thoroughly satisfied that farmer Thomas Paddock was telling the truth. He was considered a man of excellent character, so townsfolk refused to believe any trickery was involved, especially after he offered a reward to anyone who could explain the mystery.

In short, to the people of North Pownal, the stone throwing began and would probably end in mystery.

*

Admittedly, all this happened more than a century ago.

And sure, a buck went a lot farther in those days.

But Farmer Paddock's limited resources only permitted him to offer a *one dollar* reward. I can't help but wonder how much true scientific zeal that magnificent prize might have inspired.

Still, whatever their motive, there were a number of investigations. Thomas Paddock's farm was close to town and just a little more than a mile from the railroad station, so investigators from near and far had easy access to the bedeviled site. Many people testified that mysterious stones fell from nowhere, struck the ground, then tumbled along as if propelled. If handled, they were found to be oddly warm, in contrast to the air.

Observers stated that stones hit the roof with sufficient force to break shingles. Sometimes they'd strike near the eaves, then defy gravity by rolling up the slanted roof and over the peak.

And poor Farmer Paddock remained in "a state of profound affliction."

In late December the venerable *Rutland Herald*, always cautious about matters spiritual, warned its readers "not to place that implicit faith in [the story] which they would, had they witnessed the phenomenon themselves."

Whether inspired by scientific curiosity or Mr. Paddock's generous reward, an intrepid group of investigators from nearby North Adams, Massachusetts, made their way up to Pownal.

Feigning a belief in Spiritualism, and affecting a wide-eyed credulity, they interviewed Farmer Paddock, his family, and their two hired hands.

It turned out that the most frequent witness to the phenomena was a hired boy named Jerry.

Though Spiritualists might have suspected Jerry of being a medium, the ghostbusters had a different suspicion.

So it was Jerry whom they watched most closely.

As the group stood around the farmyard waiting for something to happen, one of the investigators engaged Jerry in conversation, saying how much he believed in spirits and how happy he would be for an opportunity to witness a wondrous display of falling rocks.

At length, Jerry grabbed his pail and headed off toward the barn to begin his chores. Not long afterward, a stone, arcing from the direction of the garden, hit the roof of the house and fell to the ground.

"Ah-ha!" said the farmer, "did you see that stone?"

No, replied the investigator, "but I heard it hit the house. Let's find it!"

Everyone searched but to no avail until Jerry returned from the barn and almost instantly pointed to the fallen rock. Upon examination, a bit of soil from the garden was found still clinging its surface. The conclusion was obvious: Young Jerry was the force behind the falling stones.

Interestingly, the *Troy Times*, which first broke the story, was first to print the solution. It wrapped up the Mystery of the Falling Stones this way:

Not wishing to wound the feelings of Mr. Paddock, who firmly believes the imposition so long practiced upon him to be the work spirits; and not caring to have any trouble with "Jerry" the visitors departed, fully convinced that they had solved the mystery.

Clearly they were not interested in the reward money. At the same time, I can't help but wonder if they really solved the mystery. Did stones actually roll up hill? What caused the heat so frequently reported? Why couldn't witnesses duplicate the indentation made by the twenty-pound rock? In truth, we'll never know.

In any event, it is fun to imagine: What might have happened on the Paddock farm when their next newspaper arrived?

Treasure!

We may have to fight dead men and devils
before we get fairly hold of it.
—Daniel P. Thompson,
May Martin, or The Money Diggers

One day in the summer of 1800, some boys from the sparsely populated town of Pocock, Vermont were exploring near the base of South Mountain when they heard a puzzling commotion. It wasn't the familiar sound of a woodcutter's ax. The loud, rhythmic blows were more like the concussion of steel on stone. When they went to investigate the boys saw a solitary individual laboring amid the trees and rocks. Surrounded by freshly tumbled stone, the perspiring stranger repeatedly assaulted the mountainside with a heavy pickax.

The bewildered youngsters approached him timidly. When the stranger saw them he stopped abruptly and glared at them.

Their polite inquiries were met with rude words and threatening gestures. The stranger raised his ax menacingly and, in the most peculiar accent the boys had ever heard, told them to be off about their business or suffer the consequences.

The frightened youngsters ran home and told their fathers what had happened. Men met and discussed who might be up on South Mountain and what he might be doing. The local storekeeper recalled that a stranger—an old man, "rough and uncanny"—had entered his establishment a week or so ago. This furtive newcomer purchased some supplies, mostly edibles, and promptly vanished. Though he'd been more than normally close-mouthed about his identity, he'd had to talk in order to conduct his business. And—the storekeeper recalled —he'd spoken with a funny sounding brogue, heavily accented. "He weren't a Frenchman," the storekeeper said with conviction. He wasn't an Irishman, German, or Dutchman, either. But just what he was . . . well, that remained to be seen.

The boys' fathers and older brothers decided to go out to the ledge and confront the mysterious outsider. If he had to go around frightening children, then he definitely wasn't up to any good.

A group of them—armed—made their way up the mountainside and back to the spot where they boys had discovered the solitary laborer. He was easy to find, they just followed the impact of his ax against stone.

The oddly dressed outsider was no less surly when faced with a band of townsfolk. He told them to leave him be. Said they had no business bothering him.

I suspect the men were a rugged and potentially ornery lot; they were not to be put off. So when they reminded the stranger that he was trespassing and told him he'd better explain himself or they'd run him out of town, he had little choice but to relent.

The tale he told changed the history of the region.

He said his name was DeGrau, that he was a Spaniard, and that he had visited the town many years ago with his father, who was a miner. His father and a group of associates had been prospecting all through New England. But here they had discovered a rich vein of silver. They left to purchase mining equipment and returned a year later to begin their mining operation.

Eventually they had acquired a massive amount of high-grade silver, which—right there on the spot—they smelted into silver bars. That fall, when they prepared to leave, they found they could carry only a small percentage of the silver bars they had amassed.

So they decided to hide most of their treasure, then return for it later. They walled the silver up in a cave shaped like a brick oven. Afterward they disguised the entrance with earth and vegetation.

Before heading off to their faraway homes the miners discussed their return plans. When they came back later to pick up the rest of their fortune, they all agreed, they would have to be all together.

For one reason or another they never coordinated the return trip. Besides, they had carried away so much wealth that there was no pressing need to replenish their personal coffers. Over the years the original miners died off until the Spaniard—now getting on in years—was the only one left.

The villagers decided that the Spaniard was neither an impostor nor a mental case, and his story *did* have the ring of truth. In short, they believed him. But the terrain was not exactly as the Spaniard remembered it from his childhood. Possibly that was because the devastating earthquake of November 18, 1755, had permanently altered the face of the land. But undaunted, the Spaniard dug and poked and prodded and eventually wandered off into oblivion, apparently without finding the treasure.

Local people picked up where the Spaniard left off. They discovered some ancient signs of a mining operation, a mysterious marked container, a few nondescript odds and ends, but no mine and no silver.

*

In the years that followed, the population grew, the town changed its name from Pocock to Bristol, and the treasure remained undiscovered. Local men were joined by opportunists from far and wide, all determined to find the Spaniard's silver.

Around 1840 a group of Canadians arrived in Bristol and a stock company was organized. Every dollar invested was supposed to yield $100 for the investor.

An affable sixty-year-old, florid-faced giant known as "Uncle Sim" Coreser directed the operations. Part of his job was to raise money to finance the project, which he did with charismatic persuasiveness.

Another responsibility was to coordinate information from local fortune-tellers, who apparently had tremendous influence on the dig. There was a woman from Pawlet whom Uncle Sim consulted quite regularly. And another "old Frenchman" conjured from his home on the eastern side of the mountain. These folks, and more like them, never had to callous their hands tossing rocks or wielding axes at the excavation site. It was enough that their paranormal vision allowed them to discern the spot where the treasure lay and the amount that would eventually be unearthed, some $3,100,000 (which would now be worth well over $50,000,000).

The conjurers were also able to offer supernatural immunity, for the preternatural dangers were many.

The treasure was known to be "enchanted." It was protected by guardian spirits, demons, really, and woe to the person who entered the cave or touched the treasure.

When it had originally been placed there, a savage dog had been sacrificed, its blood burned by moonlight. The resulting dust was then sprinkled over the treasure, which the dog would then guard as if he were guarding his own life force. The nasty animal was thus sentenced to infinite vigilance. He would spend eternity dashing around the cave, listening for intruders, sniffing at fissures in the rocks, preparing to tear trespassers to pieces.

But the dog was not all there was to fear.

Chronicler Franklin S. Harvey tells us, "A boy, with a frightful gash across his throat, paced round and round the glittering pile with a red hot iron upraised to smite with vengeful force the sacrilegious hand that dared to touch a single bar of the guarded pile."

Of course, it was Uncle Sim's job to keep such loathsome abominations at bay. This he did with magic words he'd learned from the conjurers, while at the same time he spurred the diggers on with humor and charisma.

Taking directions from the fortune-tellers, the workers dug shaft after shaft, some forty and fifty feet deep. One sank to well over a hundred. Still the silver's hiding place remained a mystery.

Where the men found the energy to continue is a mystery all its own. Their shafts caved in, and some filled with stifling gas or flooded with water. Almost as much effort went into reclaiming holes as digging them. But no treasure came to light. After more than twelve years and thousands of dollars, Uncle Sim gave up. About a decade later he returned alone. He had seen a new conjurer who showed him how, just by moving a few stones, he could open a passage leading directly to the treasure, and "by Keeser" (Uncle Sim's worst oath), he was going to find it.

But by then he must have been in his eighties, was half crippled by arthritis, trembled from a palsy, and simply wasn't up to the rigors of treasure hunting. Shortly, he "turned his face toward Canada and hobbled away."

In spite of repeated failures, efforts to find the Spaniard's silver have continued intermittently throughout the twentieth century.

In 1934 a man from nearby New Haven took up the cause. With great élan he began digging and dynamiting until little was left of the earlier excavations. His treasure-finding techniques were more modern than his precursors'. Instead of consulting conjurers, he brought along his "divining rod," which he believed would lead him directly to the treasure. But in time he too left, tired and discouraged.

The much-punished area just south of town long ago became known as Hell's Half Acre. Today it is pitted and pocked and permanently defaced from the efforts of more than two centuries of treasure hunters. Quite possibly, someone could be digging there right this minute.

Unfortunately, all the Bristol excavations have produced are questions: Was there ever really a treasure to begin with? Did one of the diggers secretly find it and covertly carry it away? Or is it still there, securely hidden, ready to inspire another hundred years of treasure hunting?

Without a find, the truth of all this will be nearly impossible to sort out. At the same time, surely some truth is revealed about the human character, for we have seen how the promise of instant wealth can inspire a lifetime of backbreaking labor and repeated disappointment.

But historical truth is smelted from different ore.

Bristol newspaperman Franklin S. Harvey, who perhaps researched the Bristol diggings more than anyone else, chronicled the events in a series of vastly entertaining articles for the *Bristol Herald* in 1888 and 1889. He had spoken to people who remembered the mysterious Spaniard. DeGrau, he said, "cannot be called an impostor, for he asked no favors of anyone."

And Mr. Harvey had personal recollections of Uncle Sim, whom he believed was also on the level. He recalls the last time he saw the old man:

"He had a few tools and was digging and prying around in his feeble way among the loose rocks. I pitied the poor old man, and freely forgave him for all the awful frights he had given me during my boyhood; for hiding behind a rock and growling like a bear; for telling me blood-curdling stories that made my hair stand on end; for ridiculing my odd and bashful ways; all doubts I may have had of his present or former sincerity were scattered in the winds."

The real key to the story's legitimacy seems to lie with the original excavator, DeGrau. Presuming that he did not find what he was looking for and furtively spirit it away would suggest that whatever it was—at least for a time—was really there.

It is unlikely to me that a band of roving miners, traveling randomly through primitive New England, would just happen to make the needle-in-a-haystack discovery of a rich silver mine while passing through Pocock, Vermont. The credibility gets more flimsy when we realize there is not much if any silver to be found in the Green Mountain State.

Easier then to suppose DeGrau and company hid something somewhere in the wilds of Bristol and then, years later, came back to reclaim it. The fact that he was Spanish might provide a clue as to what his "treasure" might have been.

Without getting into the confusing and convoluted history of the Spanish ship *Santa Elena y Senor San Joseph,* suffice it to say that in 1752, it was on its way from Honduras to Spain. It was loaded down with treasure that included forty chests of silver. Repeated trouble at sea forced it to anchor near New London, Connecticut, on November 24. Its requests for aid and repairs were met with deceit and thievery. While it was there, most of its treasure disappeared.

What happened to it remains a mystery that will never be solved. However, it is possible that thieves, carrying an unspecified amount of silver coins, made their way north, eventually unburdening themselves in the wilds of Bristol before continuing on to Canada.

If that is so, then the Spaniard DeGrau may have been the one remaining member of a pirate band who returned to Vermont in 1800 to reclaim his ill-gotten gains.

Though the prospect is admittedly remote, the scenario is within the realm of possibility—as possible, perhaps, as a productive silver mining and smelting operation in colonial Pocock.

The power of this solution is diminished a bit when we consider that several Vermont towns in addition to Bristol—including my hometown, Chester—boast essentially the same story of lost silver and wandering Spaniards.

However, the colorful tale does accomplish at least one thing: it introduces the concept of high-seas piracy to the only New England state without a sea coast. So if DeGrau was a pirate, he was a rarity indeed.

But somewhere in the human psyche there must be a longing for the unique color supplied by buccaneers and their buried bounty.

White Rocks

The "Chester Variation," as I call it, was recorded in 1861 by Albert D. Hager in his *Geology of Vermont.*

The central character was one Richard Lawrence, an elderly Chesterite who recalled meeting a stranger in town in the late 1700s.

At that time the young Mr. Lawrence observed the stranger traveling east through town on horseback. The slow-moving animal seemed uncomfortably weighted down with heavy saddlebags. The stranger stopped, tied up his horse, and looked around as if he were puzzled or in need of assistance.

Young Lawrence approached him and asked if he could be of some help.

Relating the story a half century after the fact, Mr. Lawrence couldn't recall the exact nature of the favor he provided, but he'd never forget the elderly stranger's gratitude. He said, "Young man, one day your kindness will be richly repaid."

He then went on to tell how his saddlebags were full of silver coins he had just secured from a hidden cave in Wallingford. He explained that many years ago he had come with other Spaniards to prospect in this new land. In the mountains near Wallingford they had discovered a rich vein of silver. The band had worked the mine for a long time. In the cavity they had created in the rock, they constructed a partially concealed work area where they smelted the ore and turned it into coins.

When they had made money enough, they decided to return to their native land to enjoy the rest of their lives among the rich and famous. The only problem was, they had no way to transport all the silver back to Spain.

With the help of pack horses they carried off almost all the coins, but they had to abandon a large quantity of coins and a fortune in silver bars.

The flat, horizontal opening to their mine was nearly impossible to find. They disguised it as best they could and left their surplus silver with the understanding that in the unlikely event any of them ever needed money again, they could come back and take what they wanted.

Years rolled by until the old Spaniard was the only survivor of the original party. Now, as he met young Richard Lawrence on the streets of Chester, he was just on his way back to Spain after replenishing his coffers.

The old man was so taken with the youngster that he told him the location of the hidden mine. The only condition imposed was the young man could not tell of it while it was probable that the old Spaniard still lived. After allowing his elderly benefactor a reasonable time to die, Lawrence would be permitted to do as he liked with the silver-laden contents of the cave.

Lawrence proved to be as honest as the old man had suspected. He held the secret for many years.

Finally he confided his story to a few friends. Enthusiasm was immediate. Together they set out for Wallingford, fully expecting to easily unearth a rich treasure trove of precious metal, already mined and partially converted to coin.

The spot was easy to find. And it is conspicuous today. Called White Rocks, it is a precipitous range of quartz rock, the very sight of which is guaranteed to provoke the imagination. It is strikingly visible to the east of Route 7, about two miles from North Wallingford.

The men's search was diligent and systematic, but try as they might they simply could not find the door to the hidden cave. Maybe, they guessed, the opening had been covered by some rock slide.

To facilitate the search, magical "mineral rods" were procured along with the services of a conjurer who could operate them. True to form this conjurer—"con" for short—told them where the opening could be found, but reaching it would be difficult and expensive. The immense wealth waiting, however, would be worth the cost of blasting and mining.

Work commenced and continued for several months. Needless to say, nothing was discovered but the limits of their tolerance.

Albert Hager writes, "Again and yet again the work has been resumed and abandoned. At times the mining party has consisted of more than a dozen men, who have vigorously pushed the work for weeks at a time. But not withstanding all these efforts, the hidden treasure is still unreached, and we are not permitted to record the discovery of that lost cave, or the remnant of that rich lode of silver."

That was in 1861. It is still true today.

No Kidding

I realize it doesn't make a lot of sense, but during the late 1700s and early 1800s, a number of Vermonters became absolutely convinced that treasure in its most romantic sense—pirate treasure—could be found under these Vermont hills. And here's the weird part: certain get-rich-quick schemers actually came to believe some of that treasure was buried here by Captain Kidd himself.

One really has to stretch the imagination to discover a rationale for this notion. It is true that Kidd owned a home in New York City, but there's really no evidence he ever came further inland than the northernmost room of his house.

Perhaps Kidd's legend sailed a little closer to home because of a persistent rumor that one of his gold-heavy vessels sank in the Hudson River. This legend gained strength because of an ongoing effort to raise the wreck from the river bottom. However, I suspect the vessel was a ghost ship, for it never actually appeared.

Even before Kidd was hanged in 1701 he had become legendary. The fact that his corpse was hung up for public viewing probably kept tongues wagging. And the colorful captain remained fixed in the popular imagination through numerous history books coupled with the fiction of Edgar Allen Poe and Robert Louis Stevenson.

In spite of all this, it is still an odd notion to think *any* legitimate pirate plunder might be hidden in this landlocked little state of ours. But the towns of Middlesex, Bellows Falls, Wallingford, Rutland, and Waitsfield have all been combed in search of Captain Kidd's booty.

Of course, human nature repeatedly demonstrates that it doesn't require logic or especially solid evidence to convince a dreamer that untold riches are just waiting to be found.

For example, one of my favorite Captain Kidd stories took place in Waitsfield around 1800. In this story the dreamer was a young woman named Nancy Savage, daughter of Samuel S. Savage.

Three nights in a row, Nancy dreamed that a large pot of Captain Kidd's money was buried near a ledge just east of their house. At that time the common wisdom was that anything dreamed three nights in succession had to be true. So, on the strength of his daughter's dream, Mr. Samuel S. Savage commenced digging.

The account of the incident in Abby Hemenway's *Vermont Gazetteer* says, "It never entered the heads of any of the family . . . to ask how Captain Kidd should chance to be burying money 200 miles and more inland, [at a time when only Indians] inhabited all the wilderness."

Anyway, because the location of the loot had been supernaturally disclosed, certain prescribed rituals had to be observed while digging for it. First, no one should speak during the excavation process. Second, one among them should sit and read the Bible as the others dug. This was presumably to keep away any demonic intruders and to neutralize any spirits that might be guarding the swag. Nancy did the reading while her father and brother took turns digging.

The excavation continued for several days. Then, when jabbing his crowbar into the ground, Samuel hit the pot he was looking for. He distinctly heard money chink and he held his crowbar tightly against the pot so he wouldn't lose it. Then, wordlessly, he beckoned his son to come dig it out.

Unfortunately, no matter how he waved or contorted his face, the poor man could not make his son understand what he wanted. At length Sam Jr. broke the silence to inquire:

"Wha' cha want, Pa?"

Instantly the pot of money moved away as if sucked into the bowels of the earth. Though Sam Savage spent years trying, he could never locate it again.

Hemenway's account concludes this way, "The most ridiculous part of the matter, is . . . that Mr. Savage believed all this as long as he lived, and was never ridiculed out of it."

A Vermont Pirate

It's a wonder we have any pirate stories at all, since Vermont is the only New England state without a seacoast. It is absurd to believe Captain Kidd or his treasure ever really crossed the border into what's now Vermont. But there are slightly more credible tales of buccaneers and buried treasure. One of the most persistent involves Vermont's very own resident pirate.

You may have heard of him. There are a number of landmarks that bear his name, among them a bay, a state park, and for a while there was even a restaurant named after him.

I'm talking about the infamous Captain Stephen Mallett.

According to legend, Mallett, like Kidd, was a real pirate, a high-seas swashbuckler who gave up his evil ways and retired to—of all places—Vermont. He built a home and ran a rough tavern somewhere on what is now Mallett's Bay. Inevitably, as with any pirate, along with stories of dark deeds and derring-do there are also stories about lost maps and buried treasure. Supposedly Captain Mallett buried his treasure on Coates Island in Mallett's Bay.

Trying to ferret out the truth in all this is an exercise in frustration. Every story I read about Captain Mallett is annoyingly brief. Inevitably each includes some variation of the sentence, "Not much is known about Captain Mallett nor the deeds which have won him a vague sort of fame."

We know, of course, that he was a Frenchman. The confusion is that sometimes he's called Stephen Mallett, sometimes Pierre Mallett, and occasionally Jean-Pierre Mallett (or, perhaps more properly, Maillet, Mallet, or Malet).

And we know that he was *real*.

Vermont historian Ralph Nading Hill describes Mallett's land as the remains of a French settlement, suggesting Mallett moved there under a French grant long before the American Revolution. Hill writes, "Captain Mallett was apparently a man of considerable independence of spirit; he feared no one and acknowledged allegiance neither to the English King nor to the American colonies. It seems that he never accepted the Treaty of Peace which gave control over his lands to the English; his sympathies were on the side of rebellion, for he welcomed spies and smugglers into his home all through the Revolutionary period."

Sounds like the perfect description of a pirate, all right. But what real *piracy* did he ever commit? Again, it's hard to say. In 1939 Winooski mayor Albert Gravel researched Captain Mallett's story and discovered that a Pierre Mallett had "absconded from France with the regimental funds [from] Napoleon's army." However, an organization of people claiming to be Mallett's descendants deny this story, saying he acquired his wealth honestly.

Other tantalizing possible pieces of the Mallett jigsaw puzzle have turned up over the years. William Coates, who lived on Captain Mallett's treasure island, once found some brass buttons he believed belonged to the pirate.

And supposedly a wooden leg was discovered by Jeb Sharrow and some friends who were digging for artifacts on Mallett's Head. Thought to be the pirate's prosthesis, it was scientifically dated to the 1700s. Although brass buttons and a peg leg certainly contribute to the image of a pirate, nothing conclusively links these artifacts to the captain.

So what about the treasure? Well, if it has ever turned up the discoverers kept it pretty quiet.

Some years ago several marked trees were supposedly found on Coates Island. These might have provided a clue to the treasure's whereabouts, but sad to say they were not discovered until after they'd been destroyed in a storm.

Truth or fiction? I suppose it doesn't really matter. To me it is wonderful just to think we have our own colorful version of Long John Silver who was kind enough to leave a fortune in buried loot for some lucky Vermonter to find.

*

Of course, digging is not the only way to acquire treasure.

For example, about thirty years ago, literally thousands of French citizens joined forces and tried to get their hands on Captain Mallett's loot. It was the latest development in a quest that has been going on for over a hundred years.

According to them, Jean-Pierre Mallet died in Winooski, Vermont in 1818. But because he had no children, the captain's vast property holdings—stretching from Lake Champlain all the way to Chicago—were not claimed.

Although he had no relatives in this country, he had plenty back in France. In 1957 Helene Ayoubi organized some 22,000 people, each claiming a relationship to Vermont's Captain Mallett. They called their organization the World Union of Mallet Heirs.

According to Madame Ayoubi, Jean-Pierre Mallet was born in Limousin, France. He came to America and fought with the Marquis de Lafayette in the American Revolution. For his services to the new country, the grateful Continental Congress rewarded Mallet with a huge farm in Vermont.

Allegedly, he cleverly multiplied his newfound fortune in several ways: first, by discovering oil on his land. Then by marrying a Louisiana woman who soon inherited a bunch of gold mines. And finally, the enterprising captain bought a string of slaughterhouses in Chicago.

But, so the story goes, after Mallet's death in 1818, soon-to-be President Andrew Jackson somehow expropriated everything. This illegal seizure was allegedly in retaliation for Napoleon's blockade of the United States during the war of 1812.

In 1965, Mallet's alleged descendants laid claim against the U.S. Treasury for $512 million. Today those confiscated holdings would be worth twice that, or more. Since the fortune was seized illegally, the "World Union" argued that the U.S. Treasury should have been retaining the money in trust for the rightful heirs.

Needless to say, the U.S. treasury denied all knowledge of Captain Mallet's missing millions.

And unfortunately, Vermont could do nothing to bolster the French case. Our probate court records held absolutely no evidence of Mallet's money or land.

Early in 1966 Madame Ayoubi was indicted for swindling the 22,000 members of the World Union of Mallet Heirs. After listening to her elaborate story in court, the judge asked, "What documents do you have to prove the existence of the inheritance?"

Unfazed, Madame replied, "I don't have any documents. That's why I founded the Union—to find the documents."

The weary judge ruled that before proceeding, Madame would have to submit to a psychiatric examination.

Who can say where truth lies? Maybe Madame really is related to Vermont's own Captain Mallett. If so, it might prove only one thing: that piracy runs in the family.

But when all is said and done, perhaps the only real treasure will be the truth someone eventually digs up, truth that will reveal everything about Vermont's mysterious Captain Mallett.

Digging Deeper

Surprisingly, we still have not exhausted all Vermont has to offer about pirates, wandering Spaniards, hidden riches, and related weirdness. I presented the Bristol excavations as a treasure tale, but—if you prefer— it is also a ghost story. The details seem to confirm some supernatural law: Where there's buried treasure, there's likely to be ghosts.

To me the Bristol treasure tale's most gothic element is the associated belief that a murdered boy and his demonic hound hold eternal vigil in the lightless bowels of the mine shaft, forever guarding against would-be treasure hunters. Franklin S. Harvey wrote, "As these patient toilers hewed their way through the ledge and drew nearer to the object of their search, they could hear the boy sigh and groan."

As a lad, Mr. Harvey was often present on such occasions. "I can't say I ever heard the howls and groans," he wrote, "but who is to dispute the statement of a dozen gray-haired men, all of whom were ready to say they did hear them?"

Over the years the saga of the boy and his hellhound evolved a bit. Though they continued to appear in local folklore, their story began to take on less sinister and far more poignant tones.

In today's rendering they are truly sympathetic characters as, together, they commenced a pleasant hike one fine fall afternoon. The Bristol boy whistled happily as the dog, a companion of many years, loped along at his side. The reason for their woodland sojourn has been lost. Maybe the boy was gathering spruce gum. Maybe he was hunting. Most likely, he was simply indulging a boy's curiosity by exploring the abandoned cavities on Hell's Half Acre. No doubt he was speculating that maybe, just maybe, a fortune in silver lay beneath some nearby and overlooked rock or under one of the many rotting wooden platforms.

But as night began to fall, the boy didn't return home.

His worried parents called his name and organized search parties, but to no avail. The boy and his dog had vanished completely.

Some time later, maybe after the snows of the next cruel Vermont winter had melted, a local man wandering through Hell's Half Acre, noticed something among the ledges and pits and caves and rubble—the skeleton of a dog near the opening of a shaft.

The man probably did not have to look into the pit to know what he would find there. The scenario would have been easy to reconstruct: The boy had fallen into the fifty-foot shaft. Alone and terrified, he had died there, unable to escape. His faithful dog, refusing to leave the boy's side, waited at the opening fifty feet above him. In time he, too, died in the woods, and nature took its course.

Then supernature clicked in.

Today, when the moon is right and the shadows are long, local folks and puzzled outsiders swear they occasionally hear "something" in addition to the woodland sounds of wildlife, water, and wind. Some say they hear faint cries. Cries for help. Or the unearthly wail of a dog.

Sound far-fetched? It does to me, too. But enough people have heard the unexplained sounds so that particular excavation in Hell's Half Acre has come to be known as "the Ghost Shaft of Bristol Notch."

The Lair of the Beast

Another treasure tale, though full of gothic touches, failed to pick up steam the way the Bristol story did. This one, attributed to the *Poultney Journal*, was reported in 1899. It concerns a "Startling Find" made by a trio of hunters from Fair Haven, Vermont.

A nightmarish odyssey began when James Kelley, Fred Copeland, and Albert Austin grabbed their guns, called their dog, and headed out for a day's hunting. They had heard odd tales about a strange wild animal that had been spotted by some lumbermen near Bloody Ledge. The witnesses claimed the creature made plaintive, wailing sounds that could be heard for miles.

Being curious sorts, the three hunters wanted to see the peculiar beast for themselves.

Within sight of Bloody Ledge their dog picked up something's scent and forged ahead. Soon the trio heard growling and shrieking from deep within the woods. When the fighting stopped, the men listened in terror as something made its way through the forest toward them. It was their dog. The poor animal was limping and covered with blood. Its head and back were lacerated in a frightful manner. Obviously, this was a the work of a large and ferocious animal, but what? A bear maybe? Or a catamount? Or possibly something far worse . . .

In time the dog's courage returned and once again it picked up the scent of the beast. It tracked its prey to a hiding place among the boulders on the east side of Rattlesnake Hill.

The men decided to smoke the monster out. They built a fire and watched its thick black smoke vanish into a hole behind a huge bolder. Moments later the men saw the smoke billowing out of a crevice several yards away. The knew they had discovered a tunnel or cave.

For half an hour they let the smoke do its work. Then the men timidly entered the beast's lair. Copeland led the way, holding a makeshift torch. All were surprised to find themselves standing in a large cave, twenty feet wide by one hundred feet long by ten feet high.

And they soon realized they were not the first to stumble upon this hidden spot. At one corner they saw a large iron kettle. Nearby, resting against the wall, were five grinning skeletons. Panicked by this frightening discovery, the hunters made a hasty exit.

In minutes, after working up their courage again, they reentered the cave. This time they discovered a pile of old coins that they guessed were Spanish. Exploring further into the cavern's darker regions, they found a sizable, tangled pile of rattlesnakes. Luckily, the snakes were in a torpid state and could be handled without danger. Within an hour the three men had secured nearly half a bushel of rattles for which they would later receive a $750 bounty. They packed up the coins, too, and found they were worth almost $3,000.

Three thousand seven hundred and fifty dollars—not bad for a day's work.

But they never found the animal they had been chasing. Who knows what *that* might have been worth?

The article goes on to say that the skeletons were brought into town and examined by a Professor Norman, who declared they were Indian bones.

He said they probably came from an incident in 1725 when a band of white men under Captain Titus had come up the Connecticut Valley and attacked the Indians near Rattlesnake Hill. He theorized that the Indians had carried their wounded into the cave where they died. However, he had no explanation for the Spanish coins. They had been there a long time, he speculated, because the most recent date was 1705.

The article concludes by saying that this strange discovery triggered an epidemic of treasure hunting around Fair Haven. Unfortunately, nothing extraordinary was found.

The monster, the skeletons, and the gold make a wonderful story, rich in delightful gothic touches. But, alas, it is most probably little more than a story. The last century is known for its many journalistic hoaxes. Some caught on and took root, like Allen Morse's yarn about freezing and thawing elderly hillfolk. But most such tales have faded into the shadowy caverns of time. Luckily, I rediscovered this one. But I experience a real sense of loss when I think about all the wonderful Vermont tall tales that are gone forever.

Vermont Crude

Some readers might suspect another tall tale, or possibly the presence of some menacing supernatural entity, when reading about certain odd occurrences that took place in the northern part of the state.

For example, Mr. and Mrs. Lawrence Bellrose had a new well drilled at their house in Swanton. They struck water at 650 feet and had the fresh supply hooked into the plumbing of their house. "One day a fuse blew out in the cellar and a strange hissing noise was coming from the water storage tank," Mrs. Bellrose recalled. "My husband went down cellar to see what was wrong. He struck a match and the room lit up with a ball of fire."

In nearby Alburg Center, Robert Carpenter's kitchen faucets lit up and burned like torches.

And on a neighboring farm, the hired hand tossed a cigarette butt into a cattle watering trough and caused the barn to catch fire.

What these three bizarre incidents have in common is a rare phenomenon known as "fire water"—water that seems to burn like gasoline.

Of course the water itself isn't combustible, as we can see in the case of a St. Albans man who burned over a field beside his house. The fire went out quickly, except for a slight crevice that continued to burn. In fact, it went on burning for several months.

What I'm describing is nothing supernatural. It's *natural* gas. Sometimes people strike gas when they're drilling for water; it seeps naturally from the ground and, if ignited, can burn for a long time.

Natural gas deposits are not rare in Vermont. But back in the early 1950s a retired St. Albans businessman named Douglas Kelley realized that natural gas is often one of the first hydrocarbons noticed before striking petroleum.

As a result, Kelley launched what he hoped would be Vermont's oil boom. With a group of adventurous associates, Kelley became a pioneering Vermont wildcatter. Then, on April 19, 1957, New England's first heavy drilling for oil began on Isadore Yandow's St. Albans farm.

Kelley's effort won coast-to-coast publicity. Local landowners fantasized about riches as the rest of Vermont dreamed about prosperity, new industry, and jobs for everyone.

Drilling continued for months. A four-man team worked seven days a week, twenty-four hours a day, and in exhausting twelve-hour shifts. The cost—some $250,000—should have financed three wells, not just one. They struck methane. They hit plenty of water. And when they finally reached 5,000 feet they gave up altogether. No one bothered to tell them that even in southwest America's plentiful oil fields, only one out of nine wells becomes a commercial producer.

But human beings are never quick to abandon their dreams. In 1959 and 1960 two more wells were drilled at Mallett's Bay in Colchester, lending remote credence to the story that Captain Mallett did in fact make part of his substantial fortune by discovering oil in Vermont.

Anyway, before the modern drillers reached 10,000 feet they ran out of money. All they gained was natural gas enough to supply twenty to twenty-five homes.

World-renowned geologist and Rutland native Earle Taylor figured "where there's gas there's oil." He formed the Cambrian Corporation and did a comprehensive geological survey and photogeological study of Vermont. The survey, costing well over $100,000, showed promising results. There was a good possibility of natural gas and maybe oil strikes in Addison, Chittenden, Franklin, and Grand Isle Counties. Over the next two years the corporation began leasing thousands of acres of land.

In 1962 and 1963 the corporation persuaded Belgian and American Petrofina, one of the largest worldwide oil concerns, to come in and run the operation. Drilling began on Harry Hutchins's farm in South Alburg. Hutchins said, "They drilled to a depth of just short of a mile . . . using an honest-to-goodness oil rig, a rotary drill with a tower 160 feet high."

The professionals were sure they were going to strike oil. Right up until the end they kept saying, "It's looking good."

Then something mysterious happened. They stopped drilling and left without explanation. To this day no one knows why they stopped. No one could get a straight answer out of Petrofina.

And with that, Vermont's oil boom ended without fanfare.

All the gas and oil wells are now securely capped and the rigs, for the most part, are long gone. Last I knew, a single remaining oil rig sat abandoned near a farmhouse in St. Albans. Below it, I'm sure, there is a shaft that stopped just a few feet short of a limitless supply of Vermont crude.

The Biggest Bore in Vermont

Digging for water, natural gas, and even oil in Vermont seems like a perfectly reasonable thing to do. Even hunting for long-lost pirate pillage and Spanish silver seems comparatively rational when contrasted with the exploits of a bunch of good old boys from Montpelier.

Their extraordinary enterprise involved boring a hole through one thousand feet of solid rock in order to find—

But wait, I'm getting ahead of myself again. It will make slightly more sense if we start at the beginning:

Back in the summer of 1827, Daniel Baldwin of Montpelier convinced sixty of his neighbors to put up about $35 apiece for a new business venture. That's a total initial investment of $2,100—a tidy sum in those days.

Using water-powered machinery with steel drills and spruce pole shafting, their intention was to bore a hole to the depth of a thousand feet, where they were convinced they'd find their prize.

Work commenced on August 8, 1827, and continued for two years and five months.

At a depth of four hundred feet they struck water—but that wasn't what they were after.

Then, on January 4, 1830, when they had reached 850 feet, everything came to a halt. The drill got stuck. It became so firmly embedded they could proceed no further; no available power could start it again.

But even if the desired depth of a thousand feet had been reached, I suspect the result would have been exactly the same.

The real question is: Why were these Montpelierites digging a one-thousand-foot hole to begin with? If they weren't looking for buried treasure, natural gas, or black gold, what were they up to?

Well, it all has to do with the price of salt.

In those days—before railroads and canals permitted easy transportation—salt was an essential but very expensive commodity. It cost three to four dollars a bushel—a hefty chunk of change in 1827 Vermont.

Unfortunately, there were no salt mines in the state and, as we have said, Vermont is the only New England state without a sea coast, making desalinization out of the question.

In short, there was no convenient source of this indispensable article.

Baldwin somehow got it into his head that if they just drilled down far enough they'd hit sea water. So he and his associates decided they'd start digging. When they struck salt water they could start a new business: salt manufacturing.

To be fair, Baldwin's folly was not quite as knuckleheaded as it may sound. Many communities in western New York had mineral springs that furnished an abundance of salt. Even Saratoga, only about one hundred miles away, had springs in which salt was a considerable component. And a study of the geology of the Montpelier area suggested conditions *might* be favorable for discovering salt beneath our capitol city.

As bogus as all this may sound, there is no information that suggests this fanciful venture was any type of scam. All the investors and participants apparently believed in what they were doing. No one complained of having been swindled, and, in spite of their eventual failure, all concerned were able to keep their good reputations in the community.

Since then, no one has ever taken up the challenge of salt manufacturing in Vermont, though I can't understand why not. In an age when we have the Made-in-Vermont stickers on such products as Mexican salsa and even Indian chutney, does the Vermont Salt Company seem that far out of line?

Mr. Trombley's Deep Freeze

This is the story of a Brandon farmer who dug a well, but unearthed a mystery. In November 1858, Abraham Trombley began digging for a new water supply. He had sunk a hole to about fourteen feet—well past the frost line—when, to his amazement, he struck frozen ground. Puzzled, he kept digging through foot after foot of frozen gravel, rounded stones, and big lumps of clear ice that simply shouldn't be there.

Frustrated but curious, he kept hacking away; the frozen layer turned out to be fifteen feet thick! Then, at thirty-two feet, he finally struck water.

Next morning Mr. Trombley went out to fill a bucket from his new well. But a two-inch layer of ice had formed on the water's surface. Night after night the same thing happened, so every morning Mr. Trombley's son had to climb into the well and chop through the ice to get drinking water.

By summer Trombley knew the ice was permanent. No matter how hot it became, the well always froze overnight. A glaze of ice even formed four or five feet up the sides. Brandon residents were fascinated by the mystery: why was it so cold under Trombly's property?

Soon the ice well became a popular local attraction. Hundreds of curiosity seekers visited the farm and a *Burlington Free Press* article turned the phenomenon into national news.

Perplexed, Boston's highly respected Society of Natural History launched a thorough investigation. An expedition of three scientists came to Brandon to get to the bottom of the frozen well.

The leader, Charles T. Jackson, was vice-president of the society. He had studied geology at the Sorbonne and had served as Maine's first state geologist. He was well suited to tackle Vermont's arctic oddity— or so everyone thought.

Jackson and his colleague John H. Blake spent the first day studying the geology of the area before turning their full attention to the well. They compared temperature readings against normal wells in the area. They analyzed the water and found its mineral content unremarkable. They even wanted to sink a second well nearby, but farmer Trombley refused because it would disrupt his potato crop.

The scientists returned to Boston scratching their heads.

During a second expedition in August they dug another well and at twenty-nine feet struck ice. Now they realized the underground mass of ice was big. But they still had no idea how big or why it was there.

Three hot summers passed and the ice stayed firmly in place. In 1862 Jackson and Blake submitted a report on their findings: it was full of exotic theories but no explanation. A decade later the ice still had not melted and the men gave up for good.

Vermont's state geologist, Edward Hitchcock, had conducted his own investigation. His assistant, the self-taught and apparently brilliant Albert D. Hager, theorized that the surrounding clay insulated the ice deposit like "a mammoth refrigerator." This proved to be, in effect, true.

But where had the ice come from? That was still a mystery.

Hitchcock came closest to deciphering the mystery. His theory was perhaps influenced by the fact that he was not only Vermont's state geologist, but also an ordained minister. He therefore believed in the biblical flood—a flood that had carried icebergs to New England and carefully deposited one within Brandon's insulating clay.

How long had the ice been there? He said we could only guess by "piling tens of thousands of years upon one another."

More up-to-date thinking agrees that there's a huge mass of ice under Brandon; otherwise, Trombley's well wouldn't have frozen year after year. But it probably isn't an iceberg. More likely it's part of a gargantuan continental ice sheet—one of unimaginable proportions. Similar ice deposits may have formed kettle ponds like Spectacle Pond in Brighton and Silver Lake in Barnard. Others ice deposits, like Brandon's, ended up in clay. Indeed, a second such well was reported in Sudbury at about the same time.

In his article in *Vermont Geology*, Kevin Dan says it beautifully: "Hitchcock, Jackson and the rest . . . had been staring the Ice Age in the face without knowing it."

And since Brandon's buried mass of ice had lasted tens of millions of years, can Mr. Trombley's Ice Well still be around? Kevin Dan tells us, "The Brandon frozen well came to a decidedly unpoetic end in the 1930's when heavy equipment working nearby disturbed the protective clay layers and the underlying glacial relict. It possibly survives today, smaller perhaps, yet still there."

Oddities in Stone

As you may have already guessed, I enjoy reading nineteenth-century newspapers. I like to get an idea what life was like here in Vermont before the turn of the twentieth century.

In the old days even no-nonsense newspapers like the venerable *Rutland Herald* routinely published what they called "Oddities." Essentially these were short, curious stories intended simply to fill up space.

But by studying these oddities it is possible to get a sense of what piqued our forefathers' curiosity long before the days of Robert Ripley and TV's *Unsolved Mysteries*.

Water from a Stone

For example, a stone "oddity" was reported in the *Burlington Free Press* on December 30, 1870. This geological anomaly was situated in Sheffield, on land owned by William Gray. It was a large granite boulder. The unusual thing was that the top of the boulder contained what the paper called "a spherical excavation" that was constantly filled with water.

There was no visible inlet, yet even in the driest days of summer the stone bowl was always full. What makes it more curious is that it was never known to run over; it just filled up and stayed full.

Mr. Gray said that he occasionally dipped the water out, but the bowl immediately refilled, even though it hadn't rained and there was no identifiable source of the water.

Stoned Frogs

Another odd life-sustaining property of stone is evident in a pair of stories about Burlington.

In the summer of 1786, on the intervale by the Winooski River, a Mr. Lane decided to dig a well. The earth through which he dug was comprised of a fine river sand. Twenty-five feet below the surface Mr. Lane unearthed what appeared to be a large number of small rocks. Upon removing them he discovered they were not rocks at all, but frogs—alive—"in a torpid state . . . bedded in the earth like small stones."

After being exposed to the fresh air they revived for a time, leaped around happily, but soon became "languid, and died."

Considering the depth at which they were found, Jedediah Morse, in his *American Universal Geography* (1805), concluded, "These frogs must have been buried in the spot where they were found, by some extraordinary inundation of the river, while in that state of torpor in which they always pass the winter in those climates, and have continued in that situation for centuries."

Weird to think that frogs can lie buried without air or nourishment for centuries. That they can then be revived is weirder still. Indeed, one has to wonder if an untold number of live frogs can be part of the bedrock of Burlington.

On October 12, 1807, Moses Catlin was digging a well near his house about a hundred yards south of the University of Vermont. The ground was hard and gravelly. When the workers had dug about five feet below the surface they found six live frogs nearly identical to those just discussed here. Two of them lay together; the others were separate. All were covered with small stones.

On October 13, in the same well, two more were found, again packed among small stones. On the 14th, when the well had dropped to a depth of eleven feet, five more live frogs were discovered packed in hard gravelly earth.

The workmen continued to dig to a depth of eighteen feet, but no more animals were found.

Scientists at the time had no explanation for frogs that could survive while packed solidly in soil in the bowels of the earth. I guess times haven't changed all that much.

Hard as a Rock

A different kind of stone oddity frequently appeared in Vermont papers. It seems there were a fair number of articles about petrifaction. Somehow the notion of human beings turning to stone held endless fascination for nineteenth-century Vermonters.

Take the case of Daniel Vaughn of Middlesex. In life this much-loved local man was known to all as "Uncle Daniel." He stood five feet ten inches tall and weighed less than 200 pounds. In 1846 Uncle Daniel died of "dropsy" at age seventy-eight. He was buried at home, alongside the grave of his granddaughter.

Then in 1855 relatives planned to move the bodies to a family plot in Woodstock. The remains of the granddaughter were found to be exactly as expected. However, Uncle Daniel's coffin seemed uncommonly heavy. Upon lifting the lid they discovered the man had unaccountably turned to stone. Everything but his nose was petrified. And moving him proved to be no easy task; he now weighed over 550 pounds!

A similar story comes from down south in Bennington. In 1870 a group of workmen were relocating bodies in a local cemetery. When they got to the grave of a Mrs. Bartlett, they ran into trouble. They tried to move the corpse, but it just wouldn't budge.

When they investigated they were surprised at what they found. The poor woman had only been in the ground for about twelve years, but in that time, for some unknown reason, her corpse had completely turned to stone.

The petrified body now weighs more than 500 pounds. Mrs. Bartlett, you might say, has become her own gravestone.

*

It is easy to speculate why some of these oddities held so much fascination for our ancestors. They were no doubt tied in to very real fears.

The idea of being able to get water from a stone must have been comforting: even during the most severe of Vermont's droughts, Farmer Gray's magic boulder would reliably produce drinking water.

Fears surrounding petrifaction are somewhat different. I don't think it grows so much out of the vain fear of gaining weight after death as it does from the unpleasant prospect of putrefaction in those pre-embalming days.

But the frogs? I don't know what to make of them. The similarities to Allen Morse's human hibernation yarn are obvious. But for some reason a quote from famed curio collector Charles Fort springs to mind: "You can judge a civilization by its frogs." Trouble is, I just can't figure out how it applies.

For further confusion, there's the saga of the stone "something" two boys and a man found on the banks of the Connecticut River . . .

The Petrified Indian

The mystery of the petrified Indian began in January 1871 when George Parsons of Springfield, Massachusetts, got an unaccountable craving for rabbit stew.

He was visiting Turners Falls at the time, so he rounded up a couple of local lads, they grabbed their dog, and the whole crew lit out on a hunting trip.

As they made their way along the Connecticut River bank, not far from the famous dinosaur tracks, the dog suddenly let out a howl and began sniffing and scratching at a hole in the ground. The spot, as Mr. Parsons would later recall, was "forty rods from the bank of the Connecticut River, some six miles northeast of Greenfield, and roughly about twelve to fifteen miles from Brattleboro, Vermont."

For a while the trio stood watching the agitated animal, thinking he had cornered some kind of game. Soon Parsons and the boys started digging in the frozen gravel.

All activity ceased at once when they realized what they had found: a bare, brown, human foot.

Fearing the worst, they put off further excavation until the following day. They came back with proper digging tools. Working together they quickly exposed the form of a young boy lying face down against the earth.

One hand had been flattened under his weight. The other hand, and one leg, were firmly attached to the rock ledge on which the body rested. A thin gray mold covered the form, but it vanished in the air and sunlight. Clearly the figure had been buried a long time.

In order to free his discovery, Parsons had to break one foot and one finger. The three then lifted the surprisingly heavy figure on to a blanket.

Parson described his trophy as a stone statue of a boy about six to eight years old, perfect in every detail right down to its fingernails and eyebrows. But why, he wondered, was a statue buried near the Connecticut River?

Parsons took his discovery home, where local experts hypothesized a slightly different scenario. They speculated that Parsons had not found a statue, but rather the actual body of a boy, hundreds—maybe even thousands—of years old. He had presumably fallen, struck his head, and died. In time, they guessed, mud had covered him and hardened. Over the centuries, minerals from the water had replaced bones and flesh. In other words, Parsons had found a petrified human being who'd had smooth skin, well-shaped limbs and cranium, wide-set eyes, and a forehead that showed him to be of an intelligent race.

Encouraged by this historical hypothesis, Parsons built a display case and began show off his petrified prize—for a modest fee—at the American House in Greenfield.

John W. Stewart, then governor of Vermont, examined the exhibit and proclaimed, "Unquestionably, this is an Indian." Professor Webber of Middlebury College disagreed, pointing out that the lad did not have the high cheekbones or elongated features of the local Native Americans.

So what was he?

With the questionable—and conflicting—opinions of these "experts," the mystery deepened. Was the stone boy a member of some forgotten civilization? Possibly a representative of the lost tribes of Israel? Today we might even suspect he was a space alien.

Anyway, crowds of sightseers grew. Mr. Parsons moved his adopted boy to larger quarters and raised the admission fee.

Journalists picked up the story, quickly turning it into big news. The petrified Indian boy captured the public's imagination . . . and sympathy.

People printed up informational pamphlets and clergymen preached about it from the pulpit. Historians tried to define its significance and theologians wracked their brains for its meaning. Some, through miraculous contortions of logic, even interpreted the stone youngster as an argument advocating temperance.

In time—for reasons we can only suspect—Parsons sold his petrified prize to Brooks Whitney for eight to ten thousand dollars.

Whitney took it on tour and made a fortune. Perhaps sensing what was coming, Whitney traded it to Abner Woodward for a hundred barrels of whiskey.

While displaying the petrified Indian boy in Boston, the events Whitney so cunningly avoided struck Woodward with full force. Some shrewd Bostonian who had heard about the recent Cardiff Giant hoax began to smell a rat. He dug a fingernail into a crack in the petrified boy's ankle and scraped out—you guessed it—plaster of Paris.

The petrified Indian boy had been a hoax all along.

Woodward was fined for obtaining money under false pretenses. He paid up, grabbed his plaster sidekick, and headed for Canada, where he made back the expense of the fine and then some.

It is at this point that we lose the trail of the little Indian boy. Some years later it showed up at the Sheldon Museum in Middlebury, Vermont. Sheldon's diary for February 16, 1884, gives only a cryptic entry that reads, "Mr. Frederick A. Leland has given me permission to place in the museum the petrified Indian boy that has caused so much talk a few years ago."

That's all it says. And that's all we know. But the boy has resided there ever since.

Yet mystery still surrounds the little figure. To this day we don't know who perpetrated the petrified hoax, or why he chose to do it. We don't know exactly how the statue was produced or when it was placed in the ground. We don't even know with any certainty how it ended up at the Sheldon Museum.

All we know for sure is that regardless of its origin, this relic of nineteenth-century charlatanism still has the power to provoke curiosity and wonder.

In the Clutch of Witches

On the weekend of March 28, 1998, I was in Marblehead, Massachusetts, visiting friends. Because we were next door to Salem, our conversation naturally turned to witchcraft.

Interestingly, my companion, an eighth-generation Vermonter, is descended from a witch. Her maternal ancestor, Martha Carrier, was executed in Salem on August 19, 1692. So both of us, for different reasons, wanted to learn what we could. The next day, Sunday, we drove to Salem.

We started with a tour of the Salem Witch Museum. There imaginative dioramas recreated that horrible time in 1692 when 156 people were accused of making pacts with the devil. The resulting Witch Trials lasted thirteen months. Nineteen men and women—even two dogs—were hanged. One elderly man, Giles Corey, was pressed to death.

Clearly the Devil had visited New England. But not just Massachusetts. I saw that neighboring states had fatal experiences with witchcraft as well.

Naturally this got me thinking about Vermont. Did we have an outbreak of witch hysteria here? Were any witch trials conducted? Was anyone executed?

Of course I knew the timing wasn't right. It wasn't until half a century after the Salem trials that New Hampshire governor Benning Wentworth granted the first lands in what was to become Vermont.

When I got home I persistently poked around at my various reference materials, but failed to discover any accounts of a Green Mountain witch hysteria. However, I did discover a few interesting stories.

Pownal

For example, T. E Brownel recorded an incident in Pownal involving a Dutch woman named Mrs. Kreiger. The details of her alleged "crime" are a little sketchy, but her trial was designed to place her in a life-or-death situation to see if the Devil would come to her aid. Presumably if he saved her, she was guilty. If she died, she would die an honest woman.

They decided upon the tried-and-true "water test." Mrs. Kreiger would be tossed into a body of water. If she sank she was innocent. If she floated, Old Nick was obviously assisting her.

After much deliberation, the town fathers hit upon the perfect scheme. The poor woman was forced through a hole in the ice on the Hoosic River. With the ice sheet making resurfacing impossible, she of course sank, thus proving her purity of spirit.

Perhaps God really did have a hand in the proceedings. Some time later, when Mrs. Kreiger emerged downstream, she was pulled out, warmed up, and saved. A perfect solution.

Lincoln

The town of Lincoln also had a local witch, and a tale handed down from witchcraft times to prove it.

It seems a man came to town looking to buy a farm.

He was quickly offered an acceptable place and at a very agreeable price. In fact, the house and property were so cheap the man could hardly believe his good fortune.

When he started asking around he learned that no one else had wanted the place. And he began to hear stories: Over the past few years a number of families had moved in, but no one would stay. Everyone said it was jinxed; strange things kept happening and people just couldn't stand to live there.

The farmer didn't believe in jinxed farms and bad luck, so he went ahead with the purchase, moved in, and went about his business.

As townsfolk got more used to him, they started letting on that the real problem was his neighbor's wife. Some said she was a little tetched, some said she was out and out crazy, and still others said—in lowered voices—that she was a witch.

By then the farmer was beginning to think maybe all his neighbors were a tad peculiar. Crazy folks were easy enough to believe in, but witches were another matter. Besides, he'd had no problem with the family in question.

Then one day he started off to town in his wagon, when the oddest thing happened. One of the wheels wouldn't turn. He climbed down and examined it. There didn't seem to be anything wrong. At least nothing he could see. It just wouldn't turn. Becoming quickly irritated at the inconvenience, he gave the wheel a couple of stiff kicks with his heavy boot.

Now it worked just fine and he continued on his way.

Then another wheel seized up. A few more kicks freed that one too, but when he got underway, a third wheel locked.

Each time he had to get out and kick a different wheel until his wagon finally limped all the way to town.

Next day, after giving the axles a good greasing, he went to see his neighbor on business. The old witch-woman came to the door. "My husband ain't to home," she said. Then she pointed to her black eye and said, "See there! See what you done to me?"

The farmer, recalling the tales about her crazy antics, pretended he didn't hear, excused himself, and walked back toward his own door-yard.

But later, when he tried his wagon, the freshly greased wheels kept locking up again. Now he carried a heavy hammer with him and every time a wheel stopped turning he gave it a vigorous pummeling. They worked just fine after the pounding. In fact, that hammering seemed to solve the problem once and for all.

Next week, on his way into town, the farmer stopped in again at the neighboring farm, hoping to see the man of the house. He found the old fellow washing dishes. When he saw he had a visitor the neighbor announced, perhaps with a note of suppressed happiness, "My old woman's dead."

"Oh dear," said the farmer, "I'm awful sorry to hear that. What ailed her?"

The old man shook his head and replied, "Don't rightly know and it puzzles me. Happened right sudden-like. She got all black and blue and she died."

The farmer quickly offered his condolences and continued his trip to town.

Guilford

In the Packer Corners area of Guilford, very near the Massachusetts border, we encounter another woman with the reputation of being a witch. In the late eighteenth century, "Old Mother Honeywell" was considered a good person to avoid.

According to *The Official History of Guilford*, she was a product of the "super-religiosity" of the area. At that time "deluded souls saw as visions the mirage in the fog and mist of Weatherhead Hollow, and a mile or two away the followers of William Dorrell received the doctrine of their false prophet." So it should be no surprise that such pious Protestants saw devils in their midst.

For example, a local farmer picked out a new pair of sheepshears at the local general store. The storekeeper wrapped them in paper and the man brought them home where he placed them—still wrapped—on a shelf in his closet. Later, when a friend was visiting, the farmer took down the shears to show them off. He unwrapped his prize only to discover they were rusty, well used, and apparently old.

After taking an appropriate ribbing about his horse-trading skills, the farmer put the shears back thinking he'd been cheated by the storekeeper's sleight of hand.

A day or so later another friend stopped by. He had heard the outrageous story and wanted to see the magically transformed shears for himself. When the farmer took them out and unwrapped them, they were all bright and new! Obviously the mischief of Mother Honeywell.

A different Guilford farmer was transporting a load of hay on his wagon. Unaccountably, the wagon stopped. The powerful oxen couldn't budge it another inch.

When the farmer investigated he found a tiny mouse with her shoulder under the hind wheel. He plucked the mouse free, tossed it into the bushes, and continued on his way, puzzled that the tiny creature could halt his heavy beasts of burden.

When he told the story next day, someone who'd recently seen Mother Honeywell reported that she was suffering from a lame shoulder.

Later the poor woman was injured far more horribly when some local lad shot a white owl. At the same moment Old Mother Honeywell tumbled down the stairs of her home and was terribly wounded.

If these witch stories are beginning to sound a bit familiar, the authors of *The Official History of Guilford* have an explanation: "Probably all witches belonged to a union and had to follow a general pattern in their activities."

Stowe

According to Walter J. Bigelow's *History of Stowe*, their resident witch was a woman with the innocuous name of Nancy Sanborn. It was around 1802 that her reputation for satanic mischief began to spread. Her "evil eye" received full credit for all sorts of local misfortunes. If butter didn't properly separate from cream, that was Nancy's fault. If a hunter's bullet missed its mark, he had obviously angered Nancy in some way. Local illness and hard luck could all be traced back to Paul Sanborn's ornery missus.

But Stowe had to have someone to blame when things didn't go well and—for whatever reason—Nancy seems to have been the target. As Bigelow explains in his 1934 book, "Whatever her power really was, she has furnished early Stowe with its only story of witchcraft."

In a way, I suppose, that's good luck.

Whitingham

In the late 1700s, the wicked witch of Whitingham, Vermont, was the much-feared Mrs. Lamphear.

"At the time it had been settled . . . that witchcraft was a miserable delusion," Clark Jillson says in his book *Green Leaves From Whitingham*, "and yet . . . nine tenths of all the inhabitants of Whitingham believed Mrs. Lamphear to be in league with the devil."

Apparently she was an elderly widow, perhaps a bit eccentric, who had two sons, Reuben and Chandler. Chandler's daughter lived with Mrs. Lamphear, and apparently even she believed her grandmother to be a witch.

So, one wonders, what were the indications of this local woman's guilt? Remember, the validity of "spectral evidence" had been pretty much shot down after the Salem trials, but there was a strong anecdotal case against her.

For example, one individual claimed that when he went to his barn on a particular morning he found all his cattle on their backs. As he looked more carefully at this odd sight he realized that everything else around him seemed upside down, too. He blamed this altered perception on Mrs. Lamphear's evil influence, though, I must admit, other explanations leap readily to mind.

Other more rational Whitingham residents like Hezekiah Whitney and his sons demanded sturdier proof of Mrs. Lamphear's witchery. They got it. As one of the level-headed lads was driving a yoke of oxen, he stared in disbelief as one ox walked right through the oxbow and yoke—a solid passing through a solid—and continued to trudge on several paces ahead of its mate.

Another neighbor, James Upton, managed to offend Mrs. Lamphear in some way. He claimed she retaliated by telling him that his children would get sick and that his cat would die. Though Upton tried to laugh it off, his children *did* get sick, and the poor cat died—exactly as predicted. Perhaps to some this might be pretty convincing testimony, but Clark Jillson adds, "Mr. Upton was an intemperate man and might have seen snakes."

Julius Clark said that Mrs. Lamphear had him so completely under her spell that he was unable to leave his bed for ten years. One might suspect this is a more accurate comment on his level of ambition than the witch's skill. Yet when Mrs. Lamphear died, Julius Clark recovered immediately and lived well into old age.

Jillson's 1894 book used Mrs. Lamphear's story as an appeal for proper education and sound judgment. It is a good and necessary reminder. After all, evidence much more flimsy than what we've seen here actually got people hanged in Salem.

With that in mind, it seems especially odd to me that there should be a more recent report of witchcraft, and that it should also come from Whitingham. I don't dare speculate whether Mrs. Lamphear might still be living there, possibly under an assumed name.

Grandmother Thyme

In 1968 Josh Wallace was attending Marlboro College in southern Vermont. One day he found a note from his friend Echo, whom he hadn't seen for over a year. Echo invited Josh to meet him at "the house of Grandma Thyme in Whitingham."

Josh was surprised to discover his old friend was so near by. But why, he wondered, would he be staying with someone's grandmother?

Eager to find out, he borrowed a car, not bothering to mention that he had no license. Under cover of twilight he followed the note's directions through a maze of rural Vermont dirt roads.

Josh says, "The dark was almost total now and the road followed a slow rise. . . . I probed its strange contours . . . with my high beams, hoping for some indication of a village, four corners, or any other guidepost in my journey to Whitingham."

Soon he became hopelessly lost.

Shortly, he saw the dim lights of a solitary farmhouse. It was huge. As he drove closer he noted the absence of electrical or telephone lines. The dim interior glow, he realized, was attributable to candlelight.

Somewhat reluctantly, he walked up and knocked.

An elderly woman with a round red face opened the door.

"Excuse me," Josh said, "could you tell me how to get to Grandma Thyme's place?"

The lady smiled. "I'm Grandma Thyme," she said, "why don't you come in?"

She returned to the bread she was kneading on the kitchen tabletop. As Josh started to follow her, she said, "Go ahead, take a look around."

So he wandered off, searching for his friend. In the low light of oil lamps, he noted the floors were hand-hewn boards. *What a weird old place*, he thought. *It must be two hundred years old. Maybe more. . . .*

In the living room he found a group of people his own age talking quietly.

"Is Echo around here someplace?" he asked.

"He's upstairs," someone answered. A young woman in a long calico dress pointed the way.

Trembling unaccountably now, Josh grasped the banister and went up. Each step creaked.

At the top he found an open door and looked inside. There, in the candlelight, he saw Echo, deeply involved in painting a watercolor. "Hi, Josh," Echo said. "I'm glad you came."

"Jeez, Echo, what is this place?"

"What do you think it is?" Echo replied.

"I don't know; I'm getting the creeps."

Echo laughed. His laugh seemed horribly loud in contrast to the quiet in the old house.

"Tell you what," said Echo, "just let me finish what I'm doing here and I'll join you downstairs. Meet you in the living room, okay?"

*

But now the rooms downstairs were empty. Josh sat on the sofa and waited. He felt uneasy and more than a little bored. Echo seemed to be taking way too long to finish his painting.

In a while he got up and began to wander around, looking for someone to talk to. Though it was dark and creepy, the fresh bread smelled good, strangely comforting.

Josh stepped out the screen door and under the stars. In the distance he heard the sound of muffled voices. Apparently everyone had moved out to the barn.

He crossed the yard to join them.

Inside, by lamplight, he saw the people from the house and a few others. They were off at the far end of the barn. He could tell they were singing, or praying, or something. A growing feeling of unease warned him not to get too close. He says, "It looked very pretty in a way. Big stacks of hay, a golden flickering light, low moaning rhythms. . . ." But one thing wasn't so pretty. A skull. Somebody had nailed it high on a post. "It had both jaws pinned together and a cruel forehead with a huge snout. Maybe it had belonged to a cow. Or a bull. A goat, I finally decided. Yes, a goat."

The group still hadn't noticed him, so he examined the skull. He touched it, tugged on one of the teeth, and found it broke off in his hand.

To this day he has no idea why he did it; perhaps he just wanted to have a souvenir of this surreal evening. But for whatever reason, Josh took the tooth and put it in his pocket.

By this time he had given up on Echo. As there was no reason to interrupt the chanters, Josh decided to return to his car and get out of there.

Later, after the strange events that followed, he speculated that maybe, if he had not taken the tooth, this story would have had a very different ending.

*

Josh drove away in silence on the midnight Vermont roads. The only sounds were the squeaking of springs and the crunch of gravel beneath his tires. Feeling oddly spooked, his one thought was escape. There was no way he could know he was plunging deeper into the twilight zone.

"I drove faster," he says, "Soon I would reach campus, run straight to my dorm, lock the door, and leave the devil behind."

When he was within three miles of the college, he flicked the signal to make a left turn on to Moss Hollow Road. But, he says, "As I did that the power steering and power brakes both failed. Simultaneously."

The Ford left the road. It plowed through the underbrush, tearing up shrubs and saplings, before it ground to a noisy stop against the trunk of a tree, just a dozen feet from his turnoff.

Odder still, the tree—though seemingly in the middle of nowhere—was directly across from the property of the West Halifax law enforcement officer. He busted Josh for driving without a license.

*

In the next few weeks a trio of odd events reinforced just how weird his evening at Grandma Thyme's had been.

First, when he paid the automobile repair bill, the mechanic told him the systems failure was especially peculiar. The power brakes and power steering were on separate circuits, completely independent of each other. There was no reason for them to fail at the same time.

Later, when he was swimming alone at an isolated quarry, an oddly old-fashioned looking couple slowly emerged from the woods and joined him. The man, bearded and barefoot, wore denim overalls with a brown T-shirt. The woman had a wan smile and a long thin cotton dress; its hem rested on her naked feet. They approached and sat by the water, silently.

Josh said, "Hello," and slowly the three struck up a conversation. Presuming they were locals, Josh decided to ask them about his bizarre evening.

"I was at this place in Whitingham," he began cautiously. "It was weird. . . . They called it—"

The woman cut him off. "You went to Grandma Thyme's house."

"How did you know that?"

Her fine smile didn't change. "Grandma Thyme is my mother. My adopted mother. She raised me from when I was two. Grandma Thyme is a witch."

"I might have suspected that," Josh said.

"Well, believe it. It's true. She's a white witch. She's over three hundred years old."

What could he say to that? He just stood there as the bearded man took the hand of Grandma Thyme's daughter. They walked back into the forest, disappearing like ghosts.

The final curious incident happened sometime later when Josh tried to contact Echo regarding the odd incidents at Grandma Thyme's farm.

He phoned Echo's parents' home in Putnam Valley, New York, only to learn Echo had left the country. "He's in Jerusalem," Echo's father said.

"Jerusalem? Do you have his address?"

"Sure, but it won't do you no good."

"Is he okay?"

"Well, he joined a monastery. Greek Orthodox Monastery."

"A monastery? I didn't know he was religious."

"Me and his mom didn't, neither."

"Can I write him?"

"Sure. But it won't do you much good."

"Why?"

"Said he was taking a 'vow of silence.' Haven't had any news from him since."

The Vermont Odditorium

Fire Walkers

In their April 7, 1947, issue, *Time Magazine* reported, "In Woodstock, Vermont a fire broke out in the basement of the Wendall Walker house on Sunday; the staircase caught fire on Monday; an upstairs partition blazed on Tuesday; the jittery Walkers moved out on Wednesday; the house burned down on Thursday."

Though it must have been a bad week for the Walker family, this peculiar progression of details provides exactly the type of fuel to fire folktales. Vermont history is full of such peculiarities. And they can evolve into wonderful stories.

*

For example, there is an extraordinary old Vermont tale that reminds me of Alfred Hitchcock's film *The Birds*. As you recall, *The Birds* is about the day our feathered friends—for no apparent reason—became our feathered enemies.

Fiction, of course. But in the late eighteenth century the good folks of Barnard, Vermont, experienced a similar episode for real. We might call it . . .

The Animals' Revenge

Beginning in 1783, a strange madness seemed to seize many local critters. First, folks began to notice abnormally aggressive behavior among the wildlife. Feral creatures that ordinarily remained hidden marched brazenly out. Foxes or wolves were often seen fighting at the edge of cleared land.

Unsettled by such unnatural behavior, settlers killed the feuding beasts. Then, as if striking back, animals began attacking people.

Everyone grew frightened to venture outdoors alone. A walk to the barn was a hurried undertaking; a trip to the well could be a harrowing experience. Parents armed themselves to escort children to and from school.

In several cases, wolves walked right into town. In one instance a face-off developed between a wolf and a man on the road by the Methodist cemetery. The man saw the wolf approaching, but figured it would spot him and dart back into the woods. Instead, it pressed forward, not altering its path. Finally the man had to step aside to let the animal pass.

Not knowing how to respond to this unfamiliar animal behavior, the unarmed man leaped on to the wolf's back and grabbed it by the ears, hoping to capture it. The animal proved stronger. It easily tossed him aside unharmed and continued on its way.

Before long, even domesticated animals got into the act. Dogs growled menacingly at their masters. Kittens bit and clawed at their owners. Even docile barnyard critters like pigs and oxen displayed an odd and unprovoked belligerence.

During the evening of March 17, 1784, Willard Smith heard a commotion outside his cabin. Something was attacking his sheep. Suspecting a wolf or catamount, Smith grabbed a club and headed out to do battle. He was surprised to see the intruder was his neighbor's dog. Because it had never acted that way before, the puzzled farmer scared it off without harming it.

But it was definitely a wolf that attacked the sheep in Mr. Steward's barnyard. Upon hearing a wicked commotion, Steward and his two sons rushed outside. A savage battle ensued. Eventually they clubbed the wolf to death, but all three farmers had been bitten. After some primitive medical intervention, the two boys survived. Sadly, their father died following severe bouts with fever and eventual madness.

At this point all the villagers realized what a few had suspected right along. The revolt of the animals was nothing supernatural—it was the result of rabies.

Almost miraculously, the Stewards were apparently the only humans infected. And, as far as I can tell, Mr. Steward's was the only death.

In piecing together the events, Barnard citizens learned that a traveler had brought the trouble to town. Somewhere along, his horse had been bitten by a rabid dog. Upon reaching Barnard, the traveler put the suffering animal out of its misery and buried it near the woods. But because the grave was so shallow, wolves and foxes dug it up and fed on the horse's corpse. When they became infected, their raids on livestock spread the contagion.

The singular events at Barnard must have been puzzling at the time. They supplied yarn-spinners with material for decades. But today, I'm afraid *The Animals' Revenge* has been relegated to the limbo of lost lore. Hopefully, someone like Hitchcock will come along to immortalize this scary Vermont tale.

The Northern Army

In the summer of 1770 the "Northern Army" descended on the town of Guildhall. Though the hardy locals had battled Indians and Tories, this new band of invaders was like nothing anyone had ever seen before.

The invaders, inching steadfastly southward, innumerable in multitude, were an army of worms. Soon they became a plague of biblical proportions.

So vast were their numbers that Everett Chamberlain Benton, in his *History of Guildhall*, says they "extended from towns in this immediate locality to Northfield, Mass." To many, such an improbable flood seemed to signal the end of the world.

Guildhall's "queer visitation" started during the later part of July as the worms began to appear from the north.

Soon a trickle became a deluge—they were everywhere. Worms were so prolific that they covered whole fields. Rev. Grant Powers wrote, "A man could not put down his finger in a single spot without placing it on a worm."

He went on to provide this description of the invaders: "There was a stripe upon the back like black velvet, on either side a yellow stripe from end to end, and the rest of the body was brown. They were sometimes seen not larger than a pin, but in their maturity, they were as long as a man's finger and proportionally large in circumference."

The incredible crawlers carpeted the forests, blanketed cleared land, and polluted the wells. "They would go up the side of a house and over it in such a compact column that nothing of boards or shingles could be seen."

They entered and filled the houses. People would discover them in their larders, burrowed into bread dough, and twisted into the folds of their bedding. Clothing had to be shaken in the morning before it was put on.

In general, the worms seemed to be in a hurry to get . . . somewhere. They'd pause only long enough to eat, and to the farmers of Guildhall, eating meant destruction. Worms leveled fields of wheat and corn, thus cutting off major food sources.

Farmers tried to dam the relentless tide by "drawing the rope," as they termed it. Two men would take each end of a rope, pull until it was straightened, then pass it through their wheat field in an effort to knock the worms off the stalks. The effort proved fruitless.

They also tried digging trenches around their fields, a foot wide by half a foot deep. The trenches were soon filled; the advancing worms used the bodies of their fallen comrades as bridges, so the organic tide continued to flow.

If the devastation had been complete, the fledgling settlement of Guildhall itself would have been "nipped in the bud." The settlers would have had to abandon their town—which was just six years old at the time.

Luckily, the invaders had no appetite for pumpkins, peas, potatoes, or flax. With other crops gone, pumpkins flourished astonishingly, offering abundant, if tedious, sustenance.

Around the first of September the worms suddenly vanished. Rev. Powers wrote, "Where they terminated their earthly career is unknown, for not the carcass of a worm was seen."

Almost immediately upon the end of one plague, another seemed to begin. Everett Benton writes, an "immense number of pigeons . . . came through this section immediately upon the disappearance of the worms. Nothing could equal their number unless it was the worms which had preceded them."

Perhaps they had fed on the worm carcasses that seemed to have vanished so suddenly. In any event, the famished settlers fed on the pigeons. "They were so thick that 3 men in 10 days captured 400 dozen."

Fred Smith recalled an attempt at efficient pigeon hunting. Some locals got a big gun that would take a pound of powder and a pound of shot. They loaded it up and went into a field before daylight. Hiding behind a large pine stump, they propped the gun into position on its top.

At daybreak the pigeons began to come from all directions and congregate in the field. At the proper time a hat was thrown among them, which made them rise in the air and the gun was discharged!

The report was tremendous! It took 15 minutes for the smoke to clear away, and when the morning sun began to shine through the breaks in the clouds of smoke they were greatly surprised, astonished and dumbfounded to find that they had not killed a pigeon. They had delayed a little too long before firing the gun, the pigeons had risen a little too high. But they picked up 133 bushel baskets of legs and toes.

After eleven years of relative comfort, the same kind of worms began to reappear in 1781. The terrified townsfolk geared up for another battle with what they now referred to as the "Northern Army."

But it wasn't to be—the invaders were comparatively few in number. They vanished quickly and have never returned.

The Salisbury Flood

For many people, the scenery around Lake Dunmore has always held a special appeal. And the lake itself has long been regarded as a thing of particular beauty. The whole area is tranquil, timeless. I've even heard it described as magic.

Standing on any of the summits around the lake, a striking panorama unfolds. To the east there's the Green Mountain National Forest. To the west—some sixteen miles as the crow flies—Lake Champlain. And beyond: New York's Adirondack peaks.

It is easy to let our imaginations roam across this enchanted landscape, for it has changed little in thousands of years. It's an effortless flight of fancy to suppose we can still see Vermont as it must have appeared centuries ago when the first colonial settlers began to arrive.

And it is easy to imagine other things, too. But the fantastic sight witnessed by a group of people back in August of 1833 was no act of imagination. They really saw what they saw. And as far as I know, nothing like this spectacular and terrifying sight has ever been seen again.

Picture this if you will:

You are standing with a group of "city boarders" on Sunset Hill, an elevated piece of land just west of Lake Dunmore. Although the weather is insufferably hot, the air is perfectly clear. All of a sudden you notice something odd is happening with Lake Champlain, far in the distance. The waters are starting to rise—and fast!

As you stare in disbelief, the grayish liquid surface of the lake widens so much that the intervening hills appear to be islands.

Finally, as you watch, all these island-hills disappear as one by one they're swallowed up by the mighty flood that's rapidly swallowing this whole landscape. Soon, looking west toward Addison, Bridport, and Shoreham, and stretching out before you, is one vast body of water covering all the ground from Burlington to Benson.

Trees standing on the slope of nearby Mount Bryant are wading in water, while taller trees at its base are entirely covered and out of sight.

It's a terrifying vision, yet you watch, transfixed, feeling fortunate that you are standing on high ground, safely away from the encroaching tide.

Then, as you stare, something stranger happens. It's like the magical work of some woodland conjurer. You blink but the sight remains. Before your disbelieving eyes a great city begins to appear, forming, it would seem, from the very air itself. You recognize familiar landmarks—bridges, buildings, a tower—and you know you are seeing the city of Burlington, some forty-six miles to the north.

This can't be happening, you think. It is impossible to see Burlington from this place, even with a telescope. But now, before your very eyes, it's in perfect view. All natural points, all man-made structures, are distinctly visible with the naked eye.

*

One of the people who actually witnessed this strange event became so terrified that he believed he was seeing a "true sign" that the world was coming to an end. As he watched the water rising up the slope of the mountain, he became convinced that once again our little globe would be inundated in a great flood. The old account concludes by saying, "after all was passed, [he] begged his companion not to describe the phenomenon to others lest so strange and marvelous a story might make them a laughing stock."

Personally, I don't think anyone would have laughed. I think people would be envious of seeing such a fascinating natural phenomenon. No doubt the Salisbury Mirage was one of the most remarkable ever observed in Vermont—perhaps in all of New England.

Historically, this spectacular atmospheric refraction took place on or about the 20th of August 1833. Those who saw it guessed it was produced by the rays of the sun passing under a long, narrow, black cloud, which, one of the witnesses described, hung in the west just before nightfall.

For the fortunate witnesses, the cloud, like the vision, must have been a once-in-a-lifetime thing. And, as far as I know, nothing like this fantastic vision has ever been seen again.

The Whitingham Windows

Occasionally I run across wonderfully weird accounts of things that allegedly happened right here in Vermont. But when I try to learn more, I come up empty-handed and—at least in the following case—very disappointed.

While leafing through an old *Rutland Herald* dated October 1, 1874, I discovered this little gem, titled "Ghosts":

Whitingham [VT] is exercised over a fresh outbreak of "spiritual manifestations." The windows of Rev. N.D. Sherman's residence are mysteriously covered with etchings of a strange variety, in which believers see the portraits of dead friends. The windows in the house of his son-in-law, near by, are also being covered and great numbers of people flock to see the phenomena.

That was it! The article fails to mention how many panes of glass were involved. Nor does it give the number of portraits; it just says "covered." We can assume at least two pieces of glass contained portraits because the phenomena occurred at two houses. Of course, there were no photos.

It's a great story, but where is the evidence? You'd think such miraculous pieces of glass would be preserved somewhere.

I spent hours at the Vermont Historical Society newspaper files but learned nothing more about Rev. Sherman, his son-in-law, or the glass portraits.

A few months ago I discussed the story with a photographer from Hanover, New Hampshire, who had an interesting theory that might explain the events. He said that in the old days, when photographic images were recorded on glass plates, photographers would often sell off their used plates after the images were printed. Some of these castoff plates might have been recycled as window glass. If so, sunshine might have in effect "developed" the images and caused the excitement.

A good solution, but does it fit? We'd have to learn more about the problem to decide. Perhaps someone from Whitingham will discover a little more information about this most tantalizing tale.

Sounds Weird

Before I give anyone the mistaken impression that fascinating events only happened a long ago, let me set the record straight. The past has no monopoly on the mysterious. The events I'm about to describe are going on right now.

Certain Newark, Vermont, residents are hearing a mysterious sound, an elusive low-pitched humming often described as resembling the distant drone of a diesel engine. Weirdly, no one has any idea what it is.

Newark is in Caledonia County, part of our fabled "Northeast Kingdom." But that is as close as anyone can come to determining where the sound originates.

It is also difficult to pinpoint exactly when people started hearing the Vermont hum. Certain residents say it's been around for eight years. It first reached public attention when the *Caledonian-Record* ran a story about it in March 1997.

Oddly, as if in response to the article, the hum stopped, but only briefly. After a few days it started again, steadier, and slightly more high-pitched.

But Vermont's mysterious hum has other puzzling attributes:

First, no one knows what it is. It occurs in places where there's no electricity, so we tend to eliminate dehumidifiers, blenders, and the like. Some people accuse pump motors submerged in wells. But even during power outages, the hum keeps humming along.

Second, not everyone can hear it. Those who can, often find themselves sitting in the same room with people who cannot. To compound that particular bit of weirdness: often deaf people can hear it every bit as well as those with perfect hearing.

And third, different people describe it in different ways. In general, it's perceived as low-pitched, like an electrical motor running in another room. Sometimes it sounds deeper and seems to turn on and off at unpredictable intervals. Sometimes it fades in and out.

The mystery broadens when we realize this puzzling sonic phenomenon is not confined to Vermont. Similar low-pitched sounds are heard all over the country: New Jersey, Florida, Minnesota, Wisconsin, Michigan, New York, and Maryland. It is also present in England, and parts of northern Europe.

In the old days speculation might have gravitated toward the supernatural, as it did with the famous Moodus noises in Massachusetts. We who put our faith in science tend to look toward the laboratory. But this time science has let us down. The hum cannot be detected by microphones or special low-frequency antennas.

The most thoroughly investigated hum occurs in Taos, New Mexico. It's close enough to the sites of atomic detonations, aircraft testing, and the Roswell UFO mania to suggest it is of military origin, possibly generated by U.S. Navy "ELF" stations. But a thorough study concluded ELF could not be the source. In fact, the Taos investigation found no source at all for the mysterious hum.

On July 9, 1997, Adam Lisberg, a reporter for the *Burlington Free Press*, ventured up to Newark to investigate our local hum. He interviewed a number of people and did a fine story about the mystery. But ultimately he went away puzzled.

Apparently thousands of puzzled people can hear the hum, enough to be collectively referred to as "hummers." In fact, two hummers wrote a book called *The Mystery of the Hum*. Authors Theroux and Vassilatos cover the sound's history and myriad theories accounting for it.

Explanations range all the way from UFO interference, to stresses in the earth's crust, to epidemic ear problems. Some scientists even speculate that certain people are hypersensitive to the growing volume of electromagnetic noise from microwave communications, cordless phones, and the like. But the truth is, no one knows what causes the hum. It is, in fact, a modern mystery.

Curious Encounters

Since my book *Green Mountain Ghosts* came out in 1994, Vermont monsters have remained undisturbed. No one has landed Champ, netted Memphré, or bagged Bigfoot. But that doesn't mean people have stopped experiencing odd encounters. In fact, the Green Mountain State seems to be a cryptozoological jungle if we consider the variety of strange encounters reported over the years on land, water, and in the air. The witnesses are a varied lot, yet they all have one thing in common: They all wish they'd had a camera.

Baby Champ

Back in 1945, Edwin Bell, an employee of the Lake Champlain Transportation Company, pulled a fourteen-inch reptile out of Shelburne Harbor. No one was able to identify it. Certain witnesses thought it resembled a miniature version of the "lake sea serpent" and speculated that it might be Champ's offspring. Others said that, except for its small jaws, it looked like a diminutive alligator. Less imaginative individuals dismissed it as some kind of ordinary salamander.

Little Alligators?

Robert E. Pike of Swanton, who grew up on Isle La Motte, was present when a weird set of bones was recovered from a farm pond in the 1940s.

The pond was at the edge of some marshy land near the bridge to the mainland. Everyone thought the skeleton looked like that of an alligator.

In 1945 a strange fourteen-inch reptile was caught in the harbor nearby. Witnesses said it resembled a crocodile, except that it had very small jaws. I'm not sure if anyone connected it with Edwin Bell's similar serpent. Cousins, perhaps?

The Connecticut Crawler

But what was it that Douglas and Dorothy Gove of Manchester, New Hampshire, saw in the Connecticut River in 1968?

While canoeing from Rygate to Brattleboro they spotted a small animal with bright green scales swimming along beside them. They said it was between eighteen and twenty-four inches long and probably weighed about two pounds. They kept it under observation until it vanished beneath a tree stump on the river bank. When they checked they found tracks and markings from its tail. They stopped at the state park in Ascutney to report the incident. Officials were not able to identify the tracks nor suggest what sort of reptilian creature could have made them.

Groton's Godzilla

Jane Desorda of Waterbury tells of a memorable encounter she had near the Big Deer Campground in Groton during the late 1960s.

It was in July or August. Jane and her husband, along with their three children, were going camping for the weekend. It was Friday, late in the day, probably between three and four o'clock. She recalls that there was plenty of sunshine.

They were traveling in two vehicles, Jane in front, her husband following with the camper. They drove slowly along the narrow dirt road, moving toward the bog.

Suddenly they saw movement at the roadside.

As Mrs. Desorda explained in a recent interview, "He stopped and I stopped. And here was this huge thing, I don't know what it was. It had come up part way across the road. . . . And I could see it as it went by. It looked just like a dinosaur. It came from the right side of the road. It went slowly across and just kind of slithered down into this swampy, treed, dense area on the other side. Just my husband and I saw it; the kids were sleeping. Of course the camera was in the trailer."

Though many years have passed, Mrs. Desorda was able to give me a vivid description of the creature.

"It had a long tail and an arched neck. And it had a hump. It's back was very humped. The top of the hump was probably two feet tall. All I could think of was a huge turtle that had lost its shell. The hump was too high for a turtle, though.

"Its head looked like a dinosaur, you know, the pictures you see. It was kind of a tannish color. A dark tannish color. And it was close to the ground, kind of like an alligator is close to the ground. And not very long legs. It had—all I can think of is—webbed feet. Like duck's feet. Only they were *big*. It went real slow, down into this swampy area. Into the high grass."

Somehow, when it comes to dinosaurs, the important issue seems to be size. As we talked, we tried to get an idea how big this mysterious lizard had been.

She recalled it in relation to the road. "From the end of its tail to its head was almost as long as the road was wide. Two cars could probably get by [on the road] if they went a little to either side."

That seemed to make it fairly sizable. The road would have had to be eight to ten feet wide. And an eight- to ten-foot lizard is a veritable Godzilla by Vermont standards.

I asked her what efforts she had made to identify this unusual specimen.

"We got to the campground and . . . we told them the story and they said, My God, what have you been drinking?"

But later she made a more serious inquiry. "I called UVM and I talked to a professor there and he said I'm not surprised at all, he said, because in Groton there are places no person has ever walked. He said there are some very strange things up there. Over the years people had called him, apparently. I don't remember what his name was."

Mr. and Mrs. Desorda went back the next day, but they couldn't find the exact spot the encounter had occurred. "We should have gotten out and marked it," she said. "Then come back."

Stegosaurus?

Mr. P. G. Levesque of Hartland is a native Vermonter with New England roots going all the way back to the 1660s. Around 1971 he was vacationing in Bloomfield, Vermont, at his father's 200-year-old farm. He says, "I was near the top of the ridge, walking along the road, when I noticed down the bank to my left about fifty feet away was a small animal—bigger than a large woodchuck, black shiny fur and a fat long pointed tale. The creature had the posture and mannerisms of—believe it or not—a stegosaurus or something.

"It lumbered along walking and rocking side to side, dragging its tail and with its head horizontal and sticking straight out and ahead.

"I have never seen anything remotely resembling this sort of thing. Its rear legs were like hunched up rabbit legs, but it walked heel-to-toe fashion with them, not hopped.

"I spoke with an old hermit man at the end of the road who had lived there since 1912 and he said that he had seen two or three in his life and had no idea what they were.

"We both agreed on its peculiar way of walking, shifting its head side to side in time with its gait.

"It was aware of me and headed away into the underbrush, but not with great haste.

"It was much larger than a 'quill pig' and jet black and proportioned more like an otter. Its haunches were tall and its front low, with a longish body. Its small head was far ahead and carried low on a line with its tail which stuck straight out. Picture a very small stegosaur with no armor and black fur and you're close."

Prehistoric Insects?

In 1994 I received a fascinating letter from a twenty-three-year-old woman in Alburg who assured me—to use her phrase—"Strange things happen in this town." She went on to list a few of them, occurrences with which she has direct experience.

For example, she told me about an earth-bound oddity she'd encountered. "Some years ago," she wrote, "I was biking . . . when I saw something by the side of the road. I stopped and got off my bike and approached the thing. It was perhaps eight inches in height and maybe a foot in length, resembling an inchworm. Eye-shocking orange, covered with spikes and occasional black spots. It did not move. I did, though. Knowing no one would believe me without some proof I biked home and back with my camera, pedaling like a maniac. It was gone when I returned." Her letter even included a color picture she had drawn of the odd-looking creature.

Big Bird

She also wrote, "One evening in the fall, when I was eight or nine years old, I saw a tremendous black bird. I remember playing near the swing set and looking up at a huge dark creature, flying very low. It looked to me like a prehistoric animal and for many years I maintained that it was a pterodactyl.

"Now that turkey vultures have moved into the area I suppose I should believe that's what it was—yet the feelings of unreality, of strangeness, has persisted through the years."

Bigger Bird

Talking about strange birds, a Shelburne woman told me about another fearsome feathered phantom. She looked out her kitchen window and saw a huge bird in her backyard. Its head was a good three to four feet off the ground, its neck was long and thin, and its aspect was somehow . . . unpleasant, even sinister. She had never seen anything like it. The only birds she could compare it to were the vultures she used to see in cowboy movies—but this was bigger. And decidedly stranger.

It was especially unsettling, she said, because as she looked at it, it was looking back at her, staring, never breaking eye contact.

Things got curiouser when it flew off. She figured a bird that size would need a running start. But no. This creature just rose into the air and soared off among the trees. Its flight was especially perplexing because its wingspan was from 8 to 10 feet, greater than the distance between many of the tree trunks. Yet the bird flew without colliding with any of them.

The witness told me she phoned experts at various schools and colleges, but no one had any idea what she might have seen.

Unfortunately, there were no other reported sightings in the area, so, understandably, she stopped telling people about it. She swears she saw something, but has no idea what.

Biggest Bird

During a late summer in the early 1980s Jim Guyette was visiting his mother on the family farm in Irasburg. The Guyette property was at the end of a dirt cul-de-sac, directly across Route 58 from Lake Region Road. The area was quiet and sparsely populated; no one was used to any sort of disturbance. That's why Jim was alarmed to hear an unearthly screeching coming from outside.

He ran out onto the porch, trying to locate the source of the noise.

"When I heard it again," he says, "I pinpointed it as off to the right. I looked over and saw these huge birds. They were *huge*. I hollered to everybody in the house."

Inside, young Ben Guyette heard his father shouting, "Come out here and look at this!" So he and his brother ran outside.

"There were three of them," Ben told me, "gigantic birds. It looked like one was trying to land in this big maple tree. It was just swaying the tree so much that it couldn't land. Me and my brother started walking out into the backyard, but my dad's yelling, 'Get back here; they might pick you up!'"

That's how big they were. Jim and Ben Guyette agree that the wingspan of the mysterious birds was at least fifteen feet. Maybe more. The force of those wings was so great that it made the tree look as if it "went through a hurricane."

By now the whole family was watching. Jim, his wife Jeanette, their two sons, and a family friend all saw the odd winged creatures.

Jim recalls, "They were flying north, with two in front and one behind. Like a triangle, but reversed. They were very sleek and dark brown. But the head was quite long. There was a long neck, and a long beak. I'd say the wingspan was twenty feet from tip to tip. Possibly more. And their wings were quite stiff-looking. Quite solid. They looked like bat wings, with a crick in them, not straight across. . . . I was just stunned. I wish I'd had a camera with us."

Ben remembers a very similar picture. "It was black looking with a long neck and kind of a pointy head. A big beak. The beak looked pointed. Not excessively long, but wide and pointy."

He didn't see feet or legs, nor could he distinguish any feathers.

"They had at least a good fifteen foot wing span on them. I definitely saw all three of them flapping their wings. One would flap its wings and it was starting to come down toward the tree and that big old tree was just swaying. I'm surprised it didn't snap; that's how bad it was swaying.

"There was a line of trees. But it was going for the biggest one. They tried to land and couldn't. . . . And then they all just flew off towards Butternut Hill."

What happened next was every bit as extraordinary—they vanished! Ben recalls: "When they got off over the top of the Butternut Hill it was the last I ever saw of them. It was weird, they kind of—they got to the top of the hill—it's almost liked they just disappeared. You could see them plain as day, then all of a sudden they were just gone."

His father finds it equally puzzling. "I ran around behind the house. I thought I would be able to see them, because that was the direction they were going. But they disappeared. I didn't hear another sound. Didn't see a thing. . . . I don't know where they went."

In separate interviews, I asked both men what they thought they had seen. Ben didn't venture a guess, he just said, "It didn't look like any normal bird. I'd almost say it was prehistoric."

His father was a little more speculative. "To me they looked like pterodactyl things; they had that type of a head. They were so huge."

At this point the odd encounter has puzzled the Guyette family for almost two decades. But their mysterious story could have had a very different ending. As Jim told me, "They didn't hurt us or anything, but I knew they were big enough to pick us up and carry us off. No doubt about it."

Pigmania

When it comes to over-the-top encounters, the curious events at Northfield would be hard to exceed. In fact, its difficult to believe anything weirder has happened there since the town was settled in 1785.

The strangeness began during the quiet spring of 1971, when a young man about twenty years old apparently vanished from a remote farm on Darby Hill.

A runaway?

A kidnapping?

The community conducted a search, of course, but nothing ever turned up. What had become of the blond young farmer's son? Nobody knew. It was a mystery.

By comparison, the events that followed about six months later didn't seem especially serious; no one even suspected they were related. That's when people about two miles away on Turkey Hill began to notice other things had come up missing. Not children, this time. Dogs and cats mostly. They'd disappear from the porch or yard never to be seen again. A lot of searching was going on in Northfield in those days, but nothing—living or dead—was being found.

Then all of a sudden a third event occurred. The alarming details worked their way through the community, spreading like a contagion. The odd tale became the principal topic of conversation all over town: A man living on an isolated farm on Turkey Hill had heard something in his yard. It sounded as if something—probably dogs, coons, or porcupines—was rooting around in his aluminum trash cans.

He rushed to the window and flicked on his floodlights. There, at the edge of the bright illuminated circle, he saw a figure rummaging through his garbage. It was man-sized, standing upright.

He went to the door and hollered, "Hey, git outta there!"

The figure turned, looked at him. And the man couldn't believe his eyes. He said the intruder was naked, covered with light, possibly white, hair. And—contrary to all experience and logic—the "man" had the hideous face of a pig.

The two looked eye to eye for a split second. Before the man could move, react, or rationalize, the thing by his trash can bolted down the driveway and ran into the woods. It was definitely naked, the man said, and it ran on two feet.

*

Lifelong Northfield resident Jeff Hatch is the owner of a successful automotive business in town. He recalls hearing the tale back in 1971 when he was a junior in high school.

Though he didn't give much thought to the events at first, Jeff was soon to be involved in an investigation of sorts when four of his friends had a curious encounter with the same odd critter.

He recalls being at a high school dance when four terrified youngsters burst into the auditorium. "They were white," he recalls, "Scared. Not *pretending* scared—*really* scared. I saw them and heard them. They were in tears."

The boys had been behind the school, way out on the far side of a cemetery, having a few drinks in a sand pit. That's where kids habitually hung out after dances and basketball games.

"They told how they had seen this creature in the sand pit. And it had approached them. They immediately ran back to the school, scared to death."

Again, the description of the creature's horrible countenance was the same: it had the face of a pig.

Curious, Jeff and some of his friends left the dance, charged out across the cemetery, and ran to the wooded area near the sand pit. If some kind of a weird creature was on the loose, they wanted to see it.

The frightened witnesses led Jeff and the others to the woods and pointed out the particular spot where the thing had approached them. Everyone could see where something had come through the bushes. "The grass was beat down," Jeff recalls. "Something had been there."

But now the thing had vanished.

"We never heard anything, we never saw anything. That night."

Later, in telling the tale, someone referred to the creature as "Pigman." The name, like the story, caught on.

*

Inspired by the "Pig" part of the creature's name, Jeff and his friends began to think the solution to their mystery might have something to do with that old pig farm up by Union Brook. "If there was a Pigman," the adolescents reasoned, "he must live at the pig farm. And that was the only pig farm around."

The boys made several expeditions to the farm. It was a weird place, Jeff remembers, since there was no farmhouse on the premises. Just a barn itself—which was sorely in need of repair—and a scattering of dilapidated outbuildings.

With a shudder he described what he found. "There were giant pigs there. Five and six hundred pounds—they were *gigantic*!"

The barn was open on both ends. The pigs were all in one section. A partition separated them from a little room that might have been used for storage. Upon inspecting the room, the mystery deepened. "You could see that something had laid there, had stayed there."

And it was there, too, that someone made a grim discovery. A small pile of dead animals. "Dogs. Cats. In heaps. Partially eaten, maybe . . . ?

"And something seemed to be sleeping there in the same room as the dead animals. The hay was flattened like a bed."

*

Down the empty road from the pig farm there is a mysterious area that has been known for years as the Devil's Washbowl. Situated at a deep natural depression at a "U" in the dirt road, it is shady, dark, damp, and—according to some odd reversed logic—seems to be hotter than any of the surrounding areas.

A short stream fed by many springs passes through it. Hunters in the area know that a number of caves are concealed here and there up the steep, rocky banks.

It was in this area, along the deserted road between the pig farm and Devil's Washbowl, that numerous drivers had encounters with an odd, oversized "animal." It appeared ghostly white as it darted out of sight or passed unexpectedly in front of moving vehicles.

These fleeting encounters became known as "Pigman sightings."

One terrified traveler even reported that the beast had leapt onto the hood of his car. Its beady pig eyes met the driver's before the "creature" leaped away and vanished into the undergrowth.

Descriptions were always the same. It looked like a person. Naked. With light hair and that grotesque pig-like face.

Another young couple parking at a turnoff near the Washbowl claimed that when the boy got out of the car, briefly, he was seized and brutally smashed against the side of his own vehicle.

His girlfriend heard him yell. Heard and felt the impact of his body against the car.

But he lived to tell the story. He said his assailant had been the Pigman. Said he had seen the creature clearly. It was five foot eight to five foot ten. It had all white hair and a face just like a pig. But he added this detail: the creature's hands were not like those of a pig. It had long nails like claws or talons. To prove it, he showed the slashes on his chest and arms.

This incident is notable because it is the only report of violence on the part of Pigman.

Anyway, the frequency of reports in that wet, wooded wilderness suggested to Jeff Hatch and his friends that the mysterious porcine phantom had relocated his headquarters from the pig farm to the Devil's Washbowl. And, they suspected, he might be living in one of the caves there.

To add strength to that theory, some of Jeff's friends claimed to have found piles of bones—"a little pile here, a little pile there"—in the biggest of the caves.

"There was no sign of a fire," Jeff told me, "but there was bedding in the cave. Hay. Probably from the pig farm. Obviously no hay is out there in the middle of the woods."

As far as Jeff knows the Pigman never spoke, but he did make sounds. People visiting Devil's Washbowl at night would hear odd vocalizations off in the distance. "At times they would sound like a scream. At times they would sound like a coyote. And at times they sounded like something [nobody had] had ever heard."

Jeff also saw footprints in the moist soil of the Washbowl. Though he claims no particular skill at tracking, he says the footprints seemed to be hoofed, or "cloven."

Stories about Pigman-related disturbances got so frequent that the town police actually investigated. Jeff remembers a patrol car showing up with three policeman in it.

"I vividly remember their shotguns," he told me.

When Jeff or one of his friends asked what they were up to, a policeman answered, "We understand there's something here. We're going to find out what it is."

But Jeff doesn't remember any shooting, though he definitely remembers the three officers.

*

The stages of adolescent conjecture regarding Pigman are obvious. He is, quite obviously, the farmer's son who disappeared back in 1971. The reason he "vanished" may be a little unclear. Perhaps he was embarrassed because of his abnormally grotesque physical appearance. Or perhaps he was deeply ashamed because—as was sometimes suggested—he was the unfortunate hybrid consummation of blasphemous backwoods bestiality.

In any event, this former farmer took to the woods and became the Pigman. Proof? There was, after all, the consistency of height and hair color. And, as we have seen, the timing was perfect.

For a certain interval the neo-savage hunted at night, subsisting on neighborhood pets and trash-picking. Eventually—so the story goes— he reverted completely to a feral state, lived in a cave, and hunted small game.

Jeff recalls that one of the kids in his high school class was the son of a Norwich science professor. "He [the professor] stated to us as a group that if a person was outside in the elements for an extended period of time, naked, their body would grow hair for protection."

Northfield residents who know the Pigman saga must number in the hundreds. But Jeff Hatch seems to be the local expert. For years he has been fascinated by the legend. He has collected testimony and has told the story many times. Jeff feels that there must be a kernel of truth somewhere in the details. But, he admits, he hasn't heard about any new sightings for over a decade.

It's possible, of course, that people simply aren't talking.

I mean, if you had a run-in with the Pigman, would you tell anyone about it?

Too Many Ghosts!

When I first began to conceptualize this book I had some kind of grandiose notion about how great it would be to include one ghost story for each Vermont town.

Then I came to my senses.

There are simply too many ghosts. Such a book would be huge. An encyclopedia. It would rival Abby Hemenway's *Gazetteer* in length, and would take so long to complete that I'd probably have to finish it via the Ouija board.

A compromise: Though more modest in scope, here's a short, quick tour through Vermont's galaxy of ghosts, stopping—at least briefly—in each of the fourteen counties.

I might add that these are just a fraction of the ghost tales I've collected. Vermont ghosts are a prolific species.

Addison County

In 1994 a nurse from Bristol told me of a spectral confrontation in a nearby hospital where she works the 11 P.M. to 7 A.M. shift. One night she was coming out of the medical records room in the oldest part of the building. She says, "I saw a white, see-through figure of a person pass out of one wall, cross the hall, and go into another wall . . . I couldn't believe my eyes."

Shaken, she made discreet inquiries of her coworkers and learned that a janitor had seen the apparition twice and a woman who worked in x-ray had seen it as well.

No one knows for sure whose ghost it is, but one theory is that it may be all that's left of a patient who died there of a self-inflicted gunshot wound back in the 1950s. No wonder 11 to 7 is called the graveyard shift.

East Calais

Another health care worker, this one from Montpelier, recalls a time during 1980 and 1981 when she was house-sitting in an East Calais home. On a couple of occasions she saw an indistinct figure that she presumed to be a ghost.

Years later she corroborated what she had seen in a chance conversation with two of her former house guests. While they had been visiting her in East Calais, they saw exactly the same apparition, though perhaps less distinctly.

A bit of investigation revealed a possible explanation. Local legend has it that during prohibition a man had been kicked to death in the kitchen of that house. And, according to these and several other witnesses, his ghost is still kicking around.

Belmont

A Belmont woman marvels at how matter-of-fact Vermonters are about their invisible housemates.

She told me about the time she was eating pie at a local farmer's house. All of a sudden she heard what sounded exactly like snoring.

Knowing the farmer lived alone, she asked if he suspected a porcupine might be residing inside the walls.

"Nope," he said and took another bite of his pie, clearly intending no further discussion.

But when she pressed him, he finally said, "Always happens this time of night, just about dark. Mr. Clark's nap, I guess." That was all he'd say.

Mr. Clark, she learned later, was a former owner of the farm who'd been sleeping deep in his grave for several decades.

Lake Champlain Islands

Generally Vermont ghosts seem to be a pretty benign lot. In all my research I've only discovered one malevolent local haunt. I keep hearing little bits of the story but so far have been unable to learn the specifics.

In an old newspaper I discovered an article in which an anonymous woman told about her visit to a stately old house on one of the Lake Champlain Islands. The owners used it only as a summer home.

One night while staying in a pleasant room close to the water, the woman had a terrifying encounter. She was awakened by the sound of a man screaming into her face. She could feel fingers digging into her shoulders and shaking her. But when she turned on the light she found that she was alone. Yet she could still sense the presence of a man in the seemingly empty bedroom.

Later she learned that other people staying overnight in that room were likely to suffer the same horrifying experience. Supposedly a previous owner of the island had tried to murder his wife. By strangulation. In that very bedroom.

And that's all I know.

I'm not absolutely sure of which island this allegedly happened on; I don't know the name of the house's owners, nor the real names of the witnesses.

If anyone knows more about this chilling tale, I'd love to hear it. I think.

Dover

The West Dover Inn was built in 1846 by two brothers by the name of Bogel. So recently, when weird things started happening there, former innkeepers Don and Madeline Mitchell, uncertain who to blame, attributed any disturbances to "Mr. Bogel."

The unseen fellow seems to engage in low-level antics like making noises or causing things to vanish from one place, then reappear in another.

Writer Patience Merriman got a short list of weird phenomena from the Mitchells, including electrical "lights that would flare, flicker, die and blaze on again in two upstairs bedrooms." Oddly, a third room on the same electrical circuit was completely unaffected.

On another evening, following a thunderstorm, when the air was perfectly still, a set of louvered doors banged open and shut by themselves.

"We both jumped!" said Madeline. "Then we said, oh it must be Mr. Bogel."

The Mitchells' daughter-in-law reported seeing a female ghost at the inn. According to Ms. Merriman's account, "She described the ghost as an older woman, wearing old-fashioned clothing, and sitting on a bed in one of the guest rooms. The woman vanished a moment later."

Mrs. Bogel, perhaps?

In 1995, the Mitchells sold the West Dover Inn to Monique Phelan and Greg Gramis. Even under the new regime employees still report otherworldly antics.

Cambridge-Bakersfield

My friend Althea Eaton collected a number of ghost stories about the Cambridge-Underhill area. To me the most unsettling involves a three-story Cambridge house and the family that moved into it around 1980. They, and at least twenty-four other people, had weird experiences there.

The most benign indication of invisible residents was footsteps. One Sunday in October 1989, six people were there for dinner. While everyone was seated around the table, loud footsteps pounded overhead. By then the family was used to such things, so no one even got up to investigate. But it had taken almost a decade of bizarre experiences for the family to become so matter-of-fact about such things.

Slightly more dramatic confrontations had built up their resistance. For example, two years after the family moved in, they were trying to sleep through a violent windstorm. A hall door outside their bedroom was loose in its frame and rattled every time wind blew from a certain direction.

Finally the man had had enough. He got up and, with a hammer and a single nail, secured the door to its frame. That ended the rattling. For a while.

The man didn't fall back to sleep immediately.

"I was still wide awake," he told Althea, "and the next thing I heard was . . . CLINK . . . and then I heard the latch be depressed and the door open and the latch secured and reset. Then the door started rattling again. The next morning I found the nail on the floor."

Another episode involved two nineteen-year-old boys sleeping in twin beds on the second floor. At first light they were simultaneously awakened by the odd sensation that the blankets on their beds were moving. But in reality the sheets were being pulled off and dragged toward the center of the room; the blankets remained in place. Whatever was doing the pulling was invisible to the naked eye.

Blankets are one thing, people another. A friend of the family, "a college graduate and president of a company," was in one of the bedrooms asleep in a sleeping bag. At four in the morning he awoke with a start to find himself being dragged across the room. A neat little trick considering he weighted 190 pounds and no one was in the room with him.

To me the single scariest incident occurred on the second night the family occupied the house. The husband and wife were asleep in their bedroom on the second floor when, with no apparent provocation, their dog started growling. Awake now, they checked the clock. It was ten after two in the morning.

Then they heard it.

Heavy footsteps below them on the first floor.

The sound switched abruptly to the floor above them. The footsteps were followed immediately by a loud clamor that sounded exactly like "somebody had a tin can and was banging a stick inside it."

The metallic racket went on for twenty minutes.

Not long afterward, they learned what was already well known in the community: Their new home was haunted. Apparently a former and long-dead occupant had contracted a debilitating illness. Eventually she was confined to a wheelchair. Her family had attached a flat bell to her wheelchair to ring in case of emergencies. The woman died in the house—at ten after two in the morning.

Pleasant Valley

But Althea didn't pick up on the following tale. It takes place in Pleasant Valley, a scenic community on a back road between Underhill Center and Cambridge, comprised of parts from both towns.

The story, perhaps now on the verge of extinction, suggests things were not always so pleasant in Pleasant Valley.

There an ancient red brick house was once owned by a Mr. Gleason and his son. The odd pair lived alone, keeping to themselves and rarely interacting with the townspeople. Because they had no near neighbors, not much was known about them or their private ways. Even when they ventured into Cambridge for supplies or on business, they made no small talk and retreated quickly to their masculine hermitage.

But people talked about the Gleasons. Travelers entering the general store in Cambridge asked what was wrong between father and son. Person after person reported they'd heard violent arguments while passing the old brick place. Word spread that all was not well—but folks thereabouts were in the habit of minding their own business, so no one investigated.

One dark winter night, after the father and son had been cooped up together for way too long, quarrels erupted into fighting. The older Gleason, tired of his son's taunting, had finally had enough. He grabbed a fireplace poker and dealt the boy a violent blow to the side of the head. The boy fell against a door, splashing blood over its surface and throughout the room into which he tumbled.

Mr. Gleason continued to beat his son until all signs of life were stilled. In the utter silence that followed, the crazy old man realized what he had done. He grabbed the boy by his feet and bounced him down the cellar steps to the dirt basement. There he dug a hole and rolled his son's lifeless form into it.

That done, he hurriedly packed a bag and plunged into the cold winter darkness, never to be seen again.

Curious passersby continued their occasional treks past the old brick house. Sounds of quarreling no longer violated the tranquillity of Pleasant Valley. No smoke from the wood fire darkened the blue sky. At night no light burned in the windows. Snow piled high in the walkways and against the door.

When authorities finally investigated they found obvious indications of what had happened. Young Gleason's body was discovered in the damp cellar, but no trace of his murderer ever came to light.

In the years that followed, no one was quick to claim the vacant property. Occasional occupants stayed briefly, but, rattled and pale, quickly moved on. They muttered stories about how the ghastly crime was reenacted over and over within the dark old house.

People feared the place and what they suspected it might contain. Gradually the old house fell into ruin.

Weathersfield

An equally ghastly crime is said to have left an indelible ghostly impression on another old brick house in Weathersfield. It lies on the Connecticut River Road between Weathersfield Bow and Ascutney, sitting on a knoll just off the street.

The story is not fixed with any specific date, but it took place in the days when the Connecticut River was a principal mode of transportation, just as I-91 is today.

The house's owner transported a quantity of grain down to Weathersfield Bow. There he sold it for a substantial sum of money. On the boat traveling home some transient ne'er-do-well spotted the gentleman's wad of cash.

When the gentleman got off the boat, the transient—who is identified in an old account as a "tramp"—followed him.

As the man made his way home, he didn't realize he was being stalked. When he stashed his money in a drawer, he had no idea he was being observed.

Later, when he went out to the barn, the tramp entered the house. As the intruder was in the act of transferring the money to his pocket, the gentleman's wife interrupted him. Before she could call for her husband, the tramp seized her by the throat, but a little too hard. Her neck snapped in his hands.

Fortunately, he didn't see the small child who watched the whole thing from the next room. As the boy ran to get his father, the tramp escaped.

He was later apprehended in Bellows Falls. The money was recovered, but there was no way to undo the great evil he had caused.

After that the house was never the same. Something—those who saw it said it looked exactly like blood—dripped from the walls in the room where the murder had occurred.

Terrifying groans echoed through the stark rooms on moonless evenings. Over the years the house changed tenants often. Between tenants it remained unoccupied for long stretches. Everyone in the area knew it was a haunted place.

Today the stories, like the ghost, have been laid to rest. The house has a new face and its dark past is long forgotten.

Winooski

The Winooski railroad trestle, known locally as "the Blue Bridge," is supposedly the scene of a suicide. A man allegedly hanged himself there. While historical details may be hard to find, people continue to report strange encounters. The usual scenario goes something like this: Imagine yourself walking the tracks. As you approach the bridge you see someone crossing the trestle on foot, coming toward you. By the time you reach the structure, the other figure has vanished.

Puzzled witnesses invariably say something like, "There was no place for him to have gone. If he'd've jumped off, I would have seen it."

Maybe.

But this much is true: it is a dangerous bridge, with no guard rails to protect against a potentially fatal drop. Quite possibly, well-meaning parents invented the "ghost" to frighten children away from a deadly playground. If not, then "the Blue Bridge," like Emily's Bridge in Stowe and the Hartford Railroad Trestle, may be a real gateway to another world.

Holland

Laurence S. Cramer tells the story of his friend's father, a logger named Tom, who was part of a lumbering operation up around Holland Pond, just south of the Canadian border.

In the 1880s, Tom lived in Morgan, so it was easy for him to go home on weekends. One cold January night he and his horse Dexter were making their way back to the logging camp. It was very late, perhaps around midnight.

Though the moon shone brightly, the temperature was ten below zero.

After every few paces the horse would snort loudly to clear ice from his nostrils. The only other sounds were the occasional hoot of an owl and the muted screech of his sled's runners scraping along the icy logging road.

The reins had iced solidly to Tom's gloves. He wore several layers of clothing, including a buffalo robe with a lighted lantern beneath it for warmth. Each time he exhaled, frost formed on his mustache and eyebrows.

He was uncomfortably cold and eager to get back to the heated bunkhouse. He hoped to catch at least a little sleep before work began next day at the crack of dawn.

Unaccountably the horse slowed, acting nervous. Soon the reason became obvious: a man was walking among the log piles near the camp. Although his face was not visible, he was nonetheless a familiar figure, easily recognized from behind. The Scotch cap, the scarf, the particular droop of the shoulders all said that it was Riley Caswell, owner of the lumber company. But why would he be out here in the middle of the night?

"If [Riley] had any failing," Mr. Cramer writes, "it was that he never was satisfied to delegate any of his authority to his son-in-law, who, through his wife, would inherit the business which the old man had watched grow into a prosperous enterprise over a period of years. At the moment he was apparently inspecting the progress of his lumbering operation."

But then Tom remembered that Riley was supposedly laid up with the grippe at his daughter's house in Derby. Still, a little thing like that wouldn't keep a man like Riley down. He probably had his son-in-law drive him to the camp for this midnight inspection. He'd never want his woods boss to get the impression Riley didn't have complete confidence in him.

Tom called out to the old man, thinking maybe he'd like a lift. But Riley ignored him.

He called again and was ignored a second time.

To hell with him, Tom thought. *If he don't want anybody to know he's up here, fine!* Tom pulled the reins and clucked the horse to move along.

He glanced one more time in Riley Caswell's direction, but the old man had moved out of sight.

Next morning Tom related the incident to woods boss John Tabor and asked, "What do you suppose old Riley was up here poking around for last night?"

"Well, Tom," John said, "there's something damned funny about this. You know, Joe Bush came in early this morning with supplies and he told me old Riley died last night around midnight."

Ryegate/Barnet

In their *History of Ryegate, Vermont*, Edward Miller and Frederic Wells wrote, "If all the tales and traditions which [linger] among the hills of Ryegate and Barnet had been gathered, they would form a volume, which in humor, pathos, and appeal to the deepest emotions of the heart, would be hard to surpass."

They then set about to prove it with a unique tale from the early 1800s. The events involve a young woman named Elizabeth McCallum, the fourteen-year-old daughter of two of the area's original Scottish settlers. Their farm was a bit northeast of Blue Mountain.

Elizabeth was a great favorite in the village. She was known to all as a lovely young woman of good manners and cheerful disposition.

On a bright summer morning her father sent her on an easy errand to the the home of a neighbor, John McNab, who lived in the eastern part of town, not far from the Connecticut River.

McNab's place was several miles away. Since most of the journey required passing through a dark, thickly wooded area, Elizabeth was permitted to take her favorite horse.

It was a lovely July morning and Elizabeth was delighted to have this errand to do on horseback. She set out with a smile on her face.

Some hours later, when she at last arrived at McNab's house, she was in a state of agitation and wonder. Something strange and marvelous had happened in those woods. She was able to describe the spot with precision—it was a spot Mr. NcNab knew well.

Elizabeth told of how, when she approached that particular spot— virtually in the middle of nowhere—her progress was arrested by an unfamiliar sound. It was music, she insisted, strange and beautiful music. It seemed to come from every direction, from all around her, filling the air, enveloping all other sounds.

She and her horse stopped and remained very still, listening in amazement. When at last the beautiful music faded away, they continued east.

John McNab and his family were quite taken by this facinating account from so trustworthy a young woman. But he was puzzled; he could offer no explanation as to what she had heard or where such sounds might have originated.

Elizabeth stayed for lunch and some conversation.

About mid-afternoon she mounted her horse and set off along the same trail, returning to her home.

*

That evening Elizabeth's parents, John and Ellen McCallum, were ill at ease. Though it was a warm, pleasant evening, all was not right. Their daughter should have been home hours ago. Now it was after eight o'clock; nighttime was descending rapidly. And still Elizabeth was nowhere to be seen.

Where could she be?

As darkness thickened, waiting became impossible. Mr. McCallum summoned a few of his nearest neighbors. Everyone grabbed lanterns and set out along the darkened path toward the McNab place.

Within an hour they found the horse, without its young rider.

Then they found Elizabeth. She was lying beside the trail, not too far from the grazing animal. The young woman was dead. No marks nor bruises could be discovered on her body. There was no blood and no broken bones. In fact, there was nothing nearby nor on her person that could give the searchers any kind of a clue about how she had met her end.

Later, John McNab and his wife told Mr. and Mrs. McCallum about the music Elizabeth said she had heard. Recalling Elizabeth's minute description, Mr. McNab was able to say that her body had been discovered lying dead at the exact spot where she had heard the mysterious melody.

Today her gravestone can be seen at the churchyard in Barnet Center. It bears the following inscription:

> Elizabeth, dau. John and Ellen McCallum
> Died July 28, 1812, aged 14 years

Though it says nothing about the mysterious music, I can't help but wonder if it can still be heard sometimes, resonating in the forests around Blue Mountain?

Shaftsbury

Specters haunting graveyards are among the most common of myriad types of ghostly apparitions, even here in Vermont. But it was uncommon to see anything strange in the Center Shaftsbury Cemetery. That's why Bob Williams, curator of the local historical society, was surprised to hear that some kind of a footloose phantom was prowling among the headstones. "The witness," Bob Williams says, "is an extremely stable, level-headed individual whom I have known for several years.

According to Mr. Williams, twice in June 1996 the cemetery caretaker, Mr. Merle Bottum, "plainly saw, in broad daylight, what he presumed to be the ghost of Gardner Barton Jr., who died in 1847 at the age of fifty-six." His grave is approximately in the middle of the cemetery.

Merle was riding his power mower when he saw the mysterious apparition. The first time it was standing behind the Barton family tombstone. During its second appearance it was walking directly toward the caretaker.

Merle said the figure was dressed in dark clothing and looked like the character "Doc" played by actor Milburne Stone on the old *Gunsmoke* television series.

Mr. Williams asked Merle Bottum if he was frightened of the apparition.

"No," Merle said, "it would have been interesting to talk to the man."

Bob Williams admits that despite his "rock-hard credentials as a rational social scientist," this matter intrigues him.

It intrigues me, too, just because of its mundane, undramatic nature and the rare fact that the apparition was seen during the day.

As far as Mr. Williams knows, there have been no other ghost sightings in the Center Shaftsbury Cemetery. I can't help but wonder if these may be the first of a series. Perhaps the citizens of Shaftsbury are about to witness the birth of a whole new cycle of ghost stories.

West Newbury

In the September 1938 issue of *The Vermonter* magazine, Miss Esther M. Hood of California told the fascinating tale of a cross-continent psychic experience.

She wrote about her mother, who had grown up in West Newbury, Vermont. "I can assure [your readers]," she told the editor, "that the story is entirely true." But Miss Hood offered no explanation; she only gave "the facts," letting readers then—and now—judge for themselves.

After the death of Miss Hood's father, Dr. Hood, the family had been plagued with troubles.

Her mother was grieving terribly, couldn't sleep, and was nearly exhausted. Then an accident pushed her one step closer to collapse. While trying to rescue her dead husband's canary from a hungry cat, the elderly woman took a severe fall and went into convulsions. Afterward, weak and lethargic, she complained that she had no more reason to live.

Assuring her that the bird was all right did no good. All other encouragement failed as well. Their family doctor determined that Mother's heart was dangerously weak; whether she lived or died was solely a matter of her own will.

For days the old woman wasted in a near coma, hardly eating, rarely speaking.

Her mother's situation was taking its toll on Miss Hood. She had recently lost her father; now it looked as if her mother would die too. She was extremely depressed and nearly worn out.

Then one night, after falling into a deep sleep, she woke with a start at about three o'clock in the morning. Someone was in the bedroom with her!

Terror vanished when she saw it was her father. He was, she wrote, "as natural as in life, only many times more vivid." She describes the apparition with remarkable clarity. "The vision," she says, "was a full length portrait of [my father], etched in light upon the darkness of the room. I closed my eyes several times but the picture remained for two or three minutes. Then, he smiled and vanished."

Later, she remembered that they'd had some kind of conversation, but she couldn't recall precisely what was said. All she could remember was that her father had told her, "Get the last [issue of] *The Vermonter*. That will solve your problems."

She ransacked the house looking for the magazine, finally discovering it among a clutter of papers in a box in the corner. The magazine, she said, was still in its sealed mailing envelope.

She opened the envelope and right away saw the cover photo: it was the old Meeting House in West Newbury, Vermont—the church her mother had attended as a child.

Miss Hood woke her mother and showed her the picture. At first the sickly woman didn't seem to understand, but as her mind grew more focused, a smile brightened her face. Miss Hood wrote, "All at once her eyes *glowed*."

"That's it all right," Mother said. "I never thought I'd see the old church again in this world!"

Over the next few days, Miss Hood and her mother repeatedly reviewed the pictures and read about the town. Together they recalled the West Newbury Church Choir and some of the people Mother had known growing up back in Vermont: Moses Brock, Hannah Sawyer (the best alto outside of Boston), and the Reverend Connell, a good friend even though he was from "that other church."

Miss Hood's mother's health improved, and it was all attributable to the dreamlike appearance of her father's spirit, a nostalgic journey back to the old hometown, and a copy of *The Vermonter* magazine.

All this makes me wonder has its successor, *Vermont Life*, received any similar endorsements from the spirit world?

St. Albans

Mr. Raymond Shepard of St. Albans is ninety-three years old. Yet he has vivid recall of an incident he experienced when he was a boy of ten. Nothing remotely like it has happened in the subsequent eight decades of his life. As he told me in a July 1998 interview, "People don't believe in ghost stories, but this is what actually happened."

Back in 1915 his family lived in a large house on Aldis Street. It was the next to last house on the right, one of two that were architecturally identical, and not far from the railroad yard where his father worked as a fireman.

Once or twice a week his parents would go to the silent movies at the Empire Theater in town. While they were away, Mr. Shepard and his brother Harold would stay home to keep an eye on the baby.

Harold was three years older, so he was more or less in charge. After the parents left, Harold locked the front door behind them. Then he ran upstairs to check on the baby, who was sleeping comfortably in his crib.

"This particular night," Mr. Shepard told me, "Harold and I were sitting around in the dining room, which was just one side of the parlor. And we sat there and played these old cylindrical-type records.

"And just while I was changing a record I heard some footsteps. I didn't pay much attention to it. I did get up to look through the parlor to see if it was the baby walking downstairs. There was nothing. So I went back and changed the record, then we went and popped some popcorn. And we sat there eating popcorn and listening to music."

After the song ended the boys heard the same sound again. Louder. More distinct. It was unmistakable this time—someone was coming down the stairs.

Raymond said to Harold, "I bet the little bugger's got out of his crib and he's coming downstairs."

So he got up and waited behind the heavy drapes that separated the parlor from the front hall. "The curtain was closed," Mr. Shepard says. "I wanted to surprise him, let him know I knew he was coming. We heard him walking. The stairs were creaking. The sound got down to where I figured he was about to the bottom. I pulled the drape open, quick like that, and said, 'What are you trying to do, surprise us?'

"And there was nobody there."

It seemed impossible. And scary. With that both boys began to worry.

"We finally got our courage together to go up and see if the baby had got out of the crib. So the both of us went upstairs. We were more or less scared then. And we went into the bedroom and the baby was sound asleep. Never had been out of the crib at all."

At that point their fear escalated.

"We swore somebody had been walking down the stairs. We came back down. We both started crying, hoping the folks would come home."

As they talked about it, the brothers worked themselves into a good scare. By the time their parents got home they were too frightened to unlock the front door. "We were scared to go past the bottom of the stairs in the hallway."

Raymond and Harold told their parents why they were so frightened, and the whole matter was put to rest. For a while.

*

Sometime later the family was entertaining guests in the living room. Another brother, Henry, was positioned in such a way that he could see through the dining room and all the way into the kitchen beyond.

All of a sudden movement in the empty kitchen caught his eye. Mr. Shepard recalls, "He looked and when he did he saw a sleeve—of a nightgown or dress—in the door waving. He got up and he walked towards it. As he got close to it, it disappeared."

Puzzled, Henry walked into the kitchen and looked around, trying to figure where the thing had gone. In a moment he saw it again. It had reappeared in the hallway. He saw it in front of a door that was about halfway between the kitchen and the front door.

It was the doorway leading to the basement.

But when Henry got to the cellar door, the sleeve had vanished again.

The bewildered boy searched the cellar but could find nothing that might account for the odd vision.

When he told people about it, they were equally mystified. But, Raymond Shepard said, "We got proof from the neighbor lady who lived next door."

During a chance conversation with their next-door neighbor, Henry described the sleeve and the odd series of ruffles that he had unmistakably observed.

The lady seemed to go white as he spoke. Finally, with wonder in her voice, she said, "That's just the gown that I put on the baby when it died. What you describe is identical to the gown that we put on the baby."

She went on to explain how the people who had lived in the house before the Shepards had had a baby who died there. She—the neighbor with whom Henry was talking—had personally dressed the baby for burial. She recalled the gown she had used.

One can imagine the chill the Shepard family experienced when they got that news. But the real kicker came some years later, after the Shepards had moved on to another St. Albans home.

News got out that the new occupant of the house had found something gruesome in the cellar. There, buried in the earthen floor, they had discovered the body of a baby: the baby the neighbor had dressed for burial. Unbeknownst to her, they had buried the child in the cellar.

Mr. Shepard recalls, "They dug in the cellar, they dug the box up and reburied it." This time properly, in the cemetery.

*

Raymond Shepard has had a long and productive life. He married a local girl and they raised a family. He worked forty-one years in the oil delivery business. Had a second career at G.E. in Burlington. Then generated retirement income as an elementary school bus driver. But never, in all that time, did he experience anything to compare with the odd occurrences in his own house.

"That's the God's honest truth," he said. "Somebody was trying to tell us the baby was in the cellar."

Island Pond

"Things in cellars" may be an epidemic terror in old Vermont homes.

Mildred Gibson of Island Pond experienced a similar near-confrontation with a subterranean something. Though well into her retirement years today, Mrs. Gibson recalls an incident that occurred in 1912, when she was nine years old.

"My mother allowed me to stay overnight with my friend Anita," Mrs. Gibson says. "Anita and her mother had just moved into a small house on Back Street. Anita's mother left us alone in the evening while she visited a neighbor."

The two little girls looked forward to a few unsupervised hours, when, "Suddenly," Mrs. Gibson says, "I heard what sounded like a heavy chain being dragged in the cellar."

Both girls became frightened. No one—nothing—should be down there. Their consternation escalated when they saw the trapdoor to the cellar begin to open.

"Terrified, we ran to the neighbor's home." But no one dared to investigate. "The girl's mother wouldn't go back into the house," Mrs. Gibson says. "We slept at the neighbor's. Mother picked me up the next morning."

Though Mrs. Gibson never saw what manner of creature was emerging from that hole in the floor, she soon suspected it might be a ghost. Her friend's new house was well known to be haunted.

Shortly afterward, Anita's mother vacated the "haunted" house and moved to better—and perhaps less crowded—quarters. Years later the place was torn down.

"I don't really believe in ghosts," Mrs. Gibson assured me, "but these are true incidents."

Fairlee

I have always loved stories about ghost ships—tales of phantom vessels like the Flying Dutchman that appear out of nowhere, then vanish into the misty night. And I have always felt a little cheated that we apparently have no ghost ships here in Vermont. Perhaps that is the consequence of having no seacoast.

Still, I would have thought Lake Champlain would be a likely prospect. With all the Revolutionary War battles and Prohibition-era rum-running that went on, you'd think there'd be at least one legend of at least one ghostly galleon somewhere on Vermont's greatest lake. But no.

Then I discovered I was looking in the wrong lake.

The honor of hosting Vermont's only ghost ship goes to tiny Lake Morey over in Fairlee. The story involves the area's most noted citizen, Captain Samuel Morey himself, after whom the lake is named.

In the early 1790s, Morey, a brilliant and prolific inventor, designed a steam engine that he adapted for use in navigation. By 1793 he was operating a fully functioning steamboat up and down the Connecticut River.

News of this revolutionary invention spread and was met with enthusiasm, so Morey packed up his brainchild and brought it to New York City for exhibition. There it was observed by Robert Fulton, who later journeyed to Morey's home in Fairlee for a lengthy consultation.

According to historian George Dangerfield, Fulton felt "other men's original ideas, in the realm of steamboats, existed only to be borrowed." So Fulton "borrowed" Captain Morey's idea, patented it, and soon became rich and famous as the alleged "inventor" of the steamboat.

Morey, realizing he had been had robbed, grew discouraged and depressed. In 1807 he sank his steamer, called the "Aunt Sally," at some unknown location in the lake.

While the history of all this may be a little hazy, the ghostlore is even more ephemeral. According to many old tales the heartbroken Morey died soon after, but his ghost still walks the shores of the lake.

As Florence A. Kendall wrote in her 1928 poem:

> People tell of other people
> Who on still and sultry eves
> Felt an icy breath go past them,
> With no rustling of the leaves.

Not only did the captain leave his spirit behind, but also the spirit of his creation, "Aunt Sally," hangs around as well. It is said that she appears each year on the anniversary of the night he dispatched her to the deep. The ghost of the "Aunt Sally" is seen to rise from its watery grave and float on the waters of Lake Morey.

With the shade of Captain Morey standing silently on her deck, the antique steamship glides soundlessly through the water without so much as creating a ripple. If it is a clear night the boat and its sole passenger will be shrouded in mist—steam, most likely—and thus they are obscured from perfect observation.

The ghostly boat will continue on its way until it either fades from sight or sinks again to that undiscovered spot that is its final resting place.

Unfortunately, I have not been able to find much in print about the legend and legacy of Captain Morey's ghost and ghost ship. However, in a 1928 issue of *The Vermonter* magazine, I discovered Ms. Kendall's poem. Elegantly and succinctly she tells the legend and says Captain Morey's midnight ritual is likely to go on forever. As she explains, the ghost ship and the captain

> Shall be seen upon the waters
> Till upon the roll of Fame
> Man shall cross out Robert Fulton
> And replace it with his name.

And this leaves us with a final mystery: Is Ms. Kendall's poem merely a retelling of the story, or is it in fact the source of the entire ghost ship legend?

It is a "chicken or egg" type of problem, and of course I can't say which came first.

However my instinct tells me that at least in this case—out of all the stories in this book—fiction might well be stranger than truth.

THE END

This book would never have happened if it weren't for all the people who helped me. Some gave me a lead, some contributed a whole story, others helped in other ways. So, in alphabetical order, I'd like to thank the following folks: Peggy Atkins, Cindy and Doug Baird, Lynne Ballard, Tom Bassett, Steve Bissette, Rick Blount, Eric Chittenden, Brian and Allison Citro, Jack Coleman, Wendell Coleman, Joan Connor, John Coon, Richard Costello, Lee Crawford, Robert Cullinan, Tom Davis, Jim Defilippi, Edith Foulds, Deborah DeGraff, Caroline DeNatale, Ed Desany, Jane Desorda, Brandy Dillensneider, Barry Estabrook, Tina Ferris, Linda Fitch, Marie Geno, Paul Gillies, Susan Greenhalgh, Robert Gussner, Jim and Ben Guyette, Jeff and Lea Hatch, Lou and Gwenn Hill, Genevieve Jacobs, William Jenney, Nancy Jeski, Michael Johnson, Dina Kane, Rita Knapp, P. G. Levesque, Adam Lisberg, Linda Malachuk, Ken and Marcia Manner, Jim Marsden, Evan Pringle, Helen Renner, Nancy Rucker, Gregory Sanford, David Schmoll, Brian Searles, Jim and Ray Shepard, Barbara Sirvis, Carolyn Stacy, Trina Stephenson, Josh Wallace, Ida Washington, Kathy White, Marion Whiteford, Bob Williams, and Christi Yates.

Thanks to Mildred Gibson and Jeanette Pyle of the Green Mountain Folklore Society for some last-minute assistance, and to Jim Davidson at the Rutland Historical Society, who did so much to help me bring Solomon Jewett back from the dead.

A special tip of the hat goes to the wonderful people at the Fletcher Free Library here in Burlington. Also, Karen Campbell and the staff of Special Collections at the University of Vermont Library have supplied invaluable help and wonderful resources, including Richard Sweter-litsch's Folklore Archives. Of particular interest were papers by Sarah Freymann, Kristin Mann, Rob Mocarsky, Kate O'Brien, Douglas Reed, and Mary Wheatley.

Jane Beck and the good people at the Vermont Folklife Center deserve a lot more than this humble pat on the back. They and their neighbor the Sheldon Museum are terrific resources and great places to hang out and learn.

And once again, thank you Betty Smith, Sam Sanders, Brendan Walsh, and all my friends at Vermont Public Radio.

There are others I should mention here who by request or oversight must remain anonymous. I sincerely apologize to anyone I've forgotten.

I tried to mention as many sources as possible within the text, if doing so was not disruptive to the story. In the interest of giving credit where credit is due, here—in no particular order—are some of the books I used in my research: Carl Sifakis's *Great American Eccentrics*; Alton H. Blackington's *Yankee Yarns* and *More Yankee Yarns*; *Mischief in the Mountains* edited by Walter Hard and Janet Greene; B. A. Botkin's *Treasury of New England Folklore*; Ruth Brandon's *The Spiritualists*; Ann Braude's *Radical Spirits*; Samuel Adams Drake's *New England Legends and Folk Lore*; Eastman and Bolte's *Haunted New England*; Charles Fort's *The Books of Charles Fort*; Judson Hale's *Inside New England*; Olga M. Hallock's *Huntington, Vermont*; Everett Chamberlain Benton's *History of Guildhall*; Miller and Wells's *History of Ryegate*; the *Official History of Guilford*; three by Ralph Nading Hill—*Lake Champlain Key to Liberty*, *Contrary Country*, and *Yankee Kingdom*; Ida Washington's *History of Weybridge*; Spencer Klaw's *Without Sin*; *A Plymouth Album*; *Mysterious New England* edited by Austin Stevens; John Lovell's *Those Eccentric Yankees*; Edwin V. Mitchell's *Yankee Folk*; *The Gazetteer of Vermont Heritage* by D. Maunsell and his colleagues; Robert E. Pike's *Drama on the Connecticut* and *Tall Trees, Tough Men*; L. S. Hayes's *History of Rockingham*; Caroline Larsen's *My Travels in the Spirit World*; Franklin S. Harvey's *The Money Diggers*; Peter Jennison's *Roadside History of Vermont*; the Federal Writers Project book, *Vermont*; Bertha S. Dodge's *Tales of Vermont Ways and People*; B. Radcliffe and S. Rogers's *Natural Wonders of Vermont*; Lee Dana Goodman's *Vermont Saint & Sinners*; Abby Hemenway's *Vermont Gazetteer*; the Bristol Historical Society's *History of Bristol, Vermont*; Curt Norris's *Ghosts I Have Known*; Clay Perry's *New England's Buried Treasure*; *Mad & Magnificent Yankees*, edited by Clarissa Silitch; Maudean

Neill's *Fiery Crosses in the Green Mountains*; Barney Fowler's *Adirondack Album II*; Clark Jillson's *Green Leaves from Whitingham*; and Walter Bigelow's *History of Stowe*.

Journals, periodicals, and newspapers consulted are too numerous to list completely. However, I am especially in debt to the *Rutland Herald, Burlington Free Press, Bennington Banner, Newport Daily Express, Times Argus, Vermont Journal, Brattleboro Reformer, Mountain Villager, County Courier, The Banner of Light, Vermont Life, Yankee, Fate, Time, The Vermonter, Vermont Geology, Vermont Affairs, Green Mountain Whittlin's,* and the invaluable *Vermont History*.

GEOGRAPHICAL INDEX

Library of Congress Cataloging-in-Publication Data
Green Mountains, dark tales / [collected] by Joseph A. Citro.
  p.   cm.
  ISBN 0–87451–863–6 (alk. paper)
  1. Tales—Vermont.   I. Citro, Joseph A.
GR110.V4G76   1999
974.3—dc21   98–33105